Death

at the

Forest's Edge

Miriam Winthrop

CaliPress

Death at the Forest's Edge is a work of fiction. Names, characters, and places, and locations are the product of the author's imagination or are used fictitiously. Any resemblance to actual events, locales, or persons, living or dead, is entirely coincidental.

Death at the Forest's Edge is grounded in careful research. However, in support of the storyline, certain details have been changed.

1 Literary Fiction/International Mystery and Crime
2 Literary Fiction Themes/Friendship
3 Mystery Characters/Amateur Sleuth
4 Mystery Settings/Islands

To Cali

Death at the Forest's Edge

1

It was by chance that Dawn reached the far edge of the forest that day, by chance that she left behind the only world she had known for five of her six years. Heavy rain had swollen the stream that separated her house from the vineyards where her mother was working, so she meandered eastward through the thickening trees looking for a good ford. She—and everyone she knew—thought of the dense ring of laurels and junipers that surrounded them as their own, although it did not actually belong to them. They even referred to themselves by the same name used by those who had abandoned the area a century before: *Comunidade dos Reis na Floresta,* the Kings' Community in the Forest. The hamlet had originally been named for the three kings who had travelled a long distance to find the newborn Messiah, just as—the people of Dawn's community were often reminded—they had travelled a long distance to find the lives they had been searching for.

It was also by chance that Dawn's nine-year-old sister, Melody, had agreed to come to the forest that day and not refused to leave the garden where she spent most of her time. Before leaving for the vineyards, their mother had told them to stay together, and Dawn knew that meant she was expected to watch out for her older sister, which she did on that day by looking around every few minutes to find where she had settled, cross-legged on a fallen log, her cap of bright red hair glowing in a shaft of sunlight.

Dawn liked feeling the cool forest air waft through her pale blond curls and listening to the hushed sounds her feet made as they sank into ground spongy with moss and decaying vegetation. She liked the way fallen leaves made hilly landscapes where they piled against tree trunks and how filtered sunlight painted patches of soft yellow everywhere and the scent of new growth in the air. Most of all, she enjoyed the quiet and the solitude. And—as young children often do—she lost all sense of time and place.

She was deep into the forest when she sensed a change. She could no longer see any of the houses of her people or the brighter greens of their fields or Melody. She felt a quickening in her chest and an unfamiliar prickle on her skin. Of its own accord, her head swiveled one way and another to home in on birds scratching and papery leaves whispering and what might have been soft footfalls. She walked on, more slowly, more alert, and a thought came to her: someone was watching.

At that moment, a truck happened along the stretch of road that bordered the forest's edge, and Dawn heard the unfamiliar rumble of its engine straining uphill and the music of an entire band spilling through its windows. Curiosity took her further, to where her world ended and the other world began, and there she stopped. For a long time, she just stood and watched the hillside across the road, and the villages so different from what she knew, and the expanse of deep blue ocean beyond the island of Terceira.

Uneasy, she turned around. By chance, a breeze picked up the corner of a red kerchief and waved it at precisely the moment she stepped back into the forest. It looked so much like the red kerchief her father had worn when he left that morning. Perhaps he had come back early and would join her.

Dawn took a few more steps before she realized her mistake. Terror rooted her to the ground as firmly as the trees towering over her. She cried out. *Papa. Mama.* The quietness of the sound she made surprised her. She tried to fill her lungs with air, but her dry mouth only hung open.

Instinct took hold, and her legs began to move, tearing one way and another, scrambling terror-driven over boulders and through shadowy tunnels in the undergrowth, until she tripped on a vine.

The last time she screamed, it was silently to herself.

Light from the morning sun made a buttery yellow parallelogram on the wall of the kitchen, where nine-year-old Liliana was making breakfast. She lined a basket with clean dishtowels, filled it with warm sweet rolls—the first she had ever made on her own—and carried it to the table. They were certain to be good. She shared her mother's talents as a baker, just as she shared her mother's thoughtful nature. With dark hair and eyes, though, her looks reflected her father's Portuguese heritage. It was only in her skin, a blend of rose and gold, that one saw her mother's Dutch ancestry.

It was a special day at Casa do Mar, her home on the Azores island of Santa Maria in the middle of the Atlantic Ocean. After a year of sacrifice and hard work, her family was going to put finishing touches on the second guest cottage of their rural hotel. The sweet rolls were a celebration—and a bribe to her father, who preferred to start his day much later.

Liliana's mother, Catarina Vanderhye, came into the kitchen sniffing the warm, caramel-scented air and smiling. "Those smell wonderful, my lovely daughter." She carried herself with an air of serenity, a woman who took pleasure in what she had built her life around: family and community. In her forties, she wore simple clothes on her comfortably rounded body. With peaches-and-cream skin that was the envy of many women, deep green eyes, and thick titian hair, most would call her quite a beautiful woman. "Your sweet rolls should get Papa out of bed," she said, kissing the top of Liliana's head.

"I'll take the basket to the other end of the barn, so Papa can see them." While the former dairy was slowly being transformed into a rural hotel, the family was living in two small spaces at either end of a very large barn. On the southern side, close to where a green foothill dropped off to the ocean, were bedrooms for Liliana, her eight-year-old brother, Toni, and her parents. On the other side were the old kitchen and a bathroom

3

so small that only one person could fit in at a time and a tub was out of the question. That was the space Catarina most looked forward to changing. She loved taking baths.

Taking the sweet rolls through the barn wasn't necessary. A happy face—one might even say the face of a man so happy that he must be oblivious to any of the harsher realities of life—appeared in the doorway. Anton Cardosa was a large man, close to six feet six inches, a rare sight on islands mainly populated with those of Mediterranean descent, and his love of good food could be seen in his build. With an almost perpetually mischievous smile and bright brown eyes under a cap of curly dark hair, his face—and perhaps his joie de vivre—often made him seem more boy than man.

"Are you on your way to bed?" Catarina teased. Her husband was known for the late hours he kept.

Anton lifted a pair of puckish eyebrows. "I smell something delicious."

"The sweet rolls are for those of us who are working this morning. We have a lot to do."

He hung his head. "I really should help, then," he said with mock seriousness. She chuckled and handed him a long wood spoon. No further discussion was needed. He took it to the two-burner stove and started to make hot chocolate for the children.

Catarina opened the Dutch door to the outside and went to get Toni, who was running back and forth across the meadow with Sombra, the small black dog who had been Anton's present to his wife on their last wedding anniversary. Two irrepressible bundles of energy, they had been playing since six-thirty that morning. Like his papa, her son loved adventures, both real and imagined, and Casa do Mar was a playground for him and his friends, the abandoned outbuildings and the old chapel providing a backdrop for their escapades. At a year old, Sombra still had the look and temperament of a puppy and when she saw the open door, she charged ahead to the kitchen, scampered back and forth several times to herd Toni inside, and finally turned soulful, pleading eyes on Catarina, looking hopefully at the table with her tail wagging.

"Quickly, wash up," Catarina urged her son. "Papa has the hot chocolate ready." With chestnut curls, light olive skin, and large dark eyes, it was easy to see that he would look much like his father one day, but his mother hoped for several more years of seeing his child's face. Time does pass quickly, she thought. It seemed like just a year ago that Liliana was learning to ride her tricycle, and Toni was learning to walk. She placed two steaming pots on the table, one filled with strong coffee and the other with rich milk, and the family settled in for breakfast.

They had named the cottage Casa das Flores, for its location in a field speckled with yellow buttercups, lavender borage, and deep blue pimpernels. Once a carriage house for the carts that took fresh milk to market, the exterior looked as it would have in the nineteenth century. It had, however, been completely remodeled by Beto, the tyrant of a contractor who shared Anton's determination to preserve the traditions of the Azores. Every one of the black basalt stones and oak beams had been returned to its original place, mortar had been mixed and applied as workmen of past generations had done, and the windows had been reclaimed from an old whaling factory.

Inside, the air was still and the smell of paint hung around them. A film of gray—some ordinary dust and some settled from the remodeling—covered every surface. Catarina threw open windows for cross ventilation, and the family got to work putting the furniture in place and unpacking boxes. They vacuumed and polished, cleaned windows and hung drapes, plugged in lamps and screwed in bulbs. They made the beds with new sheets in shades of blue that Catarina had selected to match the changing colors of the seascape outside. They removed the plastic wrapping from two easy chairs upholstered in fabric she had chosen for its traditional motifs and placed a book of short stories on the table between them. Liliana dug up narcissus from the meadow surrounding Casa das Flores and replanted them in the window boxes around the cottage, and Toni brought a platter from the kitchen, ready to hold a loaf of his mother's sweet bread and fresh fruit for guests. By afternoon, it looked exactly like what Catarina, with her artistic eye, had pictured: a homey welcoming space that paid tribute to their heritage.

Casa das Flores had been rebuilt using craftsmanship of the past, but it would also meet the expectations of visitors in the twenty-first century. Beto arrived to help set up the television and music system. A short, stocky man with weathered skin, his thick black hair sprouted from cheeks, eyebrows, arms, and along the neckline of his tee-shirt—everywhere but from his bald head. The family watched as he threaded cables and electrical lines through holes he had left between stones, and pressed a button to light up the large flat screen. Their own television was old and small, and was kept in Anton and Catarina's room because they had no living room, so occasionally, when their first guest cottage—Casa do Bosque—was not occupied, they had enjoyed family evenings watching television there. Each of them imagined being able to see personal favorites on the new television: Toni's American adventure shows, Liliana's movies set in times past, Anton's beloved soccer matches, and Catarina's British detective series.

A lot was riding on this second guest cottage. A little over a year ago, Anton and Catarina had invested every penny they had saved to make a rural hotel from five derelict buildings on a few acres of land at the water's edge. So far, prospects for success were bleak. The meager revenues from Casa do Bosque did little more than keep it up, and the first payment on the loan for Casa das Flores was due in one month. If they didn't make that deadline, their rural hotel would almost certainly be lost, and their own home would be in jeopardy.

Their best hope for the future of Casa do Mar appeared in the doorway. Lori Moore completed their family. In her late thirties, the American woman's striking looks attracted attention nearly everywhere she went. Tall and beautiful, she had long, blond hair and golden green eyes that in a certain light nearly matched her hair. "I'm just in time for pictures," she said, waving a camera.

"Lori!" Liliana was the first to greet her. They had a special bond.

A few seconds later, she had been hugged by everyone. Even the gruff Beto had given her two scratchy kisses on her cheeks.

"Any news?" Anton raised an eyebrow.

"Yes, and I think it's good news. There's interest in booking both guest houses for two weeks."

"Two weeks?" Delight and relief came through in Anton's voice.

"Two weeks, Sombra!" Toni exclaimed, dancing around. Sombra barked her excitement.

Lori had come into their lives just a year earlier, conflicted over which direction she should take her life, and the fit had proved ideal. They were the family she had never had and always wanted, and she had been the salvation of their dreams— for Casa do Mar and for the preservation of their heritage. They had shared major life events, celebrations, danger, and hope, and had helped each other in so many ways. Now at the end of her leave as a public relations executive, Lori was helping her friends get Casa do Mar on its feet. She had set up a website, created brochures, approached nearly everyone in her network of contacts, and more recently she had added something that was generating a lot of interest. For the almost two million people in America and Canada who were descendants of the Azorean diaspora, Casa do Mar was now offering both individualized research into their roots and personalized visits to the villages of their ancestors. She was very good at what she did.

Catarina's children had reached an age when they preferred different books, so the bedtime ritual took longer than it had in years past. Toni had his imaginary world of superheroes that allowed him to fall asleep with images of himself as a courageous champion of right, and Liliana had hers of girls from different times and different places. They would leave those worlds behind soon enough, Catarina thought with some sadness, just as they had left behind the eagerness to hear the very same pages night after night. Sitting on Toni's bed, she could see those books she had read aloud so many times that she could recite them by heart, sitting on the shelves of the bookcase that had held her own books when she and Anton were at university together, and she felt the passage of time sharply.

On this night, Toni wanted to hear the next chapter of the book she had read the night before, the story of a boy who battles space invaders with the help of his talking dog, something she was glad he enjoyed. There was a lot to be said for being a rational adult—and a lot to be said for not being a rational child. She hoped both her children would keep small pockets of fantasy in their adult selves, as wellsprings of creativity and imagination, sources of music and art, and the starting point for exploration and invention.

Normally, Toni fell asleep within minutes, exhausted by a nonstop day, but tonight anticipation was fighting exhaustion. His eyes nearly closed three times, then snapped open again, the last time with a murmured question, "What time do the boats come in?"

"In the morning."

"Can I go to the marina to see them cross the strait?" Toni loved watching the annual competition of old whaling boats from the different islands.

"You'll be in school," she said stroking his curly hair. "I'll take you afterwards."

"Oh." He was asleep.

Catarina went to her daughter's room. Lori was already there, reading aloud from an English biography of Laura Ingalls Wilder. Liliana spoke often about becoming as fluent in English as her mother was and going to Oxford University, something her mother had given up to be with Anton. Bedtime reading brought Lori a special, very personal pleasure. As much as she'd wanted, she hadn't shared the ritual with her own mother. She ended with a well-known quote of Wilder's, "Home is the nicest word," and felt her own emotion rise.

Both women kissed Liliana goodnight and followed the beams of their flashlights through the dark barn. Midway Lori stopped and switched off her flashlight. They stood by one of the open side doors and lifted their heads. Since her first night on the islands, the veil of sparkling stars—so bright that it seemed like the Milky Way had split the dome overhead in two—had been her favorite sight.

Lori broke the silence. "What a lovely person Liliana's becoming."

"She's becoming more her own self and beginning to live in her own world, one where I am a guest."

"She'll always be part of your world."

"She will always be at the center of my world. That is what makes it so hard. The holes at the center of my world will grow as they grow."

That had not been the case for Lori's parents. A late-in-life addition to their contented family of two, she had never been at the center of their world, and she had been as easily ignored as a child as she had been shed when they moved on in life. "Don't think of them as holes," she suggested, "anymore than you think of the stars as holes in the sky. The places the children fill now will be bright with memories, and they will fill other places as they grow. You'll have more not less."

The call came as the three adults were ending their day the way they often did, together in the kitchen, talking over the day's events and the future of Casa do Mar. It took Anton several seconds to find the right phone. He had three, one for each of the different parts of his life: one as the owner of Casa do Mar; another as husband, father, and friend; and a third as Minister of Culture. It was the third phone that rang close to ten that night. The hour wasn't unusual for Anton; what was unusual was to receive a call from the Presidente's office at that hour. His first thought was that his one-year appointment—and with it his chance to create a living historic trust showcasing the culture of the Azores—was not to be renewed. After a decade of planning, uprooting his family, and risking their future, was it all to end? As he answered, he was rehearsing a plea to let him continue.

It was the Presidente, himself, who spoke. "It's João Moniz."

His distant voice told Anton he was on a speaker. He noted that there had been no greeting, no apology for calling at the late hour, no inquiries about his health. "Hello, senhor Presidente, what can I do for you?"

"I have in my office Manuel Silva and Luis Gomes.

What could possibly involve the Presidente, the Minister of Justice, and the Head of the Judicial Police at this hour?

"An American child has been missing for two days."

Anton's normally high eyebrows disappeared under his curly hair.

"The maternal grandparents are German and Swedish, and the paternal grandmother is American."

That might explain why he had been called into the matter, thought Anton. His responsibilities included relations with visitors who had ancestry on the islands.

"I've already been contacted by lawyers—"

"Lawyers? Why are lawyers involved with this?" Anton hadn't been able to stop himself from interrupting the Presidente.

"Manuel here, Anton," the Justice Minister answered. "There's an issue of custody, and jurisdiction isn't clear. At this point, we don't have the authority to question or hold the parties who weren't in the Azores when the child disappeared, and even if we did, there's the matter of public relations."

The Presidente elaborated, "The press may go away eventually but even if the girl is found quickly, the stigma may remain."

Anton was beginning to understand why he had been called.

"Motions for custody had already been filed," continued Manuel. "The mother wants to leave; the father wants to keep the children here."

"Keep the children here? Not take them to America?"

"That's another complication. The family has been living on Terceira for five years, in a...I'm not sure what to call it."

The Presidente's voice came back on the line, and it was sober. "Anton, they've been living in a version of what you want to create on Santa Maria."

Anton heard his heartbeat thumping in his ears, something Catarina had told him was a sign that his blood pressure was too high, so he should stop what he was doing immediately.

"That's probably not relevant right now. What we have so far is the involvement of American, German, and Swedish nationals, with an odd interest expressed by a Qatari." The Presidente sighed deeply. "We also have responsibility for a young child. We don't want another Madeleine McCann," he said, referring to the disappearance of a young child who was abducted while on vacation with her parents in Portugal. Anton and Catarina had been living in Lisbon at the time, and the case had affected both of them. Every time new evidence was found, their hopes had risen, and every time those hopes had been dashed.

"I don't want this to become a media sensation. The grandparents have threatened to go to the press. One of them even dropped the names of celebrity reporters." There was a long silence, and he said what Anton was thinking, "That could put the child in greater danger."

"What would you like me to do, sir?" Anton spoke as he folded up his laptop and stacked the papers he had been working on. He intended to be ready to leave as quickly as possible.

"Effective immediately, you are relieved of all other responsibilities. I want you to go to Terceira and manage the situation—the investigation, public relations, and private negotiations."

Anton didn't ask about the extent of his authority; he wanted the freedom to determine everything from agreements between the families to ransom payment.

Luis Gomes spoke up, "The custody case and the whole issue of removing the child from the Azores have already created a lot of tension between the police and family members, and there is certainly a lot of animosity among the family members. We need someone new to the scene, someone who has credentials as a facilitator."

The Presidente had the last word. "Fix this, Anton, and I'll make sure funding for the historic preserve is yours."

It wasn't a gift; it was a threat. Anton knew he would have to make this right or lose what he had dedicated his life to.

2

By the time Anton left Santa Maria the next morning, Dawn Bennett had been missing for almost three days. Carlos Bettencourt, the pilot of the small Cessna and Anton's friend, had taken him between the nine islands of the archipelago on many occasions. Much like the gondoliers of Venice or the taxi drivers of London, the young pilot provided a convenient, pleasant way to get around, and his services were in high demand to show tourists views unlikely to be matched by anything they had ever seen or would ever see again: the iconic Ponta do Pico rising from the floor of the Atlantic to pierce the endless blue water, seaside plains against soaring cliffs, steep forested slopes, dolphins frolicking in lagoons ringed by offshore craters, foam-fringed black sand beaches, and lush green hills painted lilac, blue, white, and pink by hydrangea blooms.

An attractive man, Carlos could have been cast as the romantic lead in a 1960s film. Tall, slim, and impeccably groomed, even when flying a good friend at the last-minute, his black pants were pressed, his leather shoes were shined, and his starched shirt was snowy white. Much to Anton's delight, he had been seen at Casa do Mar more and more recently, coming to Santa Maria to visit Lori and sometimes to take her to a nearby island for dinner or to see a movie. Used to the far more casual dating scene in New York City, she had been intrigued and flattered by him, and the modern American businesswoman almost reluctantly admitted to herself that she enjoyed his formal invitations, courtly manners, and deference to what she would enjoy.

Usually, a flight with Carlos was an opportunity to do what Anton did so well and enjoyed so much—socialize. This time, with the disappearance of a young child in a place where crime was exceedingly rare, they had done little more than exchange greetings. With the exception of the brief times he allowed himself to look down on his beloved Azores, Anton spent his time in the air studying the files he had brought with him.

He started with a summary prepared by Gomes.

Dawn Bennett, age 6, did not return home on Tuesday, the 3rd. She had been with her sister, Melody Bennett, age 9. Her mother, Janine Maier Bennett, an American citizen, reported this at the local police station on Thursday, the fifth. She gave her permanent address as Comunidade dos Reis na Floresta, Terceira, where she returned after filing the report. She left no other contact information.

Ten days ago, Agneta Maier, a Swedish citizen, and her husband, Horst Maier, a German citizen, first appeared at the Justice Ministry in Ponta Delgada with their lawyer, Franz Maier, in connection with hearings to determine jurisdiction for custody of Dawn and her sister, Melody. They have since returned six times. Mention was made of press releases and negative publicity if custody was not quickly settled in their favor. Similar demands were made on behalf of the girl's father, Alexander J. Bennett, at the same time. No further demands have been made by either party since the 1st.

The Judicial Police was also recently approached by a law firm based in Doha, Qatar, asking for information on the Bennett family. All attempts to contact the firm this week have been unsuccessful.

Anton made a few notes in the margin. Why was Dawn Bennett's disappearance not reported sooner? Where is her father? Why were the intense legal activities apparently suspended after the

1st? Why was a Qatari law firm interested in the Bennett family—and currently unresponsive?

He then turned his attention to the substantially larger file that Lori had prepared. The barebones account provided by the Judicial Police had been enough for her to uncover quite a lot about the Bennett and Maier families, and her research occupied the remainder of his time in the air. He started by looking into the big blue eyes of Dawn Bennett in a recent photograph that had been included with the custody papers filed in Ponta Delgada. Masses of light blond curls topped a cherubic face, fat-cheeked and highly colored. He was drawn to her smile, so filled with delight. The picture had been taken in a forest and looking between the trees, he saw slivers of green and blue that certainly could be the ocean and grass of Terceira.

Dawn was the daughter of Alexander J. Bennett—known as AJ—and Janine Claudia Maier Bennett. Born six years ago in Nigeria, where her parents were volunteers for an irrigation project, by the time she was one year old, she had also lived in Estonia, where mother had taught English, and in a small town in Maine. While in Maine, AJ Bennett had worked the land for a collective of organic farmers, and Janine had sold jams and condiments made from its produce. It was during their time in Maine that Janine had become an American citizen and acquired a new passport.

A second daughter, Melody, was three years older. Born in Germany, she had lived the peripatetic lives of her parents until the family settled on Terceira five years ago. Lori had found several pictures and public records of Melody, her surname changing from Maier to Bennett when her parents married. Over the years, her tall body had become increasingly attenuated, her almond eyes darker, and her lips and mouth thinner, but the color of her hair remained the same shade of orangey-red. And every picture showed a face that was composed almost to the point of appearing lifeless.

Lori's research included both an overview of available records on Comunidade dos Reis na Floresta and a behind-the-scene analysis that was typical of her thorough work. The community had been in operation for seven years, the brainchild of Wallace Jenkins, a retired history professor from Maine, and at first glance it seemed to be close to what Anton envisioned: a group of people who incorporated the traditions and ways of the past into their everyday lives. But while Anton conceived of a place that preserved the best of his culture while also affording his people the best of the present and future, Jenkins had planned a complete break from the rest of the world. Despite the Terceira community's more stringent commitment to living as people had a century earlier, it had recently developed a web presence that was updated regularly and seemed to have an open posting policy.

Jenkins had bought remote land on the island of Terceira and, along with a few followers, reclaimed a long-abandoned hamlet that had once occupied the area. Over the years, some residents had left and others had joined, and as near as Lori could determine between thirty and forty people now lived there, both in family groups and as single individuals. Two months ago, citing personal reasons, Jenkins himself had posted that he was retiring as leader of the group. She found the records of his departure from the Azores and his purchase of a modest condominium in Naples, Florida soon thereafter. A man by the name of Pat Millikan, who had been with a similar group on the Azores island of Flores, had assumed leadership, but Lori hadn't found anything on him. *Doesn't seem like a Kool-Aid type of place,* she had commented next to a detailed account of life in the community that had been written by a former member. Anton understood the reference to the Jonestown commune where so many had committed suicide by drinking cyanide-laced Kool-Aid at their leader's direction.

For whatever reason, Janine Bennett no longer wanted to live there. In the past two months, an avalanche of papers had been filed in Ponta Delgada, Dresden, and Palm Beach, all with the goal of establishing which parent the Bennett girls should live with. One twist to the custody battle caught Anton's eyes. AJ claimed that he and Janine had agreed to raise their children as people had a hundred or more years ago, and his petition was based on that oral contract. An interview in the *Bristol Cooperative*

Gazette, dated just a week before the family left for Terceira, supported what he said, quoting Janine, "We want our daughters to be freed from the technology that has led to so many of the problems of the modern world." In the picture that accompanied the article, a beaming Janine stands by AJ's side, holding an infant Dawn. The caption read *The Bennetts Promise Their Children a Safer, Happier Life*.

In opposition, the legal papers filed in Janine's name by her lawyer, Franz Maier, stated her desire to give Dawn and Melody what was not possible at Comunidade dos Reis, specifically referencing technology such as the Internet, rapid communication, and CT scans. She also claimed that denying access to certain technologies at a young age could have irrevocable consequences, denying Dawn and Melody the ability to use or even understand them later in life, and her lawyer argued that as parents neither she nor AJ had the right to make that decision for their children. Every one of the twenty-three briefs had been taken care of entirely by grandparents and their lawyers, acting on Janine and AJ's behalf with powers of attorney. Each motion had led to a rebuttal that was just a bit more antagonistic than the one before, the last two pointing to the impossibility of shared custody, Janine's lawyer saying that to remove the children from school for six months every year would compromise their progress, and AJ's lawyer saying that to spend so much time outside the community would expose his daughters to dangers they were not equipped to deal with. Anton's heart sank when he read one line: No reasonable person would agree that anything the past offers is preferable to everything the present offers.

Anton and Carlos walked along the tarmac together, silent. As they approached the small terminal, their pace slowed and they looked at each other with atypically somber expressions.

Carlos lifted his trademark dark glasses to the top of his head and said, "You will find her, my friend."

All Anton could do was nod and walk away. *I hope you're right.*

Anton knew the regional chief of police, Victor Rocha, if only casually. They had met when Anton had his first job with the government and Rocha was a trainee on the police force. He remembered him as not particularly bright and with a higher opinion of himself than was warranted. In the first ten minutes of their conversation, he decided Chief Rocha had only matured into his character, a bit more dull-witted and a bit more confident of his abilities.

They exchanged a few of the pleasantries that often start tense conversations. The weather was good. The flight was uneventful. The landscaping in the park was nice. When the time came to share details of the investigation, however, it became clear that the police chief wasn't at all happy with the role Anton had been given. Powerless to deny police assistance when orders came directly from the Presidente, he nonetheless had no intention of engaging in cooperative teamwork.

"We'll have to talk to the child's mother as soon as possible," said Anton, making an effort to let the Chief know he saw this as a joint effort.

Rocha only uttered a noncommittal *mmm*.

"She can let us know where and when the child was last seen."

"If she knows."

Anton suspected Rocha had left his remark somewhat cryptic to point out that he knew more about the situation than a latecomer could. He raised his eyebrows to ask for more information.

"I wouldn't be surprised if she had no idea where the girl was that day or who she was with," Rocha continued. "You know, they're a strange lot at the...they call themselves a community. It was a mistake to sell the land to them, a mistake to allow them the live there. All of them. Together. And not a single one actually born here. They have some odd notion of returning to the old ways, and that includes letting their children wander around."

Anton thought about letting the Chief know how he, too, believed in the value of *the old ways*, but he remembered what

Catarina had taught him about how much could be learned by quietly listening, so he let him ramble.

The Chief continued lecturing on the dangers of allowing such a place to exist. "And I'm not alone. There are many others here who feel the same way."

Anton waited a full ten seconds after the rant ended before asking, "What did the mother say when she came in?"

"I wasn't here, but I do have the report that was filed. In my position, one has to delegate responsibilities. It's good management." What he lacked in intelligence, he made up for in pomposity.

"Exactly when did she come in?"

Chief Rocha reached for a folder on his desk so unhurriedly that it looked like a slow-motion film to Anton. "She came in..." he paused and scanned the top sheet in the folder for long seconds, "...yesterday morning."

"And when was the last time she had seen her daughter?"

He looked over the four sheets of paper in the folder, all fully filled out, but said nothing.

"Who took the report?" Anton asked with a snap in his voice.

The Chief raised his eyebrows and pursed his lips haughtily. "Officer Andrade did. He knows I like everything done by the book, so everything is in order." He looked over the tops of his eyeglasses as if daring Anton to challenge him on that point.

His patience was at an end. "Please have Andrade report to me immediately." Anton stood—and when he stood, his height was impressive—and added, "I'll commandeer any available office."

Rocha was not at all pleased but to show it would mean admitting he was obliged to do as Anton wanted. "I have a small space in the administrative wing that's free for a short while. My assistant, Gabriela, will show you to it." With that, he sat and turned his full attention to his laptop.

It was not a large police station, and Anton found Gabriela Viveiros easily. A tiny woman in her early fifties, her curly gray hair was cut short and her olive skin was just beginning to show the fine lines of age on her forehead and around her eyes. She was one of those indispensable people found in most organizations who, despite a lowly title and little recognition, kept everything functioning smoothly. In her case, she made all the duty roster assignments, prepared the payroll, answered both emergency and nonemergency calls, could fix most problems and knew who to call for those she couldn't, and remembered everyone's birthday with a small celebration.

Handing her his card, Anton introduced himself and explained what he wanted. She knew exactly the office space that he was to use, and they talked as she led the way into the older part of the building that housed government administrative offices. "I hadn't realized you would be working here, so it isn't set up yet. The cleaners arrive at 8 p.m., so I'll have it cleaned this evening, and you'll be good to go by tomorrow morning. I can also get you a computer and have a phone connected."

Anton thanked her, and said he'd brought his own laptop and phone with him. He decided to make use of someone who seemed to know so much. "Were you here when the woman came in about her missing daughter?"

"I was. In fact, she talked to me first. She was waiting outside when I unlocked the door in the morning."

"How did she seem?"

"Distressed. Exhausted. I don't think she had slept in a while; there were dark circles under her eyes."

"What did she say?"

Gabriela concentrated, trying to recall that morning. "I think her exact words were, 'My daughter didn't come home.'"

"And you had her talk to one of the officers on duty?"

"Norberto Andrade was the first one to come in. He sat down with her on the bench near my desk, and I brought over the form for him to fill out." She gave a half smile. "Since Chief Rocha took over, we've had a lot of forms to fill out."

He returned her smile. "I understand."

They reached the office Anton was to use. Gabriela turned the knob, but the door wouldn't open. "It must be locked," she said, looking just a bit embarrassed. "Doors are never locked around here."

"It's not locked," Anton chuckled. He knew this office and this door well. He reached up and smacked the top right corner, while turning the knob and pushing against the door with his knee.

"Well, that is clever, Minister Cardosa!"

"I've been here before," he explained. "In fact, one might say that I started right here."

After she left to find Officer Andrade, Anton arranged the furniture to suit himself, unpacked his battered briefcase, and opened the blinds. The window gave a view of the park below, lush with bougainvilleas and fuchsia, and beyond that the town and the ocean. He smiled at memories of his first time on Terceira, just after he and Catarina had received their degrees. She had taught school, and he had worked for a museum, and they would meet in that park at the end of their days apart, before going to the main square in Angra to start the evening together. That year had been a good one, during which their beloved Liliana had been conceived.

He turned around when he heard a knock. A dark young man of medium height and build stood outside the open door, hand raised to knock on the frame again. "Sir, I am Officer Norberto Andrade. Gabri...senhora Viveiros said you wanted to see me."

"Yes, come in." Anton walked around the desk and offered his hand. "Please sit down," he said pulling out the only chair.

He started to sit, then straightened up. "Thank you...I mean, no, thank you."

Anton could see the young man was flustered, unsure what to do with only one chair in the room and a superior asking him to sit, but he was a master of making others feel at ease. "What have I done? My wife would scold me for forgetting my manners," he laughed, "asking you to sit when there is only one chair. I'm so sorry."

The young man ran his fingers through short, spiky hair and exhaled with relief.

"Instead, shall we walk while we talk, Norberto?" They ended up only walking up and down the hallway, but the young man seemed happy with the arrangement. "Could you tell me about your conversation with senhora Bennett, the mother of the missing child?" asked Anton.

"She was already in the station talking to Gabriela, when I came in. That was at nine on Thursday morning."

"What was your first impression?"

He thought a moment. "That she was anxious to talk immediately." He explained, "She was drinking a cup of tea that Gabriela had made for her and the moment she saw me, she stood up and put the cup down so quickly it almost fell over."

"What would you say about her emotional state?"

"I don't know if you'd call it an emotional state, but she seemed like she was in a rush, like she wanted to say what she had to say as quickly as possible, and when she was done, she couldn't wait to get out."

"What exactly did she say?"

"She said her daughter hadn't come home—"

"When?" Anton interrupted.

"I remember because it seemed a long time to wait before reporting a missing child. She said her daughter hadn't come home on Tuesday. But it was already Thursday, sir. Doesn't that seem like a long time for a mother to wait?"

Anton nodded grimly. "It does. It does."

"Oh, and one more thing, she had her other daughter with her, a skinny redhead about nine or ten, and she kept repeating, 'Dawn needs Bobey.'"

As they finished talking and were returning to Anton's temporary office, Gabriela was approaching from the opposite direction. She had brought Anton a copy of the police report on Janine Bennett's visit. "Chief Rocha says he has some important things to attend to until late this afternoon, so talking with the mother will have to wait until then."

Anton caught Norberto rolling his eyes. Typically as relaxed a man as one could find, he felt an anger rising in him.

What could be more important than a child's welfare? "Gabriela, could you arrange for a car to meet me at the front of the police station as soon as possible?"

"Of course, sir," a gleeful nod of approval breaking her professional demeanor. "Will you need a driver?" she prompted him.

He hadn't thought of that. He had no idea of how to find Dawn's mother.

"I'd be happy to drive you, sir," Norberto said with an eagerness that bordered on a plea. Anton liked such dedication.

Gabriela had another suggestion, one that spoke of both cleverness and a hint of defiance. "Perhaps I should have the car brought to the front of the administrative wing. It's closer for you."

Everyone understood it was also less likely to attract Chief Rocha's attention.

As Norberto headed to Comunidade dos Reis, Anton enjoyed the passing views. He was particularly fond of the island, named Terceira by Portuguese explorers because it was the third island they had discovered in the archipelago. In fact, it had appeared on maps earlier, sometimes as Brasil and sometimes as Atlantis. Angra do Heroísmo—or Angra, as it was locally known— was its capital and the first capital city of the Azores. Between the fifteenth and nineteenth century, it had been where ships traveling between the Old World and the New World stopped for provisions and repairs, and the trading in gold, silver, spices, and furs that followed left it with a rich history, a wealth of charming architecture, and recognition as a UNESCO World Heritage site.

Anton sat back and savored fond memories as they passed an expansive plaza, *Praça Velha*, bordered by graceful white colonial buildings with terra cotta roofs and wrought iron balconies. The floor of the old square was a black and white mosaic of weathered stones in striking geometric patterns that were likely a legacy of the Moors. But their beauty came with reminders of a harsh environment; the white was limestone from the ocean that isolated them, and the black was basalt from the volcanoes that lay just beneath the surface. Anton remembered long, pleasant evenings in the balmy semi-tropical climate, sitting in the plaza with Catarina, enjoying music festivals, sipping wine, and making plans for the future. It had been at one of the café tables that they had first talked about how running a small rural hotel would allow them the family time they wanted.

Norberto left the city and its suburbs behind and travelled the perimeter of the island, passing village after village that had grown from agricultural settlements along the narrow coastal plains and river valleys. Anton was familiar was their layout. Each village had a white church at its heart, both literally and figuratively, and solid stone houses that met the edges of the narrow roads that fanned out from a central square. The smaller ones had only a café or two, and perhaps a few shops owned by residents. The larger ones had municipal buildings, stores, and restaurants. Most harbors berthed only small fishing boats, and where the village met the water, there were invariably boats under repair and outdoor stands that sold bait and fishing goods.

The car climbed foothills, bright green at lower elevations and darker where grass had given way to trees centuries earlier. Past the coastal plains, the terrain changed from flat meadows to dense forests, from gravelly lowlands to steep mountains. The island itself was made of the tops of overlapping volcanoes that straddled the junction of three tectonic plates five thousand feet below the surface of the Atlantic Ocean. Not unexpectedly, seismic events had plagued its inhabitants since the island was settled. Anton was a young boy when the last major earthquake struck the islands on January 1, 1980. A magnitude 7.2, it had destroyed seventy percent of all the buildings on Terceira, thankfully sparing most of the historic churches and municipal buildings.

The road continued due east towards the warmer, more humid, and less settled interior, occasionally passing a lone surviving tree of the orange groves that had supplied the British Isles for centuries, until they were wiped out by blight. Olives and pineapples thrived there now. "Most of this is a nature preserve, you know," Norberto said. A sheepish grin crossed his face. "Of course you know. I mean, you're a minister…" His voice trailed off in embarrassment.

At the junction of the two-lane highway and a secondary road, Norberto turned northward and they began to wind around the base of a hill that dominated the area. Ahead, two white churches and the top of a third could be seen, each flat facade almost defiantly facing the ocean, each catching the golden afternoon sunlight. They were headed toward the third church, its bell tower emerging from a nest of green leaves in the village of Santa Clara.

"It's the nearest village to where the child lived," said Norberto. "Once it was quieter, dying even, but since attracting some tourists, it's been doing better."

"Do people from the child's community go into the village?"

"I've heard a couple of them trade there, but most don't leave at all. They have this…" he searched for the word and—with some disdain—said, "…this *notion* that they are living as the freguesia's original community did."

Anton wanted to have a quick look at the village. If Dawn was not found close to her home, he would have to return. He had Norberto park the car on the side of the main road, and they took a ten-minute stroll to the central square, shaded by large magnolias and cobbled as most were with ancient stones. The church took up one side of the rectangular plaza. The remaining sides had four shops, four cafés, and a municipal building that housed the volunteer fire department, a conference room for the village council—two retired teachers and a café owner—and the post office, which consisted of a desk at the end of a hallway that was manned by one employee who came in two mornings a week. The businesses reflected the needs and resources of the inhabitants. Outside the secondhand clothing store, folding tables held stacks of shirts and pants, and large baskets were filled with a jumble of work gloves, children's socks, and flowered scarves appropriate for church. The repair shop apparently serviced cars, farm equipment, and small electric appliances, and the hardware store carried a wide variety of household goods. The largest of the stores, a grocery, was the only one with a customer in the postprandial hours when most people took their afternoon naps. Anton bought a soda for himself and one for Norberto, and they continued their tour.

A small school for the youngest children was across the road from the back of the church; any older students would go to larger towns. Further away from the center, increasingly larger hedged fields were planted, cows grazed, and carts stood waiting to take produce and dairy products to market. Then all signs of human habitation abruptly ended, and the forest took over.

Norberto led the way back to the car. "As far as this is from other towns, people come from all over Terceira once a week because of the bakery on the main road. It has an old water wheel and stone ovens built in the seventeenth century. On market day, visitors and locals make the trip all the way inland for the cornbread."

"Which day?"

"Market day."

"No, which *day* of the week is market day?"

"It alternates between Monday and Tuesday. This week it was…" as he spoke, he realized why Anton had asked, "…Tuesday." His eyes opened wide. "The same day the child disappeared."

Walking back to the car, Norberto pointed out the bakery near the intersection of the two main roads. "The entire valley was once owned by a Portuguese overlord, a relative of the king and reputedly as cruel as he was wealthy. In the eighteenth century, he brought in several families to work his land and had the mill built," Norberto explained.

Anton stopped midway across an old wood bridge and looked down at a rushing stream. His eyes followed its path west and uphill. "Does this pass close to Comunidade dos Reis?"

Norberto nodded. "It goes right through the forest where the child was last seen." He led the way to a circular stone terrace, called an *eira*, where grains had been threshed for three hundred years. "This place is run by a young man—the eighth in his line of bakers—who took over at the age of seventeen, when his father died in an accident. He's twenty-six now, and he's becoming quite a celebrity for his breads." The original mill house stood beside the eira, its basalt stones glistening with moisture and frosted here and there with bright green moss. Nearby was the miller's house, originally a small cottage, but with modest prosperity over the years it had been enlarged with two newer wings and modernized with large windows. The bakery itself, built in 1911, backed up against a bank of ovens built into the hillside.

Norberto's knocks at each of the buildings went unanswered, and there wasn't a sign of anyone on the property. "I think he only sells two or three times a week, sir."

If Dawn were not found by the next market day, Anton planned to return; the bakery would certainly be open, and the village was likely to be filled with locals and visitors.

Ten minutes later, Norberto pulled the car off the road near a clump of hydrangeas so heavy with pink blooms, most of the leaves were hidden. "It's the only way in, sir, just a short walk through the forest." He took the lead up a steep hill.

At the top, Anton paused to catch his breath as much as to get the lay of the land. It's time to start exercising, he thought to himself, as he had several times recently. Looking eastward, he saw the ocean he loved in the distance, and he traced the road they had travelled on as it emerged from the valley to his left, climbed past the forest, and disappeared again into dense trees. Less than a mile in front of him, Santa Clara was tucked into a fold in the hill, most of its houses clustered around the church and a few spattered on the hillside. He made out two ways the village could be reached from where he stood, the narrow paved road off the highway that Norberto had taken and what looked to be a well-travelled footpath just yards across the road from where he stood. "How long a walk would you say it is from here to the village?"

"Along the road about twenty minutes, maybe fifteen minutes if you cut across on the path. And it's only about five minutes to the nearest neighbors." He indicated the few houses on the hillside opposite where they were standing.

Norberto confidently led the way through the forest, their footsteps leaving furrows in the deep layer of leaves that brisk overnight breezes had laid down. "Have you been here before?" Anton asked.

He gave a small laugh. "Most of the kids in the area know this place. When we were boys, this was where we came to play. It was deserted then, of course, but the houses were still standing. It was *our* kingdom...until it became *their* kingdom."

Before they had gone thirty yards, he became aware of two people standing still ahead of them.

"That's the mother," Norberto whispered. "The man with her considers himself the leader of the...the little group. Pat Millikan," he garbled the unfamiliar name.

Millikan stepped over exposed roots and rocks easily, despite carrying a heavy belly over very short legs. His hair was a bit longer than was fashionable for men but other than that, he wouldn't have been out of place in a business office in the capital city. His little square teeth were straight and white, and his sharp black eyes were embedded in a round face that was deeply tanned, freshly-shaved, and glowing with some sort of ointment. He seemed uncertain of what approach to take with the visitors, changing his expression from aloof to jovial to stern, and back again.

Janine Bennett was a bit unsteady on her feet. She walked towards them slowly with her eyes on the uneven ground and her arms held a bit away from her body, as if to catch herself from a fall. She did stumble once and Millikan took hold of her arm, but she shook him off. With sun-damaged skin and dark circles under her eyes, she appeared older than her age of thirty-one. Anton saw a resemblance to her older daughter in thin features and dull, reddish-brown hair that was bluntly cut to shoulder length. As they closed the distance between them, he saw traces of the younger woman she had once been in triple-pierced earlobes and tattoos that peeked out from under both sleeves. Plainly dressed, she wore laced-up leather boots, heavy cotton pants that were drawn together at the waist, and a loose homespun shirt. He wasn't at all sure what to make of her, a woman who apparently wanted to leave behind a life she otherwise seemed to be openly embracing.

She made eye contact with Norberto and opened her mouth to speak, but before she could say a word, Millikan extended his arm and said more loudly than was necessary, "You are here about the lost child." His Portuguese was not good.

Anton addressed both Millikan and Janine, "I am. I'd like to speak with senhora Bennett..." he waited just a moment before adding, "...first."

"She's very tired. I'd prefer her to go home and sleep. I can tell you everything you want to know."

With a child in danger, Anton didn't make his usual effort to put someone at ease, especially when he suspected the man could hinder finding that child. He could tell Millikan was struggling for words and decided to take advantage of that. As quickly as he could, he shot out as many words as he could, "As Minister Plenipotentiary of the Autonomous Region of the Azores and a representative of the central government, I am electing to speak with relevant individuals in an order predetermined by me when I formally enacted the process to be followed."

Norberto almost choked with delight.

Unable to even follow what had just been said, Millikan opened his eyes wide and watched silently as Anton took Janine's elbow, led her a short distance away to a fallen oak tree, and asked her to sit. He fervently wished Catarina were with him. He was clever enough to know what to ask, but she was far better at hearing truth in the response—regardless of which words were spoken.

"I'm sorry about what you're going through," he said, taking a seat beside her.

She crossed her arms over her chest and nodded stiffly.

"I give you my word that I will do everything in my power to find Dawn..." Realizing that he had just introduced the possibility that he would not be able to find her, he added, "...very soon."

She nodded again.

"When did you last see your daughter, senhora?"

She burst into tears.

Millikan, hovering nearby, took two steps forward before Norberto stopped him with a firm palm on his chest.

Anton put a hand on Janine's shoulder. "I know this is hard, and I'm sorry." He truly meant that. Since first hearing about Dawn, his own dear Liliana had been on his mind, and he had imagined how Catarina would feel under similar circumstances. He repeated, "When did you last see your daughter, senhora?"

"It was on Tuesday, just before I went to the vineyards with everyone else. We don't pay attention to exact times here. Before joining me, she and my older daughter, Melody, were going to play." She looked up at him and said very softly, "We don't worry about our children the way others have to. They're safe…" Her voice trailed off. She took a breath and started again. "We watch out for each other, so I've never worried about leaving…"

He noted that although she was fighting to take her children away from Comunidade dos Reis, so far she only had praise for it. "*About* what time was that?"

"It was morning, perhaps a couple of hours after the sun was fully up."

Her face was stricken with guilt, but Anton didn't think she was negligent to have left her daughters to play by themselves. The islands were so safe that he and Catarina occasionally left their own children alone in the house, with only their neighbor, Maria Rosa, to check in on them. "I understand. Especially with Melody there, it should have been fine."

Janine shuddered. "Melody would not have been the best choice to have around if something happened."

"Why do you say that?"

"She lives in her own world most of the time. It's always been that way."

"Have you asked Melody?"

"Of course I've asked," she spat out. Then she quickly apologized, "I'm sorry. I'm just worried. I don't know what to do."

Anton tried to keep her on track. "What did Melody say?"

He could see her chewing on the inside of her cheek.

"Nothing. But she misses her sister terribly. She keeps asking when Dawn will be back."

He hadn't forgotten how much time had passed before Janine reported her daughter's disappearance. "Senhora Bennett, why didn't you go to the police about Dawn's disappearance on Wednesday—or even Tuesday?"

Janine froze. "I…" She clenched her hands and took a deep breath, but she said nothing more.

"Senhora Bennett, why didn't you go to the police sooner?"

Her eyes flickered in Millikan's direction. "I…It's difficult enough even when there's no trouble, when no one is watching us, and now our settlement is facing a challenge to its existence."

It didn't escape him that she was trying to defend the community she was on record as wanting to leave. He changed the subject. "Where might Dawn have gone after you left?"

"She asked if she could play in the forest before joining me in the vineyards."

Anton's heart thudded. "The forest?" Images of a frightened child flashed through his mind.

"She knows the forest so well. When Melody returned alone, everyone said to wait—that it was a warm night and Dawn had probably just fallen asleep somewhere in the forest. I could picture it in my mind, my little girl curled up next to a log on a bed of leaves." She roughly wiped a tear from her cheek and took a deep breath.

Janine's voice receded into the background as Anton began to make plans. Clearly, searching the forest was a priority. In the space of a minute, he considered how many people would be needed, what equipment would be useful, even whether dogs would be a helpful addition to the search party. And in that same minute, he became discouraged as he realized night would fall long before he could arrange for any of that.

Janine's voice broke through his thoughts. "The next morning Pat arranged a thorough search, but no one found her."

At least they looked for the child. But he would not rely on that alone; even if people from the community had already looked for Dawn, he intended to conduct his own search for any trace the child might have left behind—whether in the forest or elsewhere. "Why didn't you go to the police as soon as you knew she wasn't in the forest?"

"My fault, everything's my fault. Pat told me that she was probably with AJ and just fine, that I'd make things very bad for him, for everyone, if I went to the police." She stopped and sucked in a lungful of air.

Anton was trying tried to be patient. He looked at her steadily to let her know more was expected.

"AJ left just after sunrise on Tuesday morning. He should have come back Wednesday." She looked at Anton with dazed eyes. "I waited up all night, but he didn't come home either."

Anton clung to the hope that Dawn was with her father. "Had that happened before—AJ not returning home when he was expected?"

She seemed to think his question through carefully before answering, "Sometimes. He goes away on community business—to buy or sell—and he can't always predict when he'll be back."

"I understand that you and your husband are planning to separate."

"Yes."

"And that there's some disagreement about which parent your daughters should live with."

"Yes."

"But you didn't consider the possibility that AJ had taken Dawn until Mr. Millikan brought it up?"

"No." Anton pointedly waited and after a long stretch of silence, she said, "AJ accepted that everything would have to be done legally. He wouldn't want to take them off the island anyway." A thought occurred to her, and she tightened her lips.

Again, Anton wished that Catarina was with him. *Was Janine angry? Afraid? Was her concern an act?* He explored another possibility for Dawn's whereabouts. "I believe your parents are helping you to get custody of your daughters."

She showed no surprise that he knew that. "Yes, they're in the Azores now. I thought they might bring me more papers to sign on Tuesday, since they knew it was AJ's day to go into Angra."

He chose his next words carefully. "Is it possible they took Dawn on an outing, and there's just been some breakdown in communication about that?"

Her response was immediate and firm. "No, not them."

"What was your daughter wearing when you last saw her?" he asked, turning his attention to information he would need for his next steps in a search for Dawn.

Her face grew still as she thought back to that day. "Each of the girls has two outfits, and I saw her skirt this morning. So she was wearing her gray pants and brown shirt."

The first thing that came to Anton's mind was that those were drab clothes for a child, followed by the realization that what the community members wore might be dictated by what they could make themselves. "Do you have a recent picture of her that I could use?" The one Lori had printed was not the best.

She shook her head sadly.

"I promise to keep it safe and return it," Anton tried to reassure her.

She wrapped her arms around her middle as though she was cold and glanced back at Millikan. "I don't have anything here, but I could get you something recent."

"The picture that was filed with the custody papers?"

She reddened and gave one quick nod. She turned her back to where Millikan stood with Norberto, lowered her head, and muttered, "My parents would have that one."

"What about her passport?"

"I forgot about those. Pat takes care of them for us. But they won't do any good. She was just a baby then. Just a baby."

Anton had picked up on the tension between Janine and Millikan from the moment he first saw them together; yet she seemed to be reluctant to show any negative feelings towards him. He was *taking care of* the passports for them. It was *her fault* that she had accepted what Millikan said about Dawn's whereabouts.

"Are you comfortable staying here?" he asked, looking over her shoulder to where Millikan hovered.

"I want to stay," she said firmly. She wiped her cheek on a sleeve, and slowly dragged herself back in the direction she had come. When she bypassed Millikan, he started to follow her back into the forest. She saw him and picked up her pace. Anton signaled Norberto, who nodded, caught up with Millikan, and rerouted him to where Anton was waiting with two demands.

Millikan attempted to start a casual, friendly conversation in Portuguese.

Anton returned his greeting politely but no more, before saying slowly and clearly in English. "I want the Bennetts' passports."

His smile froze in place, although whether it was because Anton's command of English surprised him or because handing over the passports bothered him was uncertain. "You'll have to ask AJ; I'm just keeping the passports safe."

"I want the Bennetts' passports," he repeated, his voice hard and flat.

He thought through his options. "I'll go at once and get them for you."

"I'll come with you. I want to see the area where the Bennetts live."

Anton could tell that he was about to meet with resistance. Just then, he heard the slamming of a car door and Rocha's voice angrily calling his name. *I don't need this now. I need to see the Comunidade.* Before Rocha could get within earshot of Millikan, Anton ran—as well as he was able to run—to him. "Thank goodness you're here, Victor. I do need your help."

The Chief's face softened a bit. "What can I help you with?"

"I know proper procedure is to search the home area when a child is missing, but I think Pat Millikan, the leader of the group, may refuse. Perhaps a word from the *Chief of Police*," he said, giving emphasis to the title, "would help." In one sentence, he had disarmed Rocha and brought him in as an ally. Anton Cardosa knew how to deal with people.

The next few minutes showed just how inept Rocha could be. Rather than simply making it clear that the police had every right to enter the Comunidade dos Reis and then leading the way in, he spent his time with Millikan expressing his own bias against the community, bringing up unpleasant incidences from the past and grievances neighbors held against its members. Millikan tread lightly, laughing off some of what Rocha said and ignoring the rest altogether, but even without Catarina, Anton knew he was nervous from the sheen on his upper lip.

They came out of the dense forest at its western edge, where it opened suddenly onto a bright green meadow, once a mountain lake that over millennia had filled with rich volcanic soil. From Lori's research, Anton knew Comunidade dos Reis was a triangle roughly a mile long on each side. He could see two of those sides in the distance where the land rose sharply, making the property very difficult to access any way but through the forest. Directly ahead of them, fields were under cultivation and a few cows grazed. To the left, the property was not unlike Casa do Mar, consisting of a large barn and several outbuildings, but while his own home was slowly being modernized with electricity and plumbing, there had been no updates that he could see here. To the right, where Millikan led them, ten houses were grouped around a small patch of ground that had been cleared and leveled as a communal area, with a large fire pit and oven at its center. Wheelbarrows filled with newly dug potatoes and a cart loaded with milk cans stood in the middle of a narrow path that led to the fields and the outbuildings. It looked exactly like what it had once been: a hamlet of farmers and dairymen.

The cottages were built of stone, almost certainly the stones that had been cleared from the surrounding field three centuries before. About half looked to be only one or two rooms; the rest were larger, having small additions, such as lean-tos, that were more recent. They were simple and showed their age, with faded whitewash and patched roofs. Using every bit of available land between and in front of the homes, most had compact gardens with tidy rows of herbs, kale, onions, and carrots. At this, Anton smiled. It was a fast-disappearing sight that had been common when he was a boy. As he walked up to the first cottage, he saw a thin layer of soot covering all the surfaces, unusual on isolated islands where there wasn't much by way of industry or vehicles, and he realized it had come from the burning of fires and lanterns in an area that didn't use electricity. He knocked on the door.

"Go right in," Millikan said in English. "There's no one home."

"Where are the residents?" He realized the area was unnaturally quiet, and he could see only Janine, who stood stiffly near one of the larger houses, and a red-haired child he recognized as Melody, sitting on a tree stump nearby, pulling petals off daisies one by one.

He waved an arm, sweeping a broad area to the south. "Working somewhere out there."

Was that a triumphant look on his face? "We'll search the area now, and Chief Rocha will be sending officers to bring people to the station to be interviewed."

Rocha stood back, doing something on his phone, while Millikan led them from house to house. Anton and Norberto looked into each of the houses and around the gardens, but all were deserted.

"I think that's the last one," Millikan said. "Goodbye." And he turned away.

"The passports first," Anton said firmly.

Millikan looked at Janine, who didn't make eye contact, and quickly walked to his own house, glancing back twice, before hurriedly returning with four passports clutched in his hand. He handed them to Rocha—not Anton—with tight lips. "Take your time. Would you like some tea while you check them?"

"No, thank you," said Anton. "We'll be holding onto them." Walking away, he considered Millikan. On the face of things, he had been accommodating with requests, concerned with Janine's wellbeing, and welcoming with offers to show them around the hamlet. He had even done what Anton himself could not and taken Rocha's disagreeable complaints in stride. Why then, did he find himself suspicious of the leader of Comunidade dos Reis? Had he—as most people do—colored his perceptions with prejudices he wasn't aware of?

Before leaving, Anton went to say goodbye to Janine—and to ask one more question that had occurred to him. "Who is Bobey?"

"Bobey!" Janine's face brightened. "I forgot about Bobey. He's her stuffed elephant. I made him for her from an old red jacket when she was two. She carries him around wherever she goes."

"So she would have had Bobey with her on Tuesday, when she went into the forest?"

"I think so. Melody's been saying that Dawn needs Bobey." Anton nodded slowly as he took in the information. It jibed with what Norberto had reported about his talk with her at the police station.

Suddenly her face contorted, and tears streaked her cheeks, "She has to have Bobey. He's her protector."

"I know this is a difficult time for you. Do you have someone to rely on?"

For a moment, she looked puzzled. "Yes, of course. I can rely on everyone in the community."

She had only just opened the door to her house when she whirled around and ran back to Anton. Her voice may have been quiet and steady, but it was a plea. "Please find my child."

Most people have had the experience of processing so many thoughts in the space of a few seconds that looking back, it didn't seem realistically possible. That happened to Anton. He opened his mouth and his mind considered many questions. What were the chances that Dawn was still on Terceira and alive? Could he find her? Would he find her? Was it best to promise only what he knew he would deliver: his best effort? Or was it better to give a mother some hope and say with conviction that he would return her child alive and well? Was she aware of his hesitation? "I will find Dawn," he said, holding her close.

She nodded as though she believed him.

On the way back to the cars, Rocha interrupted his train of thought. "The father must have taken her," he pronounced.

Anton assumed nothing. "We'll search for Dawn tomorrow."

"They seem to have done a thorough job of it themselves."

He could tell the Chief was about to make things more difficult than they already were. "I'll need five officers."

"Only six are on daytime duty tomorrow, and I can only spare two of those."

He had done his own research, and he knew exactly how many there were altogether: eleven. If the Chief had to call in off-duty officers, so be it. "I need five. It shouldn't take long." He refrained from claiming his full authority in front of Norberto, who waited by the open car door. "They should be here at nine tomorrow morning."

"I'll see what I can do for you." Rocha turned his back and headed for his car.

"The Presidente and I appreciate it," he called after him. *This is going to be a struggle.*

Anton needed help. Before bed, he made two calls. The first was to Felipe Madruga, recently promoted to police chief on Santa Maria after more than thirty years of service during which the modest man's talents and efforts had gone largely unrecognized. The responsibility Felipe felt for the people of his island was more than the center of his life; it was virtually his entire life. Off duty, he was a lonely man, who spent his free time fishing or watching television with his beloved dog. With Felipe as his right-hand man, Anton knew he could confidently search for Dawn on two fronts.

The second call he made was to his wife. Dealing with an unfamiliar cast of characters on Terceira, he needed her gift for finding the truth in what others said. Unlike most people, who hear only a fraction of what others say, Catarina listened to everything and with all of herself, hearing the intonation, seeing a wrinkle that formed between the eyebrows or a slight downturn at the corners of the mouth, picking up on strain in the voice or pride. Her interest didn't lie in challenging what was being said or planning responses to put forward her own opinions; her interest was in listening. That was why so many went to her with secrets, and why some didn't want to talk to her at all. She could be aware of their innermost thoughts even when they were not. Along with Lori's ability make use of trivial facts to reveal a wealth of information, and Anton's own canniness in using those facts to form novel—and usually correct—conclusions, the three made a formidable team.

Reassured of the help he would need, Anton lay on his bed, and his mind imagined that Dawn was fine. She had found an unoccupied cottage and was enjoying all the food and toys inside; she was with a kind elderly couple who were planning to take her into town next market day; she had fallen asleep in a boat just before it left the harbor and was being treated like a princess by the crew, who were only waiting to make land before returning her. He knew, of course, those were fantasies, not just unlikely but unreal. After four days, the little girl with her cloud of platinum curls and her rosebud mouth was either dead or was with someone who had taken her for reasons no part of him wanted to imagine.

3

Anton began his day at Lajes Airfield. Strategically located to cut transatlantic travel time in half, it had served as a base for air operations during World War II and had been Portugal's major contribution to the newly-formed NATO alliance. Now, in addition to housing an American Air Force detachment, it served large commercial airlines and small island hoppers like Carlos' Cessna.

Anton waited on the tarmac, so close to the approaching plane that Norberto felt the need to pull him back by his jacket. Carlos opened the door and gave Catarina his hand as she stepped off. Seeing the stress on her husband's face, she gently cupped his cheek with her palm. He drew her head to his chest and held her close for a few moments. Words were not necessary.

Catarina was followed by Felipe, who looked both somber and proud to have been chosen for such an important assignment. His loyalty to Anton—the first person to have ever recognized his talents—was absolute, and he was ready to do whatever was needed.

Norberto escorted them to the car that Gabriela had claimed in Anton's name for the remainder of his stay on Terceira. On the way to the police station, Catarina guided the conversation to mundane talk of home, hoping to distract her husband from his worries. "The children were happy to see me go. They have such a good time when they're in Maria Rosa's care." Maria Rosa was their nearest neighbor, just across the narrow road that separated their two properties. She was also a nurse who filled many medical roles on Santa Maria, giving an added measure of reassurance when Liliana and Toni were with her.

"Do we have any more reservations?" he asked.

"Not yet," she gave him a playful swat on his arm. "It's been less than two days, Anton." Clearly, he was still focusing on problems. She changed to a subject she knew would interest him. "A package arrived from Ethan. He's still in Switzerland." They had met Anton's nephew, the son of an older sister who had immigrated to America, for the first time just a few months earlier, and his attraction to Lori had been clear.

"What did he send us? Chocolates?" he asked hopefully.

"No, not chocolates. And not for us, for Lori."

He showed his signature ear to ear grin for the first time since hearing of Dawn Bennett's disappearance. He had put finding Lori a good husband high on his list of priorities, and whether it was his countryman, Carlos, or his relative from America, Ethan Monise, made no difference. Marriage had made him grateful every day of his life, and he wanted the same for her.

He settled back in his seat. "Thanks for coming, Felipe."

When the Chief replied, "My pleasure, sir," he spoke with absolute truth. "We'll find the child, sir."

"How's Luis doing?" Anton asked about the young officer who had helped him on Faial recently and who he had been happy to recommend for a position on the Santa Maria police force.

"Working out well, sir. Estela is renting him a room in her house."

Anton would have characterized Norberto as a confident, efficient driver—not unlike himself. Catarina, on the other hand, would have said he was a daredevil—again, not unlike her husband. They arrived at the police station in half the time it would have taken almost anyone else. Gabriela met them by the side door with necessary supplies: police tape, scissors, markers, shovels, cameras, plastic evidence bags, even bottles of water. She had thought of everything. While Norberto, Felipe, and Anton loaded them into the car, Catarina introduced herself. "My husband isn't known for his patience," she laughed. "Having all this ready and waiting is going to make it easier for all of us today."

Gabriela smiled but with enough reservation that Catarina knew there was bad news to follow. "Chief Rocha left this for you, sir." She handed over a formal memorandum that stated only Norberto could be spared for the day's search of the forest, citing *other duties and the short notice given by Minister Cardosa.*

Anton heard the thrumming in his ears.

Catarina took a long, deep, and quite audible breath, intended to model what he should do himself. "It's simply the way Victor is. You expect people to change for the better over time, but that rarely happens. People are a certain way. Generally, what you saw in them once, you will find again." Anton had been a mischievous young man with a kind soul who had become a reliable older man with the same kind soul. He had also been the most even-tempered sort…until he was pushed too far. He set his jaw and started up the front steps to Rocha's office.

"Sir! He's not there. He left word that he would be out of the office for the next three hours."

He took the breath he knew his wife wanted him to. "Did he leave word about how he is to be reached?" he asked as calmly as he could.

"No—"

"No?"

Gabriela jumped in, "No *but*…but if you are interested, I called someone who is on leave and two part-time rookie officers to ask if they would be willing to extend their hours this week, and without disrupting Chief Rocha's plans—"

His bear hug stopped her. "Yes! That's perfect."

Catarina protected Gabriela's role in the subterfuge. "We must not forget that Anton ordered you to do this."

"That is correct." He looked at Norberto and Felipe. "I'm sure you all heard me. I gave her no choice."

"One more thing, sir." She reached into her pocket. "The Chief asked me to lock these in the safe." She handed him the Bennetts' passports that Millikan had turned over to Rocha the day before.

He winked. "I'm glad to see you're following orders, senhora Viveiros."

As the car sped towards Comunidade dos Reis at a speed that concerned Catarina but reassured Anton, he looked at the passports. The first one he opened had been issued nine years ago to Alexander Jeremy Bennett, an American born in Philadelphia thirty-two years ago. At a height of five feet nine inches and a weight of only one hundred and sixty pounds, he wasn't a large man. The picture showed an oval jaw, large green eyes, and a full mouth. Behind his ears and tucked in his blond hair there were decorative feathers of the sort that might be found in a crafts store, giving the impression of someone playful, or perhaps even intellectually challenged. According to the information Lori had found, he had travelled widely since getting the passport, and certainly the pages and pages of immigration stamps from Germany, Nigeria, Estonia, Costa Rica, and other countries substantiated that.

Janine Maier's passport and those of her two children were issued by the United States five and a half years ago. The rest of the family wore the same feathers as in his picture, tiny pink ones decorating the flaxen curls of a four-month-old Dawn. Janine's birthplace was given as Dresden and given her accent, Anton assumed she had been raised in Germany. In her picture she looked even younger than her twenty-four years, with pinkish-red hair, shaved eyebrows, tattoos, and several earrings studding her ears. Wearing a low-cut peasant blouse, she looked like a version of one of the flower children from 1960s San Francisco that he had read about. It was the emergency contact that Anton found most interesting. Unlike her husband, who had listed his mother, she had entered not a person but a location: Comunidade dos Reis na Floresta.

They were at the forest an hour before the search party was expected. Anton studied a satellite map Lori had found, a sharp image that seemed to have been taken sometime in winter, revealing details that he wouldn't have believed possible. The forest itself was a ring of trees bisected by a stream running east to west before petering out in a marshy area at the foot of a hill. In a valley at its center was a level clearing, where Comunidade dos Reis could be seen, its houses clustered close to the forest, and its fields and vineyards making a patchwork of the remaining space. The road banded one arc of the forest, and across from the forest Anton could see four farmhouses on a hill. He decided to send two of the searchers there. *Maybe we'll be lucky. Maybe.*

He walked the length of the forest that ran along the road, and with help from Felipe, he marked it off into four segments with the wide plastic tape that Gabriela had given them. His plan was to assign one police officer to search each segment from the road to the clearing, while he and Felipe crisscrossed the area to offer support.

The three officers who Gabriela had recruited arrived in a small Fiat and were given directions to both search for Dawn Bennett and to be alert to anything that seemed out of the ordinary. The first piece of evidence was found almost immediately by one of the rookie officers. The instant she shouted *Sir*, Anton had everyone stand in position, and he ran to her side, Catarina following with the evidence bags. The petite brunette was bent low over a scrap of red wool, dry leaves swirling around it in a breeze. Stopping a couple of feet from it, he looked down. "Very good, Officer Rosa. It might be from someone's clothing."

"No, sir," she said, straightening up.

"Please explain."

"It's not from anyone's clothes. It's the ear of a cloth animal, an elephant, I think."

Bobey.

Anton picked it up tenderly and dropped it into the evidence bag that Catarina held open. He put the bag in his shirt pocket, where he felt it, warm and soft, for the rest of the day, a connection to Dawn and a promise that he would find her.

The search resumed, and it went slowly. There were so many places where a child could hide—or be hidden—between small knolls of earth, in piles of freshly fallen leaves, under bushes. It was afternoon when Anton first heard, then saw, people approaching from the direction of Comunidade dos Reis. He picked out Janine in front, followed by Millikan, who was scampering as quickly as his legs could carry him. Several yards in back of them, five or six others walked, from time to time exchanging a few words and looking at each other anxiously.

Anton met the group halfway and spoke to Janine first. "You can't be here." He was thinking of her wellbeing more than any interference from her. He didn't want her there if the worst was confirmed.

"You're looking for Dawn today."

"Yes, and since we're conducting a search, it's best for you to stay back, preferably outside the forest."

"I think Mrs. Bennett told you we searched the forest." Millikan had caught up with them.

"She did. This, however, is a police investigation, and we conduct our own searches." Anton extended his long arms and started to corral the group. "I want everyone to return to the community," for emphasis, he firmly added, "now."

They left slowly but were still in sight when the same officer who had found Bobey's ear called out again *Sir*, this time with a catch in her voice. "Over here," she said weakly.

Anton told everyone to stand in place. Before he saw Rosa's chest pumping hard, before he saw what she had seen, he knew it wouldn't be good. Close to a tree trunk, in a space between two knobby roots that was filled with wind-blown leaves, he could see the cuff of a knit cap and the top of a human ear in a nest of blood-spattered blond curls.

The qualities that came to mind first when people thought of Anton—the fun-loving friend ready to share a bottle or two of good wine, the exuberant community champion, the soccer coach who led the cheering, the tender husband and father—were not always the ones they prized most. For Anton was a born leader and when a crisis arose, there was no one more valued. Those qualities of leadership became evident in the forest. He had a word with Officer Gracia, "Escort everyone out of the forest, and keep them out until I say otherwise. Senhora Vanderhye will accompany you." He sent Norberto to call Gabriela so a medical examiner could be sent and to inform Chief Rocha of the death—in that order. Officer Silva was tasked with removing the plastic tape that marked off search zones and using it to cordon off the area around the body. Officer Rosa and Felipe were asked to continue looking through the parts of the forest that had not been searched. Anton returned to the leaf-filled hollow but breezes had already covered the blond curls with more freshly fallen leaves. Maybe we imagined it, he thought desperately.

It took an hour before a black pickup truck brought the medical examiner, and the word *patient* did not describe Anton. Guillerme Nunes was a young man, tall and thin, with a long face and bulging eyes behind thick glasses. Though courteous, he wasn't much of a conversationalist and seemed to be emotionally uninvolved as he worked. He asked Norberto to bag evidence, Officer Silva to hold his voice recorder close to him as he spoke, and Officer Rosa to take pictures. Rather than feeling left out, Anton was glad to be able to concentrate on the scene and watch a competent man at work. Nunes meticulously examined and photographed the site before removing leaves from around the blond curls with his own gloved hand and setting them aside.

Anton would not wish death on anyone, but at that moment he shuddered with relief that the body didn't belong to a child but to a grown man. He remembered the shape of the head and the curve of the hairline from AJ Bennett's passport picture.

"Approximately twelve centimeters of forest floor debris was removed and bagged in…" Nunes spoke into the recorder that Silva held, "…Bag One." Norberto nodded, labeled a bag with a permanent marker, and held it open. The medical examiner proceeded methodically, removing everything that had covered AJ's body and directing Rosa to take pictures of the surface before he attempted to move him. Together with Norberto, he lifted the body out and laid it on a plastic sheet. "Livor mortis continues pronounced on the dorsal side," he said, pulling up the shirt and peeking underneath.

Anton broke in, "When did he die?"

Nunes was not happy to be interrupted. "I don't know yet," he said shortly. Regretting how he had snapped, he added, "But the man almost certainly fell against this tree and slid to the ground as his legs collapsed under him." AJ's torso had been sliced opened vertically from groin to sternum. The wound was puckered and shiny along its edges, and as the body lay there it slowly separated to reveal greenish body parts—the names of which Anton didn't know—bloated, pitted, and swarming with maggots. No one spoke. Rosa finally broke the silence with repeated digital clicks of the camera.

Anton opened his mouth, but Nunes held up a hand to cut him off. "I have nothing to tell you. You'll have as full a report as possible in twenty-four hours."

Anton appealed to him. "I know you can't say anything with certainty, but a six-year-old child is missing and your best guesses might save her life."

Nunes boney face softened a bit. "What is it you want to know," he said with a sigh.

The most important issue was whether AJ had died before or after his daughter was in the forest. "How long do you think he's been dead?"

"Four days." There were no qualifiers. No *perhaps.* No *approximately.* No *I can't say yet.* So, in all likelihood Dawn had gone missing about the same time her father had been killed. *Had he died trying to protect her?*

With the open wound that split his abdomen from navel to throat, Anton was fairly certain he knew the answer, but he asked anyway. "What killed him?

The doctor looked over the top of his glasses with raised eyebrows, as if to say *Isn't it obvious?* "Loss of blood."

Anton patiently asked, "Do you have any more details at this point?"

"Someone severed several large arteries with a knife, and he exsanguinated.

"Was he taken by surprise?"

"Likely. His clothes are orderly. No defensive wounds or bruises that I can see now. He hadn't been running away. It seems—" he held up a forefinger and repeated for emphasis, "— *seems* that he was facing his attacker when a thin sharp object...I will say a knife...was very quickly thrust in and up."

Twigs snapping underfoot announced the arrival of Rocha. He stopped short of where everyone stood, whether because he was averse to being close to the horrific sight or for another reason, Anton didn't know, but as soon as AJ's body was zipped into the body bag, he angrily approached. "Cardosa! We need to talk."

"We do," Anton said, "after I have finished my business here." Rocha screwed up his face but said nothing more.

"Do you have a name to propose for the victim?" Nunes addressed Anton.

"It's AJ Bennett," Anton informed him.

"We'll need a formal identification, preferably tomorrow."

"I'll arrange that."

"Next of kin?" asked Nunes.

"His wife, Janine Maier Bennett, lives in the community on the other side of the forest, but I'd like to spare her that. Her parents or someone else might be able to make the identification."

"You'll have my initial report by the end of the day tomorrow," Nunes said crisply. He took the camera from Rosa, told Felipe and Norberto to carry the body, and led the way to his waiting truck.

Anton turned to Rocha. "You wanted to say something?"

The Chief's second pronouncement of guilt in two days differed from his first by just a single word. "The wife must have done it." He was about to say more but first he dismissed Rosa and Silva. "You may return to the station. I'll be talking to both of you, too."

Anton's sincerity was obvious when he spoke. "Before you leave, I want to thank you for everything you've done today under difficult circumstances. I'll see you tomorrow."

"We have a problem here, Cardosa," Rocha said with a hint of condescension, "You've been going around making assumptions about who is responsible for police operations on Terceira. You circumvented my authority today when you decided you could use my officers for your own purposes. You need to understand that I have reasons for doing things a certain way."

Anton gave him a knowing smile. "Oh, I understand. I understand exactly why you do things a certain way. Now, I hope you understand: I will either receive your full cooperation willingly, or I will turn matters over to the Head of the Judicial Police." Apprehension flickered on Rocha's face, but Anton had no time for further discussion. He couldn't keep Janine in agony, wondering if they had found her child's body, and he needed to think through what he was going to say to the people of Comunidade dos Reis.

Sitting beside Melody in the Bennetts' home, Catarina watched the child as she sketched the petal of a flower in great detail. She had stopped asking Melody about what she was drawing—or about anything. The child had not answered a single question or, in fact, uttered a single word since they'd walked out of the forest together.

Janine had been looking out the window for half an hour when she turned around, deathly pale. "They're here."

Her voice had been so soft, Catarina didn't hear what she said, but the look on her face had her at Janine's side within seconds. "Let me bring Anton in to you."

Anton had remembered which house belonged to the Bennetts and was knocking on the door before his wife had a chance to open it. He looked at her first, his eyes asking how he should tell a woman that the *good* news was that the husband she clearly cared for was dead. He quietly closed the door behind him.

Janine's whimper grew to a wail and she collapsed on the floor.

"No. No," Anton said, rushing to her. "It's not Dawn."

She froze, hiccupped, and looked at him.

"It's not Dawn, but...it's—"

"AJ. My poor AJ."

Catarina and Anton picked her up and led her to the bed in the corner of the room. She buried her head in a pillow and sniffed it. "AJ," she sobbed, tears running down her cheeks.

Melody came over, seemingly oblivious to her mother's pain. "I'm hungry," she said.

Catarina knew she wouldn't be able to see everyone's faces at once when Anton announced AJ's death to the community, so she decided to concentrate on Pat Millikan. Usually, she got some sense of a person soon after meeting but in his case, she had conflicting impressions. So far, he had seemed honest yet guarded. Perhaps how he reacted to the news of AJ's death would give her a better indication of what type of man he was. It didn't. The leader's immediate response was not surprise or grief but an anger he worked hard not to show. As Anton's words were absorbed by the rest of the community, she saw disbelief followed by regret spread through the group, and she saw particular distress on the face of the short middle-aged woman who stood at Millikan's side.

Inexorably sinking, the sun had fought Anton all afternoon, now taking away the time he needed to talk to people before night stranded his team in Comunidade dos Reis na Floresta. Before leaving the forest, Anton took one last look at the peaceful scene and wondered how a violent death could have come to such a place. Then he remembered something Catarina had said more than once: people are people everywhere, so along with good, evil can be found everywhere.

Lajes Airfield had been busier than usual that day, serving as the base of operations for both a humanitarian mission to bring food to stranded Kurds and a military mission to separate warring factions on the Turkish border. Carlos and his plane had waited on the tarmac until the activity subsided, so his third passenger was less likely to be noticed. In certain situations, Lori's looks were a drawback. She may have been able to hide her blond hair under a hat and her pale green eyes behind sunglasses, but she was a statuesque woman, and she attracted attention. When they finally deplaned, she walked through the terminal wearing a hooded poncho and blended in with passengers who had just arrived from Boston on a large commercial jet. They quickly made their way to a scooter that Carlos had borrowed from a friend and headed into the hills, Lori riding behind him, her arms wrapped around his waist.

His friend had recommended an out of the way restaurant so small that no more than ten people could be served at a time and so hidden that they saw no one other than the owner-chef-waiter for the next two hours. From a bougainvillea-fringed terrace, they looked out over idyllic mist-softened landscapes and seascapes, and Lori told Carlos tales of life in Manhattan, while he entertained her with what he knew about Terceira.

At the end of their leisurely meal, they ordered espressos, put in irregularly shaped lumps of sugar, stirred slowly, and sipped. Almost to herself, she said, "I can hardly believe how much a part of my life the Azores have become in such a short time." She thought of the six miserable months between her first visit to the islands and her second, time during which she'd tried to convince herself that turning her back on a fabulous life and career in Manhattan would be absurd…until she accepted that she was simply happier in the Azores. She enjoyed quiet more than bustle, the blues of the ocean and sky more than the grays of the skyscrapers and granite, home-cooked meals more than power lunches, traditional crafts more than the latest conveniences. And above all, she loved being part of Anton and Catarina's family.

Carlos interrupted her reflections, "I'd like to show you each one of our islands."

She smiled at him. "You've made a good start. You've already flown me to four of them."

"I know. I know every island I've been to with you, and the date I was there, and what you were wearing." Her hair caught the light and glittered, and he couldn't stop himself from running his fingers through it. He'd been mesmerized by Lori from the first moment he had seen her, and had been known to lose his train of thought and even drop what he was holding when he saw her. To him, she lived up to the nickname New York colleagues had given her in jest: Norse Goddess.

"Do you know why this is called *Ilha Lilas*, the Lilac Island?" he asked.

"I would imagine for the same reason Faial is called the Blue Island: blue hydrangeas everywhere."

"Most say it's nicknamed for the exquisite pastel sunsets. I'd like to see a lilac sunset with you." He took her hand. "I'd like to do so much with you."

Lori knew where Carlos was taking their conversation, and she both looked forward to it and dreaded it. He had been open about his feelings for her, as their relationship progressed from casual family dinners at Casa do Mar to walks along the shore to romantic evenings flying over the archipelago in his plane. It wasn't as if what he wanted to say would come as a surprise. She had even given some thought to what her life would be like if she shared it with him. Her problem was that she didn't know what she wanted her life to be yet—with or without him in it. What she did know was how she felt when she was with him: flattered, cared for, relaxed, happy—and pretty darn passionate. She could only say, "I want to do so much with you, Carlos, and I want to talk about all that with you...but it can't be here and now." She kissed him lightly on the lips. "If our plan is to work, we have to leave now."

She said goodbye to him on the outskirts of Santa Clara only a few minutes after Anton and Catarina left Comunidade dos Reis to return to Angra. She waited until the rumble of his scooter faded away and set out slowly. Timing would be important. She needed to arrive late enough.

With dusk approaching, she stood at the forest's edge. She could see recent tire tracks by the side of the road and footprints going up a bank and into a dense forest, and she followed them back in time, leaving behind first the sounds of human activity and then all sight of civilization. Leaf-filtered sunlight dappled the forest with pale gold, and she could make out old paths overgrown with vines, a small shed that had rotted and collapsed on itself, and tangles of fallen branches.

The change came on suddenly; the light reddened and dimmed, the birds stopped singing, and the air cooled. Lori's worry became not that she would arrive too early but that she would still be in the forest after dark. She shifted her backpack to her other shoulder and kept moving westward towards the low sun, towards Comunidade dos Reis.

Just after she decided she must have taken a wrong turn and was about to turn back, she smelled woodsmoke and the forest opened up to a broad, flat valley. Plumes of smoke spiraled up to a lavender sky from a dozen chimneys and quivery gold windows gave just enough light to see the dark stone houses. She stopped in front of the first one, an amalgam of three smaller structures really, in front of which young children were using sticks to roll pebbles over lines scratched on the ground. She had to decide who to approach, and seeing a plump middle-aged woman look at her and hurry away, she knew she had to do so quickly. The larger the number of people who heard what she had to say, the better. But most people were clustered in twos or threes, crying or comforting one another. She chose to approach two younger women who, although distressed, were still dry-eyed and composed. By that time, the woman who had rushed away was climbing the steps of a nicely tended cottage with lanterns hanging from its porch.

"I'm Lori Moore. Have I found Comunidade dos Reis?"

The woman wearing a long, loose-fitting dark dress and head covering said in Portuguese, "You have found Comunidade dos Reis." If her heavy accent hadn't let Lori know that the woman was not from the islands, her name did. "I am Amal Hukan, and this is Kate Schultz. You are welcome here." The speaker was less than five feet tall and probably weighed ninety pounds. Lori judged her to be somewhere in her twenties, although her olive skin was crinkled like that of a much older woman. Two of her front teeth were broken, and the arm she extended in welcome was patched with the shiny, white scars of burned flesh that would never heal.

"Thank you, Amal," said Lori, glancing sideways at the short man who had been tipped off to her presence and was coming her way from the lantern-lit house.

"You speak Portuguese well," Kate said. She, too, was petite and in her twenties, but her doe eyes, upturned mouth, and high forehead gave her a pixieish appearance rather than Amal's victimized one.

Although she had a noticeable American accent, Lori did speak Portuguese quite well, much of that credit going to total immersion in the Cardosa-Vanderhye family. From her research she knew that it was the language of choice in Comunidade dos Reis, and she had a story ready. "I lived here as a child, when my father was with the military at Lajes Airfield." She wanted to be heard saying one thing before the man reached her. "I've come such a long way to join you. Wallace Jenkins told me how welcoming you would be." She made sure to raise her voice a bit at the end to be heard by others who had started to gather around her.

A squat man with longish black hair and small black eyes faced her. "Can I help you?" he asked with more than a hint of suspicion.

Lori extended her hand and introduced herself. "I'm Lori Moore. I'm expected. Are you senhor Jenkins?" She knew he wasn't.

"Jenkins? No. He isn't here…isn't with the community anymore."

A few people had surrounded her and were exchanging discreet looks.

"Oh." She made her best attempt at looking disappointed. "Could I talk with whoever replaced him?"

"That would be me. Pat Millikan. We're a private community, senhora Moore, and this is not at all a good time to talk."

"Oh, I do know about being a private community. Senhor Jenkins explained everything when he invited me to join you." She looked around at others and repeated, "He told me more than once how welcoming you would all be."

"As I said, this is not a good time to talk. There's been a death in our community."

Lori gasped. *I'm too late. The child is dead.*

"Yes," explained Kate with a lowered voice, "It was so unexpected. We all thought he was just away on community business."

He? Who?

Millikan addressed the people who had gathered more than Lori, "AJ Bennett represented the best of Comunidade dos Reis. He was generous and committed to our beliefs."

AJ? Dawn's father? Lori's head was spinning. Was there a connection between AJ's death and Dawn's disappearance? Was she even still missing? Around her, people were remembering AJ with kind thoughts and consoling one another.

"So, you'll understand, Miss Moore," Millikan said, "we're not in the position to—"

Lori knew what he was about to say, and she did the only thing she could think of: she gave a good old-fashioned swoon right into the arms of the strongest man she could see. After a minute of staying limp and keeping her eyes closed, she murmured feebly, "I've come so far. Where will I go?" Listening to herself, she almost laughed. She made eye contact with several of the people standing over her.

Millikan relented. "Perhaps you should come with me, Lori, and we can talk." As they walked to his cottage, he offered to carry her backpack and asked if she would like something to drink. "It isn't easy to get to Comunidade dos Reis. You must be tired."

"I am," she sighed. The light was now gone, and she allowed herself the thought that her timing had been good after all. A lot of people knew she would be stranded in the forest after dark if she weren't invited to stay.

Beautifully carved on a piece of wood above the open door to Millikan's house was the aphorism *Those who have should help those who have not.* He stepped aside at the open door to his house so she could enter first and then closed the door softly behind them. It was a comfortable enough space, with upholstered armchairs on either side of a fireplace, heavy drapes covering the windows, a large braided rug, and shelving built against one wall for dishes, glasses, and bottles of wine.

"Please, sit," he spoke in English. He turned around one of the chairs for her and poked at the fire for warmth.

He was several inches shorter than she, and she wanted to appear easily managed, so she promptly sat. She waited for him to assert his position as leader of the community, which he did over the course of the next half hour, giving her the impression of someone who truly cared for the people of the community and was fiercely looking out for their common interests. He asked questions about her trip that could have been merely social or could have been a way to check on her story. Then he said, "So, Lori, tell me a bit about yourself," words that would allow him to observe—and judge—her intentions. It was a technique she had used on many occasions herself.

She was prepared. "I heard about you about a year ago, through Ann Peterson," she named someone who had left the community before Millikan's arrival and whose blog about life there had been positive and detailed. "We became friendly after finding out that we had both lived in and loved Terceira."

Millikan raised his eyebrows, questioning that.

"I lived here as a child," she explained, "when my father was with the military." She was careful not to give out too many details that might be checked. "When things got difficult for me…" She let her voice trail off and hung her head, waiting for him to speak.

After a long minute of silence, he asked, "How were they difficult?"

Feigning reluctance, she continued, keeping her story as close to the truth as possible. "I made a dreadful mistake at work a while ago and destroyed my career. I couldn't find the work I need." Here, Lori sweetened her story with something that might appeal to him. "It isn't that I need the work to pay bills—I've made enough to carry me through life in style—it's that I couldn't find the type of work I need to feel good about myself."

He didn't address her remarks. "I have to be very careful about who enters our community…now more than ever."

Only her eyes and a slight tilt of her head showed any curiosity about why it was more important now than before, and she didn't ask him to explain.

"The unfortunate events that have taken place…" he prompted.

She slowly shook her head a couple of times and said in her most apologetic voice, "I'm sorry. I'm sure I should know. It's just that I've been traveling, and I don't listen to the news anyway; it's all so depressing. I promise I'll do better to keep up with things in the future." She spoke quietly and tried to show her submissiveness. Years in public relations had perfected Lori's ability to mirror personalities that others would respond to best. She could present herself as competent, unconventional, aloof, social, or a number of other types.

If what she had said had made an impact on Millikan, it didn't show. He circled her chair, looking down on her, and talked about the philosophy of the community. Some of it she had heard from Anton himself, and some of it she supported. There had been so many changes in the world over the past hundred years, and few people had taken the time to consider them. Whether they offered a better life or threatened a good life often depended on individual perspective. And now all those changes were beckoning the Azores.

"A young child wandered away and has not yet been found."

So Dawn is still missing.

"This afternoon her father was found dead, killed by someone from the outside. It's not something we worry about here. We are safe…but only within our community." He squinted, looking at her very closely, and then he walked away slowly.

During the long silence that followed, Lori thought through how AJ's death might change what she was there to do, and she decided that it only increased the urgency of finding Dawn. Someone who would kill was more likely to harm a child.

He turned back to her. "We live simply here," he said, "and we tolerate a broad interpretation of what it means to do that."

That had impressed her when she did her research. There was no set of rules by which everyone was expected to live, no oath of loyalty, no one religion or dress code. The difference between what she had been expecting and what she had found, had prompted her to note: *Doesn't seem like a Kool-Aid type of place.* "Yes. Dr. Jenkins told me that."

"You say you corresponded with Mr. Jenkins about joining us?" He had stripped Wallace Jenkins of his doctorate.

She carried with her a thread of counterfeit emails, showing exchanges with the former leader. With luck, not even Pat Millikan would have the opportunity to check on their authenticity until long after she was gone. She unzipped her backpack and handed over emails that progressed from casual exchanges through explanations of the community's beliefs to an invitation to join.

After scanning them, he looked up to find Lori nervously looking out the window.

"It's dark," she said. *And you wouldn't want to be seen sending me away from this welcoming community at this hour.*

Millikan's voice was firm. "I will not jeopardize the people of Comunidade dos Reis. They've chosen this place and this way to live, and it's their right to be left in peace and to raise their children protected from what they see as harmful."

She couldn't decide if Pat Millikan was a well-intentioned leader who took his responsibility to protect the community seriously, or a self-serving one who was more interested in protecting himself.

He returned the fake emails to her. "We don't recommend interacting with those outside the community, especially when you are new here. We don't allow the outside world to intrude at any time. We have no electricity, no running water, and we don't use so-called modern conveniences. That means no computers, no cell phones. Understood?"

"Yes. No computers. No cell phones. Nothing from the outside world to be brought in." She opened her backpack wide to show what was in it, but he didn't look.

"You will live from the work you do, whether by eating the food you grow or trading the goods you make. Your community should always be able to count on you…" He took a breath and softened. "…and you'll always be able to count on your community."

Lori let out a deep breath, smiled happily, and nodded.

"Alright then, let's find you a place to stay and get you some dinner. You must be hungry."

Lori settled into her new quarters, sharing a single-room cottage with Vera, the woman who had run to get Millikan when she arrived, and Cassie, an outgoing woman from California.

"This is a bad time for us," Cassie said. When she told Lori what they knew about AJ's death, she mentioned the *really tall man* from the police who had told the community what had happened.

Lori felt reassured just knowing Anton had been there.

Vera's account was much like Millikan's and ended with what he had said, "The danger's in the outside world, but we're safe here."

"What brought you both to the community?" asked Lori.

"Returning to my roots, I guess," chirped Cassie as she helped to make up the empty bed across from hers. "My grandparents immigrated from the Azores to what's now the Silicon Valley and became dairy farmers there."

Lori had learned not to assume ancestry on the islands meant Mediterranean ancestry, so Cassie's tall, solid build and Germanic features didn't surprise her. Although her long and very curly hair was largely gray, there was enough of its now faded original color left to know it was originally blond, and the very ends showed that she had once colored it a bright red. Sadly, her most noticeable feature was her skin, pitted and scarred by acne from her forehead to where it disappeared behind the neckline of her simple cotton shirt.

"That's interesting," Lori responded. "Which island were they from?" Since adding the genealogy package to Casa do Mar's website, that question had become second nature when talking to people with ancestry in the islands.

"Damn…I mean *darn* if I know. Hah. It's going to take a long time to break me of some habits," she said cheerily. She plumped a pillow and tossed it at the head of Lori's new bed. "Done! Not that you'll care much what your bed is like at the end of the day. We work hard around here."

"And in return we are well cared for," Vera said matter-of-factly. She spoke in unaccented Portuguese, and her shorter stature, light olive skin, near-black hair, and large brown eyes were typical of many people on the islands. She watched for Lori's reaction to what she had said.

"I'm sure we are." It hadn't escaped her notice that before Millikan confirmed she would be staying in the house, he had talked privately with Vera. She seemed to have a special role in the community. "Thank you for welcoming me into your home. Have you been here long?"

"Here? Not *here*."

"What Vera means is that she came from Flores with Pat," Cassie explained dryly.

"I thought the original group came from somewhere in New England with Dr. Jenkins."

"Dr. Millikan formed his ideas first, so his is the original group," Vera asserted. Just as Millikan had not acknowledged Jenkins' title of *Dr.*, Vera had given Millikan the title when he should not have it.

Cassie caught Lori's eye and shook her head slowly to tell her not to bother arguing the point.

"Ah, yes. I see." Lori said nothing more.

"Dr. Millikan gathered us together on Flores, and we were happy…before others made it too hard for him."

Cassie made a comment that was somewhere between concession and ridicule, "Yes, after Pat formed his ideas, his group of two and our group of thirty came together on Terceira."

So why did Jenkins leave?

"I'm going to pray," said Vera, aiming to appear serene, "that the people of Terceira will understand the good we want to do." She locked the wood trunk at the end of the bed, put the key in her pocket, and quietly walked out the door.

"She's not bad, really," Cassie tried to reassure Lori. "She's just devoted to Pat. Then again, she's very devoted to all of us. You won't find a more loyal member of the community anywhere."

"I noticed that she went directly to tell Mr. Millikan I was here," said Lori, lapsing into English. "Does she have an official position here?"

"Official? No. No one does, really." She laughed softly, "We're not like that." She sat on her bed. "Pat handles the legal issues and finances, and together with Vera he puts together the work rosters and helps us make decisions about what to plant in communal fields."

"I wonder what I'll be asked to do."

"Right now, work is pretty much covered; you're the second new citizen recently. You'll probably be able to just do group work in the fields or vineyards—if you want to eat, that is," she joked.

"Who else has joined recently?" Lori asked. "Perhaps we could learn the ropes together."

"I don't think so." Cassie sounded amused. "Helena is…well…different from you."

"How so?"

"Let's just say she's our resident herbalist and psychic."

"Ah."

"Just like when I was in my twenties, and I shared an apartment with two friends in Boston," she said, unpacking her canvas backpack. Since her arrangements with Wallace Jenkins were entirely fictitious, Lori hadn't been sure what to bring with her. She took out a few plain cotton clothes in subdued colors—a second pair of pants, a heavy sweater, two shirts, one of Catarina's nightgowns—and stowed everything in a trunk that matched Vera's. She looked around for a key, not as much to lock it as to have a way to unlock Vera's, but there was none. Finally, she put the leather work boots she had borrowed from Beto under the bed.

Lack of electricity necessitated an early dinner and an early bedtime. After Cassie extinguished the wick in the oil lantern, Lori tried to will herself to sleep, but as often happens that only made it harder, so until long after midnight, she watched smoky clouds drifting across a pale yellow moon, and thought about what she had to do and whether she would be caught before she did it.

When she finally fell asleep, it was with a hand over the powered-down cell phone tucked in her waistband.

Heading back to Angra, both Catarina and Anton scanned the sides of the road for Lori—and both second-guessed the wisdom of having her infiltrate a community where someone had been viciously murdered.

They found Gabriela waiting at the police station with a large pot of *alcatra*, a meat stew flavored with bacon, garlic, wine, and herbs. Norberto opened bottles of *vinho verdelho* from the island of Pico, Felipe cut loaves of fresh bread, and they all sat around the table in the conference room for a solid hour without mentioning one word of what they had seen that day. Instead they talked about their families and their dogs, their home villages and vacations they had taken, and if the gathering weather front would follow the Gulf Stream to hit the Azores as Hurricane Mimi.

Catarina gave Anton a small poke under the table when Gabriela served Felipe a second helping, but it wasn't until she poked him again, when Felipe poured coffee for Gabriela, that he caught on to a mutual attraction budding between the Santa Maria police chief and the woman who ran the Terceira police station. And the romantic Minister of Culture added another matchmaking mission to his list.

When Norberto offered his spare room to Felipe, Catarina asked Anton about their hotel reservations for the night.

"That's already taken care of," her husband said, and he winked at Gabriela…and she winked back.

The group turned to business after the coffee was poured. Anton had decided that his usual easygoing, collaborative approach wouldn't work with Rocha, and he wasn't going to allow the man to hinder their efforts to find Dawn. His first decision was to ask Gabriela to call every officer, rookie, and trainee into the station at ten the next morning. She didn't bat an eyelid. With input from Norberto and Felipe, he put together plans to use each one of them, while ensuring that the policing needs of the island were still covered. It amused Anton to see Gabriela and Catarina determining what materials would be needed and how to supply them; cut from the same cloth, every detail was noted on matching pads of paper at exactly the same time.

Anton stepped into his office while everyone helped to copy papers and set up for the next day, and he made a call to the Head of the Judicial Police. It was long after normal office hours, so he intended only to leave a message. In fact, Gomes was somewhat anxiously waiting to hear from him.

"I thought it couldn't get much worse for our reputation," Gomes said when he heard of AJ's murder.

"Or for the likelihood his daughter will be found safe."

"That's my concern, too. If her abduction is connected to the murder, we're dealing with someone who'll stop at nothing."

Anton felt for the scrap of red wool in his pocket and patted it. *I'll find you, child.*

"We've received another call from Franz Maier, the lawyer for the mother. I've put off answering for the second time, and I can do it again if you think that's best."

"No. We should respond," suggested Anton. "We don't want to be seen as uncaring or incompetent—especially since we are neither."

"Right. I'll take care of that in the morning and let you know how the call goes."

"Could you also fill in the Presidente on everything and let him know I'll send a full report tomorrow?"

"I will," promised Gomes. "And, Anton, thank you for taking this on."

Before they said goodbye, Anton had to say one more thing, and he had to do it as diplomatically as possible. "Given the death of AJ Bennett, I think it will be most efficient to have a single person in charge from now on."

Gomes could read between the lines. "I'll call Rocha first thing tomorrow morning and explain that I've made a decision: you are to be in sole command of efforts to find the missing child, as well as efforts to investigate her father's death."

Norberto passed Monte Brasil, rising from the ocean's floor on the outskirts of the city. A place of legends, the hill was the site of ancient manmade caves known as hypogea, once used as burial chambers. Looking at their architecture and construction, most archeologists believe they predated not only the Portuguese but Christianity.

Anton thought of the last time he had seen his daughter, stroking Sombra's black fur while she waited for her goodnight kiss. "Liliana asked for a postcard of the hypogea," he told his wife. "Don't let me forget."

She patted his hand.

Norberto turned off the main road and into a quiet neighborhood overlooking the historic center of Angra. "Just ahead to the right," Anton whispered from the passenger seat.

Now Catarina had an idea of why Anton and Gabriela had exchanged those winks over dinner. "Our old neighborhood," she said, squeezing his shoulder from behind him. She looked at Norberto, grasping the steering wheel with a tight-lipped smile on his face. He was as excited as Anton.

It wasn't exactly what she was thinking—that they would be staying in the same area where their first home on the islands had been. Anton had a bigger surprise for Catarina. With Gabriela's help, he had not only found them a place in the same guesthouse where they had lived for eleven months but, by a lucky twist of fate, the very room they had lived in.

And how Catarina loved him for coming up with the idea!

It was only one room dominated by a bed made up with well-worn but clean white linens and topped with a patchwork quilt. The bedding was new and shutters had replaced the old drapes, but the rickety table for two where they used to work and eat were the same, as were the terrible amateur oil paintings done by someone decades ago. The large wardrobe that had once held all their worldly possessions sat in one corner, and the most basic of kitchenettes filled a tiny alcove. That was it—and it had been all they needed.

For Catarina, the best part of the room had always been the bathroom with its large, deep tub. She did love her baths. Anton had asked Gabriela where to find some special soap, and she had gone out on her lunch hour and brought back a basket filled with fragrant, pastel-colored soaps and oils, which sat on a chair pulled up to the side of the tub. "It's all yours," he said with a loving smile.

Catarina's bath had been so long, Anton was asleep when she came to bed. She snuggled in close to her husband and looked up at the same ceiling that she had looked at so many times before. The cracks reminded her of a book she had read—in three languages—as a young girl: *Madeline*. The heroine was a redhead like her, but brave and outgoing, which was her antithesis before meeting Anton. It had been his faith in her that had given her the courage to break away from her oppressive parents and the life they were determined she should lead. And it had been her faith in him that had brought out the serious, intelligent side of a mischievous underachiever who had just lost both his parents. As teens, they had become each other's family and totally devoted to one another, as they were to this day. She smiled at the sound of his steady rumble. Anton's snoring never irritated her; it comforted her. She knew she was not alone in life.

4

At dawn, Lori awoke to coughing. Across the room, Vera was sitting at the edge of her bed, sheets tangled between her legs and a long white nightgown twisted around her waist. Her frizzy hair was in such disarray that no part of her face could be seen.

"Good morning, you two," Cassie said brightly as she threw open one of the two small windows.

Lori smiled back at her, trying to appear cheerful at the prospect of starting the new day, but actually wishing she was waking up at Casa do Mar to the smell of Catarina's sweet rolls and coffee. In the morning light, she could see more of the cottage. Rough-hewn beams were dark with age, thick stone walls had been whitewashed countless times, and the chimney was blackened with years of accumulated soot; it was very old. It was also clean, tidy, and filled with furniture that had been made in workshops not factories: three narrow beds and three trunks, an unfinished table and chairs, and a step stool for reaching the highest of the shelves that lined one wall.

She jumped out from under her covers, determined to embrace the chill in the room. "A brisk start to the day!"

"It is indeed, Lori," said Cassie. "A good day to start as one of us."

Lori crossed the uneven wood floor barefoot and looked through a soot-smudged window at the little community, still relatively quiet at that time of the morning. Three men were repairing a cart wheel at the border between two fields, others poured tea from kettles in the central area that served as a community gathering place, drinking without talking. Everywhere, young children were playing. There were no battery-powered miniature cars, no video games, no fashion-forward dolls with vast wardrobes. Girls made dinner for pinecone families and put pinecone babies to bed; boys ran boisterously, chasing and tagging one another; older children carried large baskets of laundry into the forest, presumably to wash the clothes in the clear-running stream. She watched Millikan come out of his house and cross the dirt square. He leaned against a large tree and within seconds was joined by others, some of whom exchanged brief morning greetings and moved on, and some who talked at length with him.

Lori realized how long she had been staring out the window. Cassie and Vera had dressed and were putting on worn boots caked with dried gray-brown soil. "I'll just be a few minutes," she told them.

"Help yourself to the mint if you want," Cassie showed her a jar on the window sill with sprigs rooting in water. "It's as good as any mouthwash in the morning." When she lifted the simple latch that held the door closed, bright sunlight flooded the room and Lori saw the extent of the damage to the woman's skin, so terrible it could be considered disfiguring, and she wondered if that had played a role in her decision to join a small, remote group of people.

"We share the outhouse in back with the women next door, Amal and Helena," Vera said before she left.

An outhouse? She hadn't thought about that when she came up with the idea of going undercover in a nineteenth-century community. Ultimately, though, she found an unexpected use for it. It had excellent satellite reception, and she got the first of Anton's texts when she turned on her phone. *AJ stabbed to death. Leave immediately.*

She replied. *Only when job is done.* And she powered off.

"Let's talk about how you want to fit into the community—and how the community wants you to fit in." Millikan's tone was avuncular not authoritarian. "Comunidade dos Reis has its own ecosystem," he said, using a word from the era he was turning his back on. "It's complex and right now it's in balance. I can't allow that to be upset. We'll take it slowly, and the community as a group will decide whether this will work for it—just as you'll decide if it will work for you."

She noticed that, although the community's language was supposed to be Portuguese, he was speaking to her in English again.

"We're close to self-sufficient. We grow most of our own food, raise our own dairy cows and chickens, make our own clothes, and build our own furniture. That being said, we do grow cash crops to trade for other things. And those who're able to contribute wealth from the less rewarding lives they fled to join us, often do so."

Was he making a pitch for money already, or just giving her an honest account of the community finances? "That's fair," she said.

"This life is not for everyone, Lori, and it's not easy."

Before her life had veered off into journalism and then public relations, Lori had thought she would study history—and her passion for nineteenth-century American history had started with the *Little House on the Prairie* books she now read to Liliana. She remembered the seemingly endless, backbreaking work that marked a farm family's life. She remembered how people were at the mercy of the vagaries of nature—weather, pests, soil exhaustion—and of the market. She remembered how survival often meant children were put to work at the age of six or even younger. And she wondered how close this imitative group was to the realities of farm life a hundred and fifty years ago.

"Thank you for being so open about it," she said.

"Do you have any skills?" He wasn't being confrontational, just asking.

Lori was prepared for the question. "All I can offer is my willingness to learn," she said meekly.

Whether by design or happenstance, Lori was to work most closely with Kate and Amal, the two women she had approached when she walked into Comunidade dos Reis. The three of them worked their way up and down one of the fields behind the houses, making holes, dropping in seeds, and covering them up with crumbly, dark brown soil. For the first ten minutes, Lori enjoyed starting her day in the warming mountain air and feeling the stretch of muscles she hadn't used since her days in the gym. After that, the heat and the pain were all she could think of.

Amal quietly kept to herself, stoically working without rest. Others talked, checked on young toddlers who napped on quilts in the shade of nearby trees, or stopped for water. Cassie and Kate introduced a number of people to Lori, including the couple who had made the trunks in her cottage and whose craft could apparently be found in several other homes. Catarina had suggested that she be alert to signs of stress such as bitten fingernails, hair pulling, muscle tension, and irritability, but everyone she met seemed to be remarkably content—with one possible exception. When Vera came over to offer her water from a pottery jug, Lori smelled alcohol on her breath, and she noticed that the woman's eyes were glassy.

"It's hot this morning," Vera said. "Not drinking enough water is a mistake many newcomers make."

Lori thanked her and tried to master the way she had seen others drink without touching their lips to the jug's spout. She tipped her head back and poured a thin stream of water into her open mouth, losing half down her chin and choking out most of the rest. "I'm sorry," she sputtered. "I'm going to need to practice."

Vera gave quite a nice laugh. "I don't know anyone who could do it on the first try. It'll come. Don't worry."

She was being far friendlier than expected, especially given her behavior the night before.

"So, how do you like us so far?"

"It's exactly what I wanted to find for my life," Lori lied.

Vera nodded with pride. "Others don't understand that this is the way mankind is supposed to live. No wonder people are so unhappy crowded together in cities, moving around in mechanical contraptions, sitting at desks for eight hours a day, and molding their bodies into what others say they should be."

Lori couldn't disagree. She had been one of those desk-bound city workers, and that wasn't the life she wanted now—but neither was this. "Exactly, Vera!" she said with enthusiasm. She returned the jug and tried not to seem too curious when she said, "You've been with the group longer than anyone, you must know a lot about it." She had used two of Catarina's tips for getting the most information from a person: starting with a compliment and ending with the chance to talk about what they were interested in. After their last conversation, it was clear that having lived in a similar community before others was a point of pride for Vera, and that Comunidade dos Reis was at the center of her life.

"I've been with Dr. Millikan since the beginning. He was the first to realize that unhappiness is caused by modern life, you know, and now he's the leader of the movement to return mankind to their proper place in God's world."

Putting aside that virtually everything she'd just said was untrue, Lori still learned something that explained a lot about Vera's actions. Her loyalty wasn't as much to the community as it was to Millikan. She had—for want of a better word—a crush on him.

After the first couple of hours, Lori fell into a trance doing the repetitive work: dig, drop, cover; dig, drop, cover. The end of the last row took her by surprise, as did the call to lunch. She was stiff, sore, and terribly sunburned. There was no doubt in her mind: she would take the comforts of the present over what the past offered. She walked back slowly, as did Kate, whose three-year-old daughter, Sally, was exploring the flowers that bordered the fields. Kate explained that on days when so many hands were needed for long hours, the community often shared a late lunch prepared by a few members who stayed behind for one reason or another. Then the afternoon was spent taking care of homes and personal business, still difficult but in a different way.

Lori watched the backs of those who passed them grow smaller as they headed to the communal lunch, most bearing right to wash up in the stream and then crossing to the central area where food was set up on a basalt outcrop. Before they reached the houses, Lori's mouth watered at the smell of roasting fish. "I can't wait to eat," she said with genuine enthusiasm.

"My husband went down to the dock and traded some of our vegetables for the fish."

"Does he leave the community often?" Lori was curious about how free members were to come and go.

"Only when it's necessary. We think it's better to keep to ourselves."

Millikan's words exactly. But was that reasonable when, as outsiders with ideas that others might see as extreme, they might be ridiculed or worse?

Kate went on with pride, "Pat trusts Reggie."

"He's also a great trader," Cassie laughed cutting across their path on her way to lunch with a plate, cup, and spoon.

"He is!" Kate called out after her. She went on, "Reggie and AJ usually took turns going to Santa Cruz for the open-air market or going all the way into Angra."

"Last week was AJ's turn to go to Angra?"

"Actually, no, but since Reggie had just made a special trip to take Helena to Angra for some of her supplies, AJ volunteered to go. Otherwise…"

They had just helped themselves to the last of the fish and vegetables when a rangy man with strawberry blond hair captured all of Kate's attention. As he walked to where they sat, Lori could see there was something off about his gait, not quite a limp but an uncoordinated movement of arms and legs. That he was Sally's father was obvious; they shared the same curly strawberry blond hair, freckles, and sapphire blue eyes, and his features were an adult's version of hers. He was wearing well-used pants and a heavy cotton shirt that had been patched more than once. In the community, things were valued too highly to be replaced easily. His eyes locked on Kate's, and he put out one of his scuffed boots, braking his forward motion, and gave her a lopsided grin.

She rose to stand by his side. "Reggie," she said, "This is Lori." She broke the name into two slow and clear syllables.

He lifted one corner of his mouth in a crooked smile. "Hello, Lori," he said haltingly.

She returned the greeting.

He scratched at the week's growth of beard on his face. "I am Reginald Frederick Bartholomew Tuttle," he said in a staccato voice.

With a name like that, his parents must have envisioned a very different future for him, Lori thought, one as a lawyer or a congressman, not as a subsistence farmer.

"I'll play with Sally," he said, squatting and holding his arms out for the daughter who looked so much like him.

She didn't go running to him. To the contrary, she slowly backed away, sucking the three fingers in her mouth.

"Sally," Kate said in warning. "It's time to play with Daddy."

Tears welled in Sally's eyes, and she pleaded *no*. It took another ten minutes to coax the child to go with him, and Lori began to wonder if the child was just being a cranky three-year-old, or if there was another reason.

As soon as the two were out of sight, Kate abruptly asked, "Why are you here?"

Lori thought she had prepared well for any question, but she was left silent for a moment because it seemed like a challenge. Did Kate suspect she was not who she claimed to be, or did she just want to know why she was interested in joining the community? Lori answered as someone who truly wanted to join the community would. "I'm hoping living this way will bring me more peace, more happiness."

Kate said nothing for a while. "That's why we're here. Peace was hard for Reggie to find out there." There was another long silence. "It isn't as much of a struggle for him here."

"It was before?" she prompted.

"Yes. Here, he's more like who he was…before."

If Reggie Tuttle was mentally unbalanced, could he have harmed Dawn? "Before?" She tried to strike the right balance between polite conversation and growing interest.

"Reggie got the worst of an IED. He was on his way home from Afghanistan for Sally's birth, when he saw the soda can. He had started to back away, and it just went off. It left him with speech and movement problems."

"I'm so sorry. That's hard on both of you." She couldn't stop herself from adding, "And Sally." She wanted to know if Reggie's medical condition explained how their daughter had reacted to him just then.

"Sally's never known Reggie any other way. She was born at Landstuhl," she said, naming the large military hospital that received so many injured military personnel. "I had arrived the day before, and I was by Reggie's bed when the contractions began."

"That must have been rough, away from home and worried about your husband."

She let out a short puff of air. "Not any rougher than I was to deal with when he first met me—and saved me—but yes, it was rough." She looked at Lori. "If you're going to be one of us, you should know that Reggie's brain was injured far more than his body. Back home, he saw danger everywhere, and it overwhelmed him. He'd have what the doctors called violent PTSD blackouts. He'd be walking down the street in the town he grew up in and he'd think a car was about to hit us. He'd yell earthquake when it was just thunder, or grab Sally off the playground when other children ran towards her."

"Were your families able to help?"

Her face was a mix of emotions: angry, sad, bitter. "Reggie is an only child, and his parents died when he was in his teens. Our family is right here in Comunidade dos Reis."

She had said nothing about her own family. "I'm sorry. Did the people around you understand?"

"Most didn't, and I can accept that; they were afraid. My fear was...for Reggie."

Lori thought she knew what Kate meant, and she waited.

"He came home from the V.A. clinic one day and told me that one of his PTSD buddies there had committed suicide. 'Smart man,' he said, 'smart man.' That made me determined to find a place where Reggie had the best chance to live the life he deserves."

Lori saw a steely determination in her. "And it's better here?"

"Oh, yes. It was better when we went to Maine, better still when we moved away from the city to work on a small farm there. Then we heard about Comunidade dos Reis, and we decided to give it a try."

"Do you miss what you had to give up by moving here?"

She gave a small chuckle, as if laughing at a joke only she understood. "Actually, I may have gotten back some of what I had given up by moving here."

Lori drew her eyebrows together to show that she didn't understand.

"I was Mennonite." She thought to herself before going on. "Do you know what *rumspringa* is?"

"I don't think I've ever heard the word."

"The word is from the German for running around. It's the time of life when Mennonite or Amish teens are not under the control of their parents but haven't been baptized as full members of the church yet, so they're not held accountable for some of what they do."

"I've read about that and seen it in movies."

A smile spread across Kate's face before Lori even finished her sentence. "It's not like the movies. A few will dress English or miss evening prayers once or twice. Even fewer will try drinking or experiment with sex. And every once in a while a teen will leave home, but that's as rare as Catholic teens becoming nuns or priests. And usually they just return and are forgiven."

"You left?"

"I did." Her pain was evident.

"Why didn't you return?"

"I did."

"And then you decided it wasn't right for you?"

"Once you become an adult in the church, misbehavior is not tolerated."

Lori understood: Kate had decided to return to her family but had done something that made them disown her entirely.

She quickly changed the subject. "So to answer your original question, yes, there are things I miss, but I got back a lot of them when I joined Comunidade dos Reis. Even if I hadn't, I'd still be here. Reggie is the best person I know. I love him, and I meant it when I said for better or worse." She looked at Lori, making a case for the man she loved. "He knows he can't cope, and he's told me to leave, to make a better life for myself and Sally without him."

Kate busied herself by scraping out the fire pit and feeding what remained to the dogs waiting nearby. "Living here is better for Reggie," she said fiercely, "and I will do whatever I can to keep us here."

Lori needed to move the conversation closer to the reason she had come to the community. "It does seem like a good place to raise a family, but... It's just that I heard about Dawn Bennett. Is safety a concern?"

"Safety just isn't something we worry about around here. All I can think is that she wandered away from the forest. Once someone is out there, anything is possible."

"What do you remember about the day she went missing?"

"It was like most market days when we're especially busy in the fields or vineyards. Our little settlement was practically deserted."

"Was anyone here to prepare lunch?"

"Actually, I was. Sally was a bit under the weather that day, and our community meal wasn't going to be until evening, so everyone insisted that I stay home with her. Amal helped me. Even taking time for her prayers, she contributes more than anyone else here."

"And everyone else was away working?"

"Both Reggie and AJ had left early, Reggie to Santa Cruz because it was market day there and AJ to Angra to do some business for the community. We were all hoping that Helena had seen something, since she works in the forest a lot, but the timing was off that day."

"What is it that Helena does in the forest?"

"Everything. She grows herbs, picks mushrooms, even ferments and dries leaves for our teas. She's one of the busiest people here."

"Speaking of tea, can I pour you some more?" Lori wanted to keep the tone conversational. She tried to think of a way of asking why Helena's timing had been off without raising suspicions, when Kate explained.

"Of all days, Helena also had to spend time on the other side of the compound making soap, and then she joined everyone in the vineyards."

"So, you were saying that only you, Amal, and Helena were here that day," she said, reaching for the kettle that rested on coals.

"And of course, Pat and Vera were working in the community office as they usually do on market day, although he did leave for Santa Clara—that's the village nearest us—about noon."

Six people, including Reggie. Lori made a mental note to give their names to Anton, along with a list of everyone else who was supposedly working in the faraway vineyards.

They started back to their own houses, personal eating utensils and plates in hand, and Kate said apologetically, "I wish I'd seen more. I was right here baking the bread and tending the fire. Dawn even came by to ask if Sally could join her."

"So you saw Dawn that day," trying to keep the conversation going.

"I watched her walk into the forest with Melody."

"And that's safe—for children to wander around the forest by themselves?" She knew she sounded critical.

Kate defended allowing that. "Dawn knows the forest well, and she loves playing there."

As they crossed the path in front of Millikan's house, Lori said, "I know this might seem terrible, but I was worried that it would be so restrictive here. That someone would control everything about our lives: when we got up, how we dressed, even if we could leave."

"It's not like that. We do rely on good advisors who understand that for some people being outside the community might be fine, while for others it wouldn't be."

"Why wouldn't it be?

"Someone might be frightened by others or tempted by alcohol or hurt by stares and remarks."

Lori knew she was talking about Reggie, and possibly Vera, Amal, and Cassie. Perhaps she was even talking about most of the community, people hurt by the world outside. *Weren't they entitled to be left in peace?*

Anton took every breath with a dreadful knowledge: of the two possible outcomes for Dawn's disappearance, the better one was that she was lonely, frightened, or suffering. Had she wandered away and died? Had there been an accident? Had she been taken by a stranger...or someone she knew?

By the time Norberto arrived at the police station with Anton and Catarina, his brother had driven Felipe in, and Gabriela had set up the only large room, where representatives of the island's freguesias met once a month, for the morning meeting. Befitting Terceira's role as the repository of so many architectural treasures, it was a beautiful space that reflected a rich history. Under a vaulted ceiling, lined with Moorish tiles, frescoed walls showed large sailing vessels arriving in Angra in the nineteenth century. The chairs, darkened with age, had come from a synagogue in Ponta Delgada, and the long table, marked with centuries of use, was originally in the dining room of a monastery.

Gabriela had made name plates, and Anton found his place at one end of the table, on which reports, folders, and maps were laid out. He didn't sit. Within minutes the room was filled to capacity with every police officer and trainee on the Terceira force.

"We are here to coordinate our efforts to find Dawn Bennett, a child of six who disappeared from Comunidade dos Reis on Tuesday," he said loudly to settle everyone into place. He took a long swallow of the coffee Gabriela had put in front of him and felt the sting of heat down his esophagus. "We will aim to meet every morning and every evening until she is found."

Gabriela wrote on her pad of paper.

"Starting today, ten officers will be on duty for the day shift. Five will share regular duties, and five will be assigned to this investigation. Remaining officers will rotate in for other shifts."

Gabriela wrote again.

"Others may be brought in as needed, but the five who start with this endeavor will stay with it until I say otherwise. No vacations. No days off. Double, perhaps even triple shifts." He knew he didn't always get the best measure of people, so he glanced at Catarina and found approval in a small nod only he detected.

"I will first ask for volunteers." Before finishing his sentence, ten hands were raised. An older officer said apologetically, "I have tickets to visit my sons in Canada."

"I understand. I know that otherwise you would join us." He did know that. "Gabriela, would you please adjust all duty rosters as needed?"

"Yes, sir." And she wrote on her pad one more time, making sure that officers who had already helped with the search of the forest were among those who were assigned to Anton.

"Felipe Madruga is the Chief of Police on Santa Maria, and I trust his judgement completely."

Felipe composed his face. Only a single hard swallow betrayed his pride.

"If I'm not available—or even if I am—his word is to be taken as Chief Rocha's word is."

Catarina noticed some shifting in chairs and saw a couple of officers exchange glances and small smirks. Their own chief was not held in high esteem.

Anton filled in the team on what he knew, the people associated with the case and what each had said, and the discovery in the forest the day before. The one thing he didn't tell them about was Lori's role in the investigation; to protect her, that would remain a secret. "We will proceed on two fronts.

Three of you will look for any sign of Dawn Bennett." He reached into his jacket pocket and pulled out a clump of folded papers—and a couple of napkins. All had notes on them, and it took a few moments to find the right one. "I'd like Silva and Gracia to return to the area of the forest. Look along the road and visit the houses on the hillside across the road. Talk to the people there. Find out how they feel about Comunidade dos Reis, and find out if they saw anything unusual the day Dawn disappeared, or any day recently. Sousa, I want you to work with Felipe. The two of you will talk to people at the marinas, airport, rental car companies, and taxi stands. If the child is not in the vicinity of Comunidade dos Reis, she must have been taken away somehow."

He held his arm out to Catarina, who sat two chairs away, the only person in the room with no official role, but for Anton the person he would rely on the most. She handed him the dossier Lori had prepared. He slipped out the only known photo of Dawn after infancy, and looked at her fat, rosy cheeks and joy-filled smile. "Gabriela, would you please run off two hundred copies of this," he said, holding it up for all to see. "High quality copies. Give a hundred to Sousa and Felipe, and a few to Silva and Gracia."

"Rosa and…" he had forgotten Norberto's last name and squinted at the name plate at the other end of the long table.

"Andrade," whispered Gabriela.

"Rosa and Andrade will support the interviews we'll conduct here today, bringing people in and helping with research."

He looked at his dear wife. "This is the time to introduce Catarina Vanderhye. She has very special talents as an interviewer, and she is fluent in several languages, which will be essential to our efforts." Catarina smiled and nodded to everyone around the table. "She is also my wife," he said with a small laugh. *And I love her so.*

An hour later, copies of Dawn's picture had been distributed, and Rosa had been sent to pick up Pat Millikan. Gabriela brought second cups of coffee to Anton and Catarina, and handed a large to-go cup to a delighted Felipe as he headed out the door.

"This is easily the best coffee I've ever had," he complimented her.

Anton found that easy to believe. Felipe had no one to cook for him, and Anton had tasted his coffee. It was easily the *worst* he'd ever had.

As Anton took his last sip of coffee, Rocha appeared in the conference room. "Cardosa! A word!" he barked.

Anton looked up as slowly as he could without making it obvious how deliberate it was. He raised one eyebrow and held Rocha's gaze. "A moment, please, Chief Rocha." He made his tone as polite as possible, highlighting Rocha's rudeness by contrast. He looked at a paper, counted to ten, and raised his head. "I'm so sorry to keep you waiting, Chief Rocha. What can I do for you?"

Norberto stood in back of the Chief, brimming with amusement.

Rocha took a short breath. "I understand you found it necessary to re-assign my officers."

"Yes." He said no more.

"Well, I hope this won't compromise security."

"My intention is to ensure security is not compromised."

"I'll be sending the central government a bill for the additional shifts."

"I'll sign off on it." Anton had let him know who was in charge, but he didn't want to put up fences. "And Victor, thank you for the support."

As soon as they got word that Rosa had returned with Millikan, Anton and Catarina went to the second floor, where he was being held in the smallest of rooms. Rosa stood at attention next to the metal chair she had been instructed to have him sit in. The room now held four people and—especially when one was a man of Anton's stature—it was a tight fit. That was done on purpose.

"Mrs. Vanderhye will conduct the interrogation," was all Anton said by way of introduction. He was familiar with Millikan's resistance to outside interference, and he intended to make clear that the man had no say in what was taking place. The team had already discussed the best approach in this case and which questions should be asked. It was to be the classic good cop-bad cop interrogation. Anton would demonstrate skepticism and inflexibility—and a harshness that was contrary to his nature—while Catarina would both reinforce that impression by deferring to him and offer kindness by contrast.

"Good morning, Mr. Millikan." She gave him a pleasant smile and waited for a response that was a long time in coming.

"Good morning," he said grudgingly.

She had opened her mouth to offer him tea when he spat out, "Why are you making things so difficult for us?"

"I don't understand, Mr. Millikan. How are we making things so difficult?"

"For one thing, you force us to turn our backs on our principles and ride in...cars."

Anton came close to telling him he could walk all the way back home, but he didn't interfere with his wife's approach to questioning the uncooperative man.

"I apologize if this creates any difficulty for you. That is not the intention. Minister Cardosa's only goal is to find Dawn Bennett."

"Then why am I here? I already told him what I know—and did *everything* he asked." His irritation was directed at Anton, and that was fine for the purpose of the interrogation.

"Minister Cardosa has instructed me to ask..." She picked up the clipboard and leafed through the pages that were attached. "...a number of questions." Her raised eyebrows and sigh were meant to let him know he had a long session ahead of him. In fact, while the top sheet had been typed up single space by Gabriela, all the other pages were blank.

"Shouldn't you be out looking for the Bennett girl?" Millikan addressed Anton.

Without moving his gaze from a point over Millikan's head, he looked at Catarina and said, "Begin."

"When and where did you first enter the Azores, Mr. Millikan?"

"What?"

"When and where did you first enter the Azores?"

He sneered as though it was the most irrelevant question he had ever heard.

"I'm sorry, Mr. Millikan. I promise to get through this basic information as quickly as I can, so you can get back home very soon."

He gestured his resignation. "May. 2015. Flores," he huffed.

"What were you doing on Flores?"

"I don't see how that has any bearing on this."

Anton said a few words in Portuguese to Rosa, as quickly and as garbled as he could make them. She reached for a pair of handcuffs that Gabriela had found in a storage closet, unused since their purchase five years before. "Yes, sir!"

"Wait," interrupted Catarina. "Mr. Millikan is only trying to help. Isn't that true?"

The man was thinking through his situation, and he decided his best option was to at least appear to cooperate. "If that's the way you want it, fine. Your loss not mine. Just ask your questions. I'll answer them and be done with you." He looked at Anton and sat back in his chair, trying to appear nonchalant. "I do have responsibilities to get back to."

His irregular, shallow breaths told Catarina that despite the attitude he was feigning, Millikan was nervous. She looked at the list of questions again. "So, what were you doing on Flores?"

"I am the elected head of an international group of like-minded people. Look, this was all cleared with *your* government." He looked up at Anton. "Don't you people talk to one another?"

He had made his role sound so much grander than it had been. Anton decided to take him down a notch with a question that wasn't on the list. "How many people were in your group?"

"The size changed over time."

"When you left Flores."

Millikan was about to be humiliated, and Catarina could see his irritation turn to anger.

"When we left, there were two of us."

"I see. Two." He gave a long pause. "Continue, Mrs. Vanderhye."

She was in fact only getting a measure of the man, noting his reactions to questions that made him uncomfortable. They already knew the answers from Lori's research.

"And why did you leave Flores?"

He dissembled. "I left to become head of our larger group here on Terceira."

"That would be Comunidade dos Reis na Floresta?"

"Yes."

"What is your role in the community?"

"I am its leader. I administer the common finances, conduct business with those outside the community, preside over meetings, direct projects, organize events and, of course, promote our ideals."

The order in which he put his responsibilities told Catarina something. "When did the Bennett family join that community?"

"They were there when I arrived."

"What is your impression of them?"

"AJ was a good man."

Unexpectedly, Catarina saw distress, even despair on his face. "Were you and Mr. Bennett close?"

He knit his brow. "Yes. We were."

"And the rest of the family?"

He considered what to say. "I don't know Janine well."

After living so closely and in a such a small group, it seemed odd that he had no further observation, but she decided to move on to what they had determined was most important to ask. "Who organized the search of the forest?"

"I did."

"Did that include assigning people to specific areas?"

"Yes, but they weren't rigid assignments. More suggestions on where people could look."

"And no one saw any trace of Dawn or of AJ?"

"No. It's a dark forest."

"Where was AJ going on the morning he died?"

"To Angra."

"What was his business there?"

"He is one of our traders."

It was an evasive response. "Do your community's profits come from trading?"

"Yes."

Catarina heard the faint sound of his tongue against his dry mouth and saw the pulsing of the artery in his neck. She knew he was hiding something—or even lying outright. His responses to the remaining questions they had planned to ask became increasingly guarded, and she soon brought the interrogation to an end—but not before Anton made clear to Millikan that he would be questioned again.

Gabriela choreographed the movement of people into and out of the police station. Just as Rosa escorted Millikan out the back door, Norberto brought the next people to be questioned in through the front door. Anton wanted to keep everyone as separated as possible. It wasn't simply to prevent them from sharing information; he wanted everyone to think they were at the top of his list of suspects.

Norberto's task had been to locate Janine Maier's parents and bring them in for questioning. He started with a list of hotels, two with over a hundred rooms but most with just a few, and he had been lucky. On his second call, he found Horst and Agneta Maier in a suite at a modern three-story hotel. He spoke directly to the hotel's manager, emphasizing the importance of keeping their conversation confidential. From the questions the man asked and the excited tone of his voice, it was clear that in a matter of hours the call would become the subject of speculation and magnification all over the island. Norberto learned that the Maiers had been in the hotel twice, staying for a week, leaving for three days, and returning five days ago—the day *after* Dawn had disappeared. Another Maier, Franz, had stayed at the same hotel for a single night, two days before Dawn's disappearance, and had returned yesterday.

Norberto stood in the second-floor hallway of the police station and shared what he had learned with Anton and Catarina while the Maiers waited—Horst in the room where Millikan had been questioned and Agneta next door. They decided that only Catarina would talk to Horst Maier, who knew little English and might be impressed with Catarina's command of German.

As soon as she entered, a man in his early sixties stepped up and extended his hand. He had a wiry body, gaunt face, drab gray hair, and a mouth that seemed incapable of smiling. "Allow me to introduce myself," he said formally in heavily accented English. "My name is Horst Maier. Janine Maier is my daughter." His words were simple enough, but his tone was haughty.

Stepdaughter, she silently corrected him. "I am Catarina Vanderhye," she said in her usual calm and steady voice. She could tell he was not only surprised by her use of German; he was not pleased. Did it remove any excuse for not answering fully? "I am working with the Judicial Police and the central government to find your granddaughter. Please, have a seat." She motioned to one of the metal chairs and took a seat opposite him, careful not to show any of the notes on her clipboard.

She had already taken his measure. He thought he was superior—certainly to her and probably to everyone—so her first task was to establish her right to question him. She lifted her chin, tightened her lips, and firmed the tone of her voice. "I will ask you a series of questions and record your responses. It is important that you answer truthfully and fully, not only to help your granddaughter but because you could be held accountable for anything you say. Do you understand?"

"Perhaps I should ask for my attorney?"

"That depends on your primary concern."

"Yes, of course I understand," he said dismissively. And although Catarina saw every sign that he was treating the interview as a game he was intent on winning, he answered all the questions that followed.

"When did you first enter the Azores?"

"On the eighteenth."

"Did you come directly to Terceira?"

"Yes."

"What was the purpose of your visit?"

Here his eyes snapped up momentarily. He was uneasy about the question. "The purpose was to visit my daughter," he blinked, lying.

"When had you last seen her?"

He sucked in his cheeks. That question made him more than uneasy; it made him angry. "I am a businessman, Frau Vanderhye, and it's difficult for me to get away."

Catarina waited, but he said no more. "So it had been a while. Longer than a year?"

"Yes."

"How long?"

He didn't like being held accountable. "Six years. But that was her fault. She was the one who made the irrational decision to leave and live in a commune. She'd always been difficult, but that…that was insane."

"And you saw her here on Terceira?"

"Yes, of course. I brought her papers to sign."

"Which papers would those be?"

"I…my daughter is…was… Well, I suppose none of that is even applicable anymore…but she was divorcing her husband and filing for full custody of the children."

"What was your role in the custody hearing?"

"Janine has never been good with the realities of life. She has no sense of business, finances, or legal matters. I had to do all that. She didn't even have pictures of the children to include with the papers I brought her to sign."

She knew the pictures he referred to. "Did you take pictures for her?"

"I had to do that, too."

"And you wanted the children to live with…" Catarina left the question hanging.

"Me. Us. All of us. They naturally belong to us. But I'm telling you, none of that matters anymore. There's no longer an issue of custody. No hearings are needed now. It's all over."

His first response was closest to the truth. He had wanted Dawn and Melody to live with him, but he was still hiding something. "Was the plan for Janine to return to Germany, then?"

"If that was what she wanted, and if she showed she was able to take care of my grandchildren." She put together what he had said with the powers of attorney that Lori's research had uncovered. His objective was never to help Janine get custody of her children. *He wanted custody.* However, he had made a point of saying—twice—that there was no longer a need for a custody hearing. *And he seemed happy about that.*

She moved on to other questions. "Have you been on Terceira since the eighteenth?"

"I left for São Miguel on the first with my wife."

"And what was the purpose of that visit?"

"Various legal matters."

His vagueness made her suspicious, but of what she didn't know. "When did you return to Terceira?"

"On the fourth."

"How was the custody hearing progressing before Dawn disappeared?"

"You'd have to ask my…our lawyer."

"Who would that be?" she asked with a pencil poised over her clipboard.

"Franz Maier," he said, handing her the man's card.

After another ten minutes of fruitless questioning, Horst Maier left with the same supercilious expression he had worn since Catarina had walked in.

Agneta Maier was a plump, well-groomed woman in her late fifties, with stiff blond hair and reddish skin. She had a tightly controlled air about her, which was reinforced by what she wore—a suit, silk blouse, black pumps, and hose that one might have seen in a business office in the 1980s.

Catarina entered carrying a tray with two cups of hot tea, a sugar bowl, and a small pitcher of cream. "I apologize for keeping you waiting, Frau Maier." She handed Anton the notes she had taken during Horst's interview to look over while she and Agneta sipped tea and made small talk. Catarina found her to be as timid as her husband had been arrogant.

Anton asked about where she had been in the past three weeks, and her account jibed with her husband's and with what Norberto had learned from the hotel manager.

"What's the purpose of your visit to Terceira, Frau Maier?" he asked.

The woman was clearly embarrassed. She clutched her handbag, shifted in her chair, and her face grew even redder. "I'm here to see my daughter. She lives here, you know."

Catarina understood. Agneta Maier was of a generation that valued privacy and guarded family dignity. She spoke softly, "Minister Cardosa appreciates how hard it is to talk about personal matters in public. He wouldn't ask these questions if it weren't important…essential…to finding your granddaughter."

Anton followed suit. "I won't pass on anything you tell me unless I need to."

Catarina added, "Raising children can be difficult. I try my best with my own, but it doesn't always turn out as you want."

Anton kept quiet. As far as he was concerned, Liliana and Toni were as perfect as any two children could possibly be, and he knew their mother felt the same way.

Catarina rephrased Anton's question. "Is there anything you can tell us about the reason you visited Janine?"

"She had written me, you know. She was planning to leave this place. She wanted to know if she could stay with us while she looked for a job."

"When did she write?" asked Anton.

"Just before Christmas. I sent her a little money, so she could buy stamps or call if she wanted to. It's hard, you see, living without any money."

"What did you tell her about coming to stay?"

She was embarrassed again. "Well, you understand, I had to talk to Horst about it."

"What did he say?"

She swallowed. "At first...well, in the end he said of course she could come. It's just that at first...well, he was just concerned about whether he could...afford it." It pained her to admit that. "His business...the market...hasn't been very good recently, so he was just worried about that."

"But in the end, he welcomed the idea?"

"Yes." She brightened. "He handled everything once custody became an issue. He even arranged to send a cell phone to the local post office for her."

"When was that?"

"Oh, not too long ago." She thought hard, unable to pin down a date, and then looked up with a happy smile. "I know when. It was just before my birthday, because Horst said it was his present to me. That was at the end of February."

"Did Janine write to you often?"

She sat back and folded her arms over the purse she held in her lap. She didn't like the question—or the answer she would have to give. For the next ten minutes, she wandered through her thoughts, "She became a real problem after... You see, Horst is my second husband... We married when Janine was ten, and she... He likes things a certain way, so... She was just so rebellious. When she left Germany for Spain and then Africa—Africa, of all places—she was far away and... Finally things settled down at home." She took a deep breath.

She hadn't answered the question, and Anton confirmed what she was trying to avoid saying. "So you lost touch with one another eight or nine years ago, soon after Melody was born?"

Agneta Maier colored deeply and hung her head. "Yes," she whispered.

"You must have been happy when she wrote," said Catarina.

Agneta said yes as though she had just realized it was true.

"What were your plans if Janine was awarded custody?"

It didn't seem to be something she had given much thought to. For a moment she just stared with her mouth slightly open. "I'm not sure. Horst said we could have the children in our house once the custody and child support issues were settled."

It didn't escape Catarina's attention that she hadn't mentioned Janine staying with them. "Raising children can be so expensive. Will AJ's death complicate the issue of child support?" Agneta's blank look was the expression of someone who didn't even have the capacity to think it through.

There was a tap on the door. Anton opened it to find Gabriela, who crooked a finger to bring him out to the corridor. She pulled the door shut and said quietly, "The Maiers' lawyer is downstairs with senhor Maier, and he demands to see senhora Maier."

While Catarina wrapped up the interview, Anton followed Gabriela to the reception area, where Horst Maier stood in a corner, talking quietly to another man. When Anton walked up, he said, "This is my lawyer, Franz Maier."

It wasn't only the shared surname that gave away their familial relationship. The two men resembled one another so closely, they had to be brothers if not twins. The only difference Anton could spot was that Horst sported more worry lines.

Franz Maier extended an arm and stiffly shook Anton's hand. "This is more than simply unusual." His English was better than his brother's. "The Maiers are foreign nationals and have been called into the police station without even a call to the consulate."

Anton raised his eyebrows and said coolly, "It was my understanding that they wanted to help us discover their granddaughter's whereabouts."

"Of course they do, but there is protocol," Franz Maier sputtered.

"I'm so glad to know that," Anton smiled, "in case more information is needed. For now, we have finished." He extended a hand, then withdrew it quickly. "Actually, I do have just one more question. "What do you know of a company called Rifai Global?"

Before denying any knowledge of the company, the Maier brothers exchanged looks that he needed no help from Catarina to decipher: *We've been caught.*

By the time Rosa escorted Janine into Anton's office, they were an hour overdue. The reason became clear when a shrill cry came from the hallway outside. Melody stood behind her mother, stubbornly refusing to move. Slender, muscled, and browned by the sun, with her short hair she could easily have been taken for a boy. She had her mother's red hair and thin features, but her father's genes were written in her beautiful green eyes.

A woman drained of energy and perhaps caring, Janine coaxed her daughter into the room. "She's been very upset that Dawn isn't with her. She doesn't understand."

On cue, Melody took in a lungful of air and expelled it loudly and slowly, calling out *Dawn*. Then, as quickly as it had started, it stopped, and she settled cross legged on the broad windowsill overlooking the park and started drumming her fingers on the glass, slowly, rhythmically.

Catarina spoke softly to Janine. "Let's talk in the hall. We can leave the door open." She looked at Anton, who nodded yes; he would watch over Melody.

They ended up in the conference room where the men and women dedicated to finding Dawn met twice a day. Over a cup of tea, Janine spoke about Melody's difficult temperament, and slowly the tension in her voice subsided and her clenched hands relaxed as she unburdened herself.

Catarina rested her hand on Janine's arm. "I'm sorry." They were simple words, but many would attest that their sincerity was comforting.

"I should have seen the problems earlier," she blamed herself as she had when talking to Anton. "Doctors never agreed on a diagnosis. She's smart, you know. Her I.Q. was tested twice, and we were surprised how high it is." She smiled weakly, pleased to have something good to say about her daughter.

"Did they think anything could be done to help her?"

"Before we came to the community, psychiatrists and other doctors predicted nothing but a troubled future for her." She held her cup tightly and pressed it against the table. "What did they know? Sometimes she's a normal child, just a bit quieter than most," she said fiercely. "It's when she's stressed that she acts up."

"May I ask if she was the reason you went to Comunidade dos Reis?"

"Not the reason we went but the reason I stayed so long. Here, Melody's calm…or she was until…" She left Dawn's disappearance unspoken. "She's happy in her own way." A hopeless look appeared on her face.

Catarina understood her torment. Melody's peace came at a cost. "Does Dawn like living in the community?"

"Like it?" she said sadly. "She doesn't know anything else."

"Did that play a role in why you wanted to leave?"

She looked shamed. "I know Melody's content here." She took a shaky breath and continued with some anger, "But what about Dawn? Isn't she entitled to know all the possibilities for her life?"

It wasn't a rhetorical question, and she waited for a response from Catarina, who could only offer sympathy.

"I even thought about leaving Melody here with AJ and taking Dawn away, but I just couldn't turn my back on my own child in the end." It was more confession than simply thinking aloud when she said, "It's my punishment."

"No, Janine. You aren't responsible for any of this."

"If you only knew the trouble I got into."

Catarina thought of the passport photo of a feather-bedecked young woman with pink hair and tattoos.

"If I hadn't met AJ, I think I'd be dead by now. I didn't deserve him. He was a good man—" Tears spilled down her cheeks.

"Yet you wanted to leave him and take his children with you."

"I know," she said sadly, "but he was a man of conviction, and his convictions were at odds with mine…with what I thought was best for our daughters."

She seemed reasonable. Had the separation only become complicated and contentious only when lawyers became involved? "Sometimes when two people are close to one another, they rely on neutral parties to resolve differences," Catarina offered.

"Neutral parties? I think AJ and I were closer to being neutral parties than our parents were. All I did was to ask my mother if the girls and I could live with her for a few weeks, so I could get a job and save enough money to start a new life. Big mistake. Before I knew it, Horst's brother had filed papers, Jacqueline was here with her own lawyer, and everything was a mess."

"What can you tell me about AJ's family?" Catarina knew that asking an open-ended question could lead to unexpected and sometimes useful information.

"AJ was raised by his grandmother, but she died when he was in his teens. Other than that, he only has his mother, Jacqueline Bennett, but we never saw much of her."

"Could you give me her contact information?"

"I remember seeing on the custody papers that she still lives in Florida, but I don't know her cell number or where she is right now. The last I heard she was in São Miguel for the depositions."

Catarina wondered the same thing she had when she talked to the Maiers. *Why the sudden interest in children who had been ignored for so long?* Perhaps the children themselves were not what their grandparents were interested in. "Did AJ have money?" she asked.

"Jacqueline set up a trust fund for him when he was very young. It gave us a few thousand every month, enough to live on but not extravagantly. We weren't here because we had no other option; we were here because we *wanted* to live this way."

"Do you know what happens to that money now?"

She thought for a moment. "I remember going to see Jacqueline before we left for Nigeria. It was really just to say goodbye, but at some point that afternoon, AJ told her we wouldn't need the money anymore, and she should take it back. She said the trust would continue for his lifetime anyway; then it would expire."

If that was true, he hadn't been killed for his money.

Janine thought aloud, "He never wanted the money for himself, but he was glad to have it in the end. The way he saw it, it overcame his biggest obstacle to getting custody of the children. He could show he had a steady income. My stepfather wasn't happy when I told him that AJ was going to file papers to prove that his biological father had been providing him a steady income since he was a year old."

"Is it possible that one of Dawn's grandparents," she avoided saying that Janine's mother was among them, "took Dawn, believing she would be better off with them?"

"Hah." She was truly amused. "The last thing any of them wants is to be saddled with either of the children."

"Just one more question, Janine. What do you know of Rifai Global?"

"I've seen the name before on legal papers. It might be the company that holds AJ's trust."

As they walked back to Anton's office together, Catarina asked her, "Do you know what you will do now?"

Janine spoke numbly, thinking aloud as though no one was there to hear her, asking and answering her own questions, and doing battle with demons from her past. "What choice do I have? I have no way to support my daughters, and with AJ gone...AJ's really gone, isn't he?" She bitterly weighed her options. "Do I go back to my mother's house? I can imagine what life would be like there. Do you know what it took for me just to ask to stay for a few weeks? Horst did exactly what I expected: he put obstacle after obstacle in my path. He didn't want to commit himself until he was certain that we wouldn't burden him. Heaven forbid that he risk his orderly life or his bank account. And I can't count on my mother. Given the choice between what I needed and what Horst wanted, she never thought twice. I was out the door the minute I said I was pregnant. Then again, I'd been far from the perfect child."

Clearly, that idea had been beaten into her as a child. "Parents take the bad with the good," she consoled her.

"Do you know what Horst said when AJ and I brought Melody to say goodbye before we left Germany? He said Melody's problems were God's punishment for my behavior."

Catarina let Janine's tears flow.

"My only friends are in the community. I can't just cut my ties and walk away. Even if I had the money, do you know what that would do to Melody? Perhaps I should just stay and accept that Dawn's future is here. But can I? Ever since I told everyone I'd decided to leave with the girls, Pat barely tolerates me. He says it's not right for me to live in the community if I don't believe in its ideals—and I get that. He told me that while I'm here, I have to live as everyone else does. That's why I hide my phone and sneak away to sign papers. That's why…" She looked at Catarina, judging how safe her secrets were with her. She said quietly, "I've been going into Santa Clara whenever I can get away, every other week or so. AJ told me about the computers in the school library that can be used after hours."

"What were you looking for?" asked Catarina, for she knew Janine had been looking for something.

"Progress." She smiled. "Do you know there's a new way of thinking about children like Melody these days, new drugs and behavioral therapies?"

Catarina smiled at the miracle of hope, reviving life and nourishing the future. When evil flew out of Pandora's Box and into the world, she remembered, hope remained. She faced Janine and held her firmly by the shoulders. "You listen to me. You are a good person and a good mother. You deserved AJ and from what I know of him, he deserved you."

Lower lip trembling, she nodded.

She smoothed Janine's hair and wiped the tears from her cheeks. "Now let's go see how your daughter is doing."

Back in the office, Anton was immersed in paperwork, and Melody sat in the same position on the windowsill, forehead pressed against the glass, still staring out into the park. Janine lightly touched the top of her daughter's head, and the child recoiled.

Anton had put a few sheets of paper and a pencil near Melody, and she had filled them with detailed sketches of eyes and fingers, flower petals and tree branches.

Those drawings reminded Catarina of something she had seen in a college lecture hall, but as hard as she chased the memory, it eluded her.

The child stared at her, grimacing.

"Your pictures are lovely, Melody."

That was when she fell to the ground in a tantrum, beating her head with her fists.

The evening debrief began with discouraging reports. Silva and Gracia had thoroughly searched the forest again, adding the road that skirted it and the banks on either side. The sum total of what they had collected was displayed in three large evidence bags, one containing an empty liquor bottle, one with a single adult flip-flop, and one with a faded homework assignment marked one hundred percent.

"We went to all four of the houses that face the forest," Silva reported. She handed Gabriela photocopies of her notes and read from the originals. "Two are owned by members of the same Leal family who've been farming that land for generations, one is occupied by the Leal widow, who lives alone, and the other by her son and his family."

Gracia, a serious-looking officer in his mid-fifties continued with their report, "When we arrived, all of them were working the land, so while they made their way in from the fields, we took the time to look around." He scratched his ear and shrugged. "Everything seemed as it should. They were cooperative. They readily agreed to allow us to search outbuildings, even their homes. They hadn't seen anything, and they were..." he tried to find the right words, "...*appropriately disturbed* to learn that a child is missing."

"What about the other two houses?"

Silva spoke. "There weren't any leads there, either. One is awaiting restoration and the other is owned by an artist who comes to paint, but only in the summer. We did look in every possible place but…nothing. Sorry."

Anton was disappointed. He had clung to the hope that someone in those houses would lead them to Dawn. "Officer Andrade, you seem to be familiar with the area around Santa Clara."

Norberto looked up at Anton. "Yes, sir."

"Would you talk to some of the residents? Ask if there are any other places nearby where a child might be hidden."

"Yes, sir."

Catarina had one more request. "Would you also find out if they know of any animosity between the settlers and other residents?"

"Yes, ma'am."

Anton nodded at his wife's suggestion. "Who's next?" he asked.

Felipe stood. "Thanks to Officer Sousa's knowledge of the island, we were able to cover the airport, all car rental companies, and most of the marinas and taxi stands on this side of the island. Although no one remembers Dawn Bennett specifically, you can imagine that with tourist season beginning, several people did report seeing a blond girl of about her age. We'll follow up on those leads tomorrow, as well as asking around at the remaining places."

"Actually," Anton spoke to Gabriela, "I want another officer to work with Sousa tomorrow." She nodded and wrote on her notepad. "Felipe, you have the task of locating Jacqueline Bennett." Catarina wrote out the unfamiliar name and handed it to Felipe. "I confirmed with Immigrations that she flew into São Miguel on the thirty-first and was there on the following four days." He passed some papers to Felipe. "These signed and notarized papers show she was in court on the third." He didn't have to remind anyone that was the day Dawn had been taken and her father had been murdered. "Immigrations has no record of her leaving the Azores."

"I'll find her, sir."

"I'd also like you to confirm what the Maiers told us about where they've been. Catarina?" She handed a summary of what the Maiers had said to Felipe. "It's quite a bit to handle so, Gabriela, would you work closely with Felipe on this?" He looked from one to the other, hoping to see them smile at the opportunity to work together, but Felipe focused hard on the papers in front of him, and Gabriela's face remained as impassively professional as always. Only Catarina noticed the slight flush to her cheeks and the tiny curls at the corners of his mouth.

Anton rose. "I want everyone else to meet me in front of the Santa Clara church at six forty-five tomorrow morning," he directed. "It's market day."

Before he turned off the lights and left for the night, Anton took Bobey's ear from his shirt pocket and lifted it to his lips. *I'm trying to find you, child.*

5

In that short time when there's just enough promise of light to know the sun will soon rise, Catarina awoke to find her husband standing over their bed, one hand massaging his scalp and the other holding the notes she had made after she last talked with Janine. He was deep in thought, so she waited quietly until he added the pages to the array of papers spread out on the quilt. She pushed herself up on her hands, careful not to disturb the map of Santa Clara he had unfolded, marked with sticky notes, and draped over the headboard. She knew he hadn't been to sleep. His normally cheery face drooped at the corners of his mouth and was swollen around his eyes.

It was pointless to scold him. Times like these were few, but Anton was a man who took his responsibilities to others very seriously and—especially when children were concerned—his determination knew no bounds. "Shall I make coffee, darling?" she asked.

"Coffee? Maybe later," he replied absentmindedly. He walked around the bed, kissed the top of her head, and drew her to him. "I love you."

"I know."

"I love Toni and Liliana."

"They know." The children had been on his mind; she had found him looking at their pictures more than once since arriving on Terceira.

"It's been six days since Dawn was taken from the forest." In an almost physical way, Anton felt her chances of survival running through his fingers.

Catarina wrapped her arms around his middle. "You're doing everything you can to bring her back to her family."

"She won't ever come back to her father." His mood changed from depression to anger, another emotion rarely seen in Anton. "How can someone—a human being—do something like this? Take a child! Kill a man! How?"

Catarina understood one reason this was hitting him so hard. Her husband accepted that evil existed, but he had always been reassured by a belief that the goodness needed to counteract evil also existed, especially on their beloved islands. Now uneasiness colored his mood. The special place he held up as a model for the rest of the world might *not* have the goodness needed to defeat this terrible evil.

"Norberto will be here in an hour to take us to Santa Clara," he said. "I'll just send my daily report to Luis Gomes and take a shower. Then I really would like to have breakfast with you." It wasn't the breakfast he wanted; it was the normalcy of being together, sipping their morning coffee, sharing small talk about their world, feeling each other's warmth, and appreciating the good things in life.

She folded the map and set the table where they had shared so many dinners. She wasn't going to tell him that everything would be fine. She knew as well as he did that by now the chance of finding Dawn alive was slim.

By the time they reached Santa Clara, there were as many people in the central square as the population of the entire village. Some had walked or biked from neighboring towns, others had driven from more distant parts of the island, and a minibus had brought a small group of tourists from Angra. Shop owners had set up tables outside to attract buyers, but most of the activity was around pushcarts, stalls, and the backs of small trucks that displayed the agricultural wealth of the area—curly kale, tiny potatoes and carrots, bright lemons and limes, juicy berries, and a local variety of fragrant pineapples. Bunches of flowers that had been cut just hours before stood next to wheels of cheese that had been aging for many months. Everywhere people were nibbling and carrying bags brimming with purchases.

Standing on the topmost church step, Anton was an impressive presence. "The village is small enough to go house to house, so I've divided it into five pie-shaped wedges converging on the square, and I've assigned one area to each of you," he addressed the search team. "You have all three of my cell phone numbers. If you come across anything of interest, call or text immediately."

Catarina gave them tips about which questions to ask and how to ask them. "Briefly let people know that Dawn was last seen somewhere nearby, without giving any details that might put false memories in their heads. Don't rush anyone," she cautioned. "Show Dawn's picture and wait patiently for comments. Try to make every question sound like what it is: our plea for help in finding a lost child—not any condemnation of the way her parents cared for her or how the community chooses to live."

"Or any reflection on safety in the area or the Department's inability to find her," Anton interjected.

"Should we take names?" Rosa asked Catarina.

"The best thing would be to introduce yourself by name. Often people will then give their own names in return. If someone gives a lead, then ask for—don't demand—some sort of contact information."

Anton distributed copies of the only picture of Dawn that existed and five copies of a map of Santa Clara, marked up to show the areas he had assigned to each officer. "Since visitors might congregate in one of the cafés, Catarina and I will take those, along with the offices in the municipal building and any place that doesn't fit neatly into one of the areas you're searching." He was momentarily distracted by a tourist taking a selfie in front of a flower-bedecked cart. "Also ask if anyone was here last week and took pictures," he added on the spur of the moment.

Anton and Catarina started on the outskirts of town with the bakery that had attracted so much favorable attention in recent years. The baker would have been standing at the crossroads last Tuesday morning, and he might have seen a suspicious stranger or a little girl holding a red wool elephant.

Even if he hadn't remembered the way, Anton could have found it by the heavenly aroma that enveloped the little complex of mill house, cottage, and bakery. Outside, the baker was standing between a long table and three racks. He rivaled Anton in height, a strong young man with serious brown eyes and curly hair that would have looked jet black if not dusted with the same flour that covered his clothes. Under the table were baskets of rolls and crusty loaves, and the racks held cornbread and enormous wheels of *massa sovada*—the sweet bread for which the islands were famous. On top of the table, special sweets were displayed: custard-filled buns, pastries bejeweled with dried fruits, strawberry tarts, and—being close to Easter—the traditional bird nests shaped of bread, each holding a hardboiled egg.

Most of the people there were residents, although there were a number of tourists, all of whom bought more than they could possibly consume and took pictures of everything their eyes could see. No one seemed able to resist tasting their purchases as they walked away—no one but Anton, who today didn't have even a passing interest in eating.

While Anton waited in line, Catarina talked to the people who milled around, catching up with local gossip on market day. After explaining that she was looking for a missing child, their first comments expressed genuine sympathy and a desire to help—but no memory of having seen anything useful. The comments that followed were more enlightening.

"From the group on the other side of the forest, you say? They're a strange lot," said one woman.

"You never know what's going on back there. They keep to themselves," said another.

"That land's always been part of our parish. It should never have been sold to them. It should have been designated as protected, just like everything around it," declared a third.

"They say one thing and do another," complained a middle-age woman who had just swallowed the last of her sweet roll. "Hypocrites."

"What do you mean by that?" asked Catarina.

"They talk about living as we used to, then they come into town and use telephones and buy prepared food."

"Who did you see doing that?"

"That so-called leader of theirs for one. He likes to spend a few hours in Nuno's café every week, eating, drinking, and using his computer."

Catarina, ever the careful listener, remembered two words the woman had spoken. "You said he's *one* person who did that. Are there others?"

"There's one woman who comes in quite a lot, buys groceries, and eats lunch on one of the benches along the square."

Catarina waited.

"And come to think of it, there's another one who I've seen around the school a few times."

"Could you describe either of them?" she asked.

She was stood still for a few moments, recapturing images she had once seen. "The first one is on the tall side. Always carries a large cloth bag and wears a scarf on her head, the same embroidered scarf every time, so I'm not sure what her hair color is. I'm sorry. I'm so bad at remembering features. You might ask Alicia at the grocery. That's where the woman shops."

Catarina prompted, "And the other woman, the one you've seen around the school?"

"Ah, her. A nervous sort. Looks over her shoulder a lot, if you know what I mean. Avoids making eye contact. Her hair was short and reddish. I remember that." She looked at Catarina and shrugged. "I'm not even sure she's one of them. It's just that she's not one of us, so I was suspicious."

And often all it takes to arouse suspicions is to be an outsider.

For a while, Catarina said nothing, making sure that was all the woman had to say. "You've been so helpful. Thank you. And thank you from the child's mother." *Thank you from the suspicious stranger with short, reddish hair, who was only at the school trying to be a good mother.*

"Well, that was pointless," said Anton, rejoining his wife. "The young baker remembers absolutely nothing."

By the time they reached the one-pump gas station on the main road, Catarina had filled her husband in on what she had heard, including how some townspeople viewed the settlers on the other side of the forest. Anton remembered that Janine had delayed going to the police because the community feared attracting negative attention, and he remembered Norberto's irritation that the land which young boys had claimed as *their* kingdom had been occupied by outsiders. *Could someone want to get rid of Comunidade dos Reis badly enough to have harmed a child?*

The owner of the gas station and the people in the cafés had nothing to contribute. The clerk who was filling in for the owner of the grocery store could say little more than what Catarina already knew: the grocer had joked about a woman who came in regularly and bought large quantities of some items.

They were halfway through the municipal building when they got their first real lead. The man behind the desk at the tiny post office looked at Dawn's picture. "Last market day? I was away at a funeral but when I got back, someone..." his voice slowed, "...someone said she had seen the prettiest little girl with *a saint's halo of golden curls.*"

Anton was about to ask *who*—and urgently—but Catarina looked him in the eyes and raised a finger to her lips.

"It was at the café..." the man continued at a snail's pace, trying to piece together the memory, "...the one closest to the church, where they have the best frosted rolls with lots of orange peel."

Anton squeezed Catarina's hand, trying to remain patient, and she gave him two quick squeezes in return. He took a deep breath.

"Wait! They weren't talking to me. I was alone." He looked at Catarina, "My wife had stayed behind after the funeral. The death was in her cousin's family."

She nodded sympathetically but said nothing.

"So I was just listening to people at nearby tables, and there was a group talking about putting together a pamphlet about the village to leave in hotels and at the airport. The young teacher—what's her name—she didn't think that was a good idea because it would bring in too many outsiders, and..." He was still trying to recall the conversation. "Padre Santos suggested that the pamphlet should just mention market day...and someone…someone said that last market day there was a little girl with *a saint's halo of golden curls.*" He closed his eyes and lifted his head to the ceiling. "Who was that?" he asked himself.

Who? Who! Anton was squirming with frustration.

"Aha! It was the retired school teacher, senhora Brum."

A break at last. He stopped and reminded himself that he might not reach Dawn in time, and he felt a lump swell in his throat.

While Catarina got directions to senhora Brum's house and thanked the man, Anton checked in with his team. Only Rosa had anything to report. She had found two visitors who had taken pictures around the village on the last market day, and both had downloaded the files to her phone right there and then. Thank goodness for technology, thought Anton.

Senhora Brum's house was just off the square in the oldest part of Santa Clara, where four narrow, cobbled lanes were lined with tiny black basalt houses and mature trees. Before they reached the front door, an elderly woman stuck her head out of an upstairs window. "There's work being done on the ground floor," her strong voice called out. "Go around."

They followed the rough path that ran alongside an uneven stone patio at the side of the house. Little sunlight reached the area, and it was noticeably cooler and damper than in the lanes. In mossy pots that looked like they had been there for a hundred years, a variety of plants had met the challenges of their environment and grew with determination. Through a small doorway, too short even for Catarina to pass through without bowing her head, they entered the dim shell of the house, with the dust of the ages hanging in shafts of pale light. Picking their way around piles of ancient debris and between stacks of new lumber reminded both of them of Casa do Bosque, when Beto had been renovating it.

"Come upstairs," senhora Brum's voice carried down the stairwell, and they followed the glow of electric light up well-worn steps to an unexpectedly large landing, now crammed with what must have been the contents of the entire first floor. A Victorian sofa was wedged against an ornate dining table, which was stacked with a hodgepodge of photo albums. Oil paintings—one of the Golden Gate Bridge—leaned against the walls, and the spaces under end tables were filled with books. The story of senhora Brum's family life was told in pictures displayed on the walls: her wedding, the birth of her children, grandchildren, and great-grandchildren, and—trimmed with faded black ribbon—the death of her parents, husband, and two children.

Senhora Brum was old, well into her eighties, but she wasn't feeble. She moved around her small space gracefully, and she cleared a heavy stack of books from one end of the sofa before either of them could offer to help. She must have been quite tall as a young woman because even now she matched Catarina's height. Her hair, smoothed into a bun at the back of her head, was white but remarkably thick for someone of her age. Of another generation, she wore a long black dress and black hose, and probably had since her husband died.

"I'm sorry I can't offer you any tea. I'm without a kitchen. My grandchildren finally convinced me to have this place modernized, so it will be easier for me when I get older."

"No tea is needed," said Catarina, who saw senhora Brum settling in for a long talk and knew this was going to be a struggle for Anton.

"They take turns bringing me dinner."

"How nice," she said with genuine warmth.

"They wanted me to live with them, but I've lived here since I was born—right in that room there," she gestured to one of the two bedrooms off the landing, "and I'm not leaving."

"I wouldn't want to leave, either. I'm Catarina Vanderhye, and this is my husband, Anton Cardosa." She heard Anton shuffling his feet and taking a deep breath.

Anna Brum introduced herself and—by way of pictures—she also introduced her entire family, going back two generations and forward three. Then she started to give them a tour of her belongings, with stories of the pieces that had been brought and sent by relatives who had emigrated to America over the years. "Almost everyone left. But someone had to stay and keep this island our home."

Catarina had heard Anton try to break into senhora Brum's reminiscences several times, growing louder each time. "Anton," she said at the first opportunity, "I must remind you to leave a picture."

He grinned with relief. "Senhora, this child is missing, and her mother is hoping someone has seen her."

She glanced at the picture. "I saw her," she said without hesitation. "Come with me." She led them to the bedroom she had been born in and moved aside a chair in front of the window that the cobblestone lane. "I sit in here a lot because of all the noise and dust. It's peaceful looking out at my neighborhood and the trees."

He clenched his hands, waiting.

She pointed out the window. "The child turned the corner there and went down toward the new municipal garden."

He looked.

"I thought it was odd that she should be going that way. I know all the families between here and the garden, and they didn't belong."

"They?" Anton and Catarina said at once.

She looked at them surprised. "Why yes, *they*. She was too young to be wandering around an unfamiliar neighborhood alone."

Anton couldn't help breaking in. "What did the person with her look like?"

She wrinkled her brow. "How strange. I know someone was there, but I was watching the girl and her angelic curls."

He was beginning to doubt the old woman had actually seen Dawn. "Was it a man or a woman?"

Puzzled, she shook her head slowly three times, unable to answer the question. Then she drew in a sharp breath and said, "Wait...I do remember something: she was holding something bright red. A stuffed animal?"

Bobey.

Anton and Catarina stood outside senhora Brum's house, looking west toward the garden that backed onto the municipal building. Surrounded by a high iron fence, it could only be accessed through a gate on the far side, making the lane a dead end, even to pedestrians.

He counted nine small houses, all similar to senhora Brum's in age and construction. "Without scaling walls, the only way to get here is the route we took from the central square," he said, thinking aloud. He took out a cell phone and called each of the police officers on the team. Within minutes, they stood in front of him. "Norberto," he said, "this is in your assigned area."

"Yes, sir."

"Were you able to find someone in each of the houses?"

"No, sir." He took out his map and the notes he had taken. "No one answered my knocks at one of the houses on the..." he glanced at the sky, "...north side of the street. Looking through the windows, it was apparently vacant, and I..." He screwed up his face and said reluctantly, "I took the liberty of entering by a side door and searching it."

Anton wasn't the least interested in protocol or legal issues. "I'll assume you didn't find Dawn Bennett. What about the other houses?"

"All were occupied by families." He ran down the list of the people he had spoken with and handed it to Anton. "No one reported seeing the child or anything unusual."

"With the exception of Norberto, you are each to visit two of the occupied houses. You will identify yourselves and say that you are searching every house on this block. Report any resistance to me immediately. After the searches are completed, Catarina will talk to the residents." He stationed Norberto at the entrance to the lane, and he and Catarina stood where it ended at the municipal garden.

Fortunately the houses were small, and their occupants were cooperative and—as far as Catarina could tell—well-intentioned. Unfortunately, nothing came of their efforts.

It wasn't until they were on their way back to the police station that a thought occurred to Anton. "Norberto," he asked, "how thoroughly did you search that vacant house?"

"I looked in every room, sir, and basement and the back garden. The girl wasn't there."

"Turn the car around. Please."

Without asking why, he did a three-point turn and headed back to Santa Clara at a speed that Anton appreciated.

"What are you thinking?" asked Catarina.

This was Anton's forte. He had distilled everything they had learned into two salient points. "We know Dawn was walking along a lane that leads nowhere on the day she disappeared. We are fairly certain that she wasn't going to any of the occupied houses on that lane. If you had just taken a child, would you wander around town on market day with her?" He answered his own question. "No. You would be heading somewhere, directly and quickly."

Once inside the house, Anton pulled a handful of evidence bags out of his pocket. "Norberto, you looked for Dawn, and I know you looked carefully. It's true: she isn't here. But she probably was at one point. Let's all look carefully for anything to confirm that."

Anton saw it first, but he knew Norberto felt derelict in his duty for not having searched thoroughly enough the first time so—good man that he was—he made sure that the young officer found it. "Would you finish in this room, Norberto? I want to look around outside again."

It didn't take long. "Sir, would you look at this?" Two letters were printed on a charred fragment of paper at the back of a mound of ashes in the hearth.

wn

"This letter isn't found in Portuguese," Norberto said, pointing to the *w*.

"Good man, Norberto. Now we have to ask ourselves how Dawn's kidnapper knew this house would be empty, and why the child was moved."

Catarina walked in with another piece of evidence that pointed to Dawn having been in the house, a single blond hair curled around her finger.

Anton could feel the warmth of Bobey's ear through his shirt. *I'm coming for you, child.*

Lori watched Millikan watching Helena, his black eyes studying her every move. Was it lust she saw on his face? Somewhere in her forties and a bit shorter than Lori, she had a certain exotic beauty, with skin the color of strong tea, sensual lips, and large almond eyes. Helena looked from person to person, possibly assessing them, but she gave her undivided attention and a warmhearted smile to anyone who approached her, and there were many. Just as with Millikan in the early morning hours, community members came to her on their way to the fields or the vineyards, and she listened, chatting with some and handing out small cloth bags—presumably filled with tea or herbs—to others.

Lori knew little about the woman who shared the cottage adjacent to hers with Amal, and she had put off talking with her. Almost a caricature of a gypsy fortune teller, she wore long flowing skirts, colorful shawls, and bangles, and—far worse to Lori—she claimed supernatural abilities. When the psychic's eyes lit on her, she steeled herself and walked over. "You're Helena?"

"I am now."

Lori had her own premonition: she was about to hear a tale of past lives.

"When I received my calling, I chose the name Helena to honor a famous spiritualist of that name."

"Ah," said Lori, relieved that the explanation had been short and simple. "What name were you born with?" She knew she didn't have Catarina's talent for slipping questions into apparently casual conversations, and she hoped she didn't sound like she was trying to extract information that would help her to look into Helena's background—which was exactly what she was doing.

"It no longer matters."

"Have you been with the community long?"

"What is long? We are all here for moments and forever."

"How wise," she commented, affecting an earnest expression. "It's just that I'm looking for someone else who's new here, so we can help each other settle in." She looked at the ground so her face wouldn't betray that she already knew Helena had only recently joined the community.

Helena watched the dogs wandering freely in the compound and the cows grazing in the meadow, but offered nothing.

Since Helena had been near the forest when Dawn had disappeared, and since the forest was where she harvested her mushrooms, fermented her tea, and dried her herbs, she could be an important source of information. Lori made another effort to start a conversation with her, "I've heard you provide medicinal plants for us."

"I'm a trained herbalist." She looked into Lori's eyes. "I am the holder of generations of knowledge on how to prepare healing infusions, tinctures, distillations, and syrups."

"How interesting. Did you do that work before you came to our community?"

Her voice was calm, and her gaze was steady. "I did."

She waited for more, but there was none. *Was this air of mystery part of an image she had created? Was she trying to avoid being identified? Or was this simply her personality?*

Millikan came over. "I see you two have met. Good. You'll find Helena is someone to rely on here. Since almost everyone else has already left, why don't you spend the morning helping her?"

Of all the places Lori least wanted to spend a morning, it was in the dreariest corner of Comunidade dos Reis. Yet that was where she found herself, in a narrow fold of land where the forest's stream drained, leaving shallow pools of muddy water and saturating the clay soil. No pretty flowers or fertile gardens were found here. Stringy algae waved in the water, lichen and grayish moss grew on sharp-edged boulders, and tall tufts of coarse grass filled the spaces in between. The air smelled of decomposing vegetation.

With the self-anointed spiritual leader of the community by her side, Lori stood in front of an absurdly large pot that reminded her of the witches' cauldron from Macbeth. Helena hitched the hem of her long skirt up between her legs and into her waistband. "It will take a while," she said, rolling up her sleeves. "I've been working on this batch for several days already. All you need to do is finish stirring it over the fire."

She handed Lori a long stick, stripped of its bark and coated with congealed soap. In the pot was a slurry of overpoweringly fragrant liquid soap. Lori recognized the smell and the goopy consistency from the pottery bowls next to the communal water pumps and the small jars Vera kept on a shelf in the cottage. She reminded herself to make the most of this time with Helena and started by trying to win her over with flattery. "I've always wondered how soap is made. I'd love to learn from the expert." What followed was a rambling, incomprehensible explanation, during which Lori patiently stirred the mixture and did her best to look fascinated. There was an entire morning ahead to ask Helena questions.

Helena left her to rummage through bushes for berries, ferret under leaf debris for mushrooms, scrape lichen off rocks, and scoop algae from stagnant ponds. Never out of sight for long, she returned every few minutes to dry what she had found on a large, flat rock and to check on Lori's progress with the soap mixture. Finally, she took the stick from her and said, "Time for a break. Why don't you sit?"

"Thanks." She wiggled her aching fingers, rolled her shoulders, and sat on a fallen tree trunk.

"It will get easier," Helena said kindly. "I got used to hard work when I was young."

Channeling Catarina, Lori resisted a strong temptation to ask her about that, and she was rewarded.

"I was born in Spain, the sixth child of a Basque and an Algerian. That means I started life as an outsider. I learned to take care of myself when I was very young."

Something about the way she said it, more to herself than to anyone else, told Lori that was the truth. "I know what you mean."

Lori had no intention of opening up about herself—she was here to help find Dawn—still, what Helena said had struck a chord. She, too, had learned to take care of herself at a young age, and Catarina had helped her to understand that—like most people—she carried the unmet needs of her childhood with her, and probably would for the rest of her life. They had shaped her, but rather than leaving her vulnerable, they had left her strong.

"Do you have children, Helena?" she asked.

"No, and I never wanted any. It's hard enough on your own, and those I care for in the community are like my children."

Lori wished for Catarina. She would know why there had been a catch in Helena's voice just then.

The stick was abruptly returned to Lori. "People in the outside world have lost touch with the spiritual life," Helena said, sitting down on the log.

Lori couldn't disagree with the premise. If the media were to be believed, a spiritual life was high on the list of coveted achievements these days. Despite that, actually living one seemed to be just out of reach for most, put aside for the next degree, the next job, the next house, the next vacation.

"There's respect for what I do here. And, of course, without interference from the chaos out there, it's much easier to connect with the spiritual."

It wasn't a novel idea. Certainly, withdrawing from the demands of modern life was offered by monasteries, meditation classes, and weekend excursions into nature.

Lori was on the verge of agreeing, when Helena uttered her next thought, "I was born as a conduit for the spiritual energy of the universe."

She silently groaned, knowing the conversation was about to turn to areas she had no respect for—and knowing that she would be Helena's captive audience for the remainder of a very long morning.

"When I was a child, some called me odd, and some called me crazy. I was only expressing the same gifts given to my mother and to most of the women in my family."

Lori's response was a noncommittal *mmm*.

"It was accepted more back then, when everything didn't have to be measured and proven. But now, because I can't explain how I pass on the universe's healing energy, I'm mocked by outsiders." Helena held Lori's gaze. "Do you believe?"

She had to be careful. She was here to get information not to share her authentic self. "I'm not sure."

"People have no problem living their lives according to what's in the Bible." She looked at Lori and waited for her to agree before continuing. "What would those same people think about me if I said I saw an angel in a bush that was on fire but never destroyed? Or that I saw a woman look over her shoulder and turn into a block of salt?"

Lori had to bring the conversation around to Dawn's disappearance. "I know you help us by bringing us special foods and making this wonderful soap, but how do you use your psychic abilities in our community?" It took some effort to acknowledge Helena's *psychic* abilities.

"Just as Pat leads the community in its physical activities, I lead the community in its spiritual activities."

"I saw everyone coming to you this morning."

"People trust me with their problems and their secrets."

Lori didn't want to seem too curious. Rather than asking about the secrets directly, she risked tempting Helena to reveal them by intimating that her gifts weren't special. "I've been lucky to have had several people in my life who were good listeners. I talked to them about problems with boyfriends, money, work.

"I'm talking about bigger things."

"Like what?" She held her breath and focused on stirring the slimy gray slurry.

"I know who goes to the outside world to use computers and telephones. I know who's hiding money and who's hiding from the police. I know Dawn is fine—"

"What? How...?" Lori's heart thumped, but her excitement was short-lived.

"Her father told me."

"AJ? But he's dead."

"Of course. The dead trust me. They tell me what they want others to know…and what they don't want others to know."

Lori suppressed the urge to walk away.

"They're still here; they come in and out of the present world until they can rest, knowing that those they love are fine. Then they go to their rest in the other world."

Listening to her, she could allow for only two possibilities: Helena was crazy…or Helena was a scam artist. She couldn't wait to relate this conversation over a cup of hot cocoa at Casa do Mar.   She made one last attempt to get something useful out of her. "I was just thinking…" she said, adjusting her face to show a high opinion of Helena's purported abilities. "Is it possible your powers could help find Janine's daughter?"

Helena eyed her cautiously. "What do you mean?"

"If you were nearby the morning Dawn was taken, the morning Janine's husband was…you know…could you have sensed something?"

Her face took on a dreamy look. "I saw the girls walk into the forest just after I brought out my last basket of mushrooms. Dawn went first, and Melody followed her. Then I came out here, and it's just too far away to have sensed anything."

Lori looked around. They really were too far to see or hear anything in the compound.

Helena bent over the remnants of the morning's fire to scoop small bowlsful of soggy soil onto the hot ashes. Deep in thought, she stood upright and looked at Lori. "Sometimes it's best to let the universe unfold without interfering."

The hamlet was quiet. After a long morning of hard work and a large meal, almost everyone napped through the early afternoon hours, something Lori had never become accustomed to. When she saw Amal walking quickly across the fields with a small bundle under her arm, she ran to catch up with her, hoping to glean something...anything...that might help find Dawn. Ahead, the slight young woman stopped at a branch of the forest's stream and bent low over the water. Lori called out to her, but she was too far away to be heard and by the time she drew closer, she realized she was intruding and stopped, trying to not make a sound.

Amal took her time, intent on washing not only her hands and face, but carefully rinsing her arms and feet, as well. She repeated the cleansing three times, and then ran her wet hands over her hair from forehead to the nape of her neck. Lori watched as she unrolled a small square woven in dark reds and blues, and stood, bowed, and prostrated herself, moving her lips in quiet prayer. When she finished, she rotated her head smoothly, looked Lori directly in the eyes, and motioned for her to join her—as if she had been aware of her presence all along.

Lori was embarrassed. "I'm sorry. I didn't mean to bother you."

"You've done no harm." She picked up the rug she had been praying on.

"It's beautiful." Lori extended her hand to touch it but stopped, unsure if it would be rude or even sacrilegious.

"Thank you," Amal said, stroking the top. Her smile was small, and the first Lori had ever seen on her face. "The design is the same as one that hung in my family's home."

"Do you have family nearby?" Even as she asked the question, somehow Lori knew what the answer would be, and she wanted to pull the words back into her mouth.

"All are dead. I am the only one who remains." Her eyes were blank.

"I'm sorry." Would saying nothing more show respect for Amal's privacy or dismiss her loss as trivial? Would questions about her family bring solace or unbearable memories? Lori touched gently on the subject, "Did you have brothers or sisters?"

Amal rolled up the rug, tucked it under her arm, and then lifted her hijab to reach into a deep pocket over her chest. She took out a creased, dog-eared picture, a happy scene of people dancing and laughing at a wedding, and she showed it to Lori.

"Your family?"

"Yes. It was my oldest brother's wedding." She continued, more to herself than to Lori, "Everyone is there except Rashid. He wasn't in the picture, so his face is beginning to fade in my mind."

Lori studied the picture. She could see Amal, probably in her late teens at the time, smiling widely with unbroken teeth and glittering eyes, waving unscarred arms to dance.

"Shall we walk back together?" All she could offer was companionship.

She nodded.

Lori lay her hand on Amal's arm, lightly at first and when she didn't flinch, more firmly. Through the thin cloth, she could feel ropes of hard scar tissue. "You've had a difficult life." It was all she could think of saying.

"As others have." She gripped the skirt of her long dress.

"Does it help to talk about it, or does that make it worse?"

Amal thought. "Nothing makes it worse. Nothing makes it better." She rubbed her nose roughly. "It simply *is*."

The conversation turned to other matters as they walked back home. "How did you come here, to Terceira, to Comunidade dos Reis?" It was so far removed from the rest of the world, Lori could see it only as a destination one aimed for, not as a place discovered on the way to somewhere else.

"My father was a professor of history at the university in Aleppo. It is…it *was* a top university with 60,000 students, a hospital, a publishing house, and so much more. We had exchange programs with universities around the world. My father was in Morocco for a term, lecturing on—" she stopped, looking embarrassed. "I'm sorry. I was carried away with my memories."

Sometimes the memories are all a person has. "Please tell me about it. I asked because I'm interested, truly."

"You wanted to know how I came to the community." Her large brown eyes looked up to Lori's. "It was because of one of my father's stories. He used to entertain us—my brothers and sisters and me—at dinner with stories."

Lori remembered the faces in the picture; she had seen all but Rashid.

"One night, the night he returned from Morocco, he talked about the Moors and how they had brought peace and prosperity to the countries of the Mediterranean during the Middle Ages. He told us about the Arab words they had left in their languages, and the plants and foods they had introduced, and the beauty of the castles and mosques they had built."

Lori remembered much of this from history classes and her own travels: open courtyards with tiled fountains and flowering plants; mosques—most of them now churches—with graceful vaulting, decorative arabesques, painted tiles, and minarets; the magnificent Alhambra. "You decided to see them with your own eyes?"

"I don't think you can call it a decision." Her voice carried no emotion. "Millions walked away from one of the oldest inhabited cities in the world, and I left my beautiful Aleppo with everyone else. None of us really had a choice."

Until then, they had only been news stories to Lori; she realized that Amal was someone who had actually lived through the daily bombings, the nightly terror, the siege, the loss of homes and family and everything dear.

"It was gone by then anyway," said Amal, still dry-eyed. "For thousands of years, Babylonians, Hittites, ancient Greeks and ancient Romans, Byzantines and later Christians, Mongols and Ottomans, Muslims, Christians, and Jews had all left their mark on my magnificent city. And in less than five years, it was dust."

Her eyes were unfocused now, dead with the memory. "We were captured. My brothers and father were killed on the first day. My mother died that night." She sounded so matter-of-fact. "I was left with my two sisters, but only one survived to escape with me, and she died of a fever. I walked through Turkey and Serbia, took buses through Hungary, and trains through Austria and Germany, working as a maid as much as I could..." She realized her thoughts were wandering and fell silent.

"Please go on," Lori encouraged her.

"To answer your question, even when I could finally stop, I kept going. I wanted to go to one of the places my father had told me about, where Arabs were once admired for creating a peaceful, tolerant society. In Portugal, someone told me about the Azores, and the isolation appealed to me." She replaced the picture in her pocket. "Maybe I just wanted a place where nothing would intrude on my memories."

Getting away from Comunidade dos Reis unseen hadn't been a problem; the settlement had many trees and few people. Lori had simply walked to the outhouse shared by the two neighboring cottages and kept walking into the forest. If asked, she intended to say she was trying to find a shortcut to the stream. The clouds had been thick and gray all day, but with warming temperatures, they broke here and there, piercing the little scene ahead of her with thin shafts of sunlight. She picked up a fleeting movement between the trunks of two trees and she stopped, foot in midair over a boulder. Another flash of blue appeared further away, then disappeared. She tried to remember who was wearing blue that day.

She was on her way to meet Anton and Catarina, but at the last minute she veered off in the direction that had caught her attention, trying to follow someone she could no longer see. She stepped carefully to make as little noise as possible and scanned the forest, her eyes spotting birds returning to their nests and branches waving but nothing more. Then the crack of a twig caught her attention, and she saw someone wearing a blue shawl hurry along an overgrown path that meandered around a massive outcrop and through a grove of lilacs.

Where the path curved downhill, the figure stepped off and continued eastward to a small grassy clearing. The woman, face still hidden under a broad-brimmed straw hat, suddenly turned around and scanned the forest in front of her. Lori darted behind a nearby thicket of bushes, unable to see what was happening. She could hear the sounds of digging and small stones hitting the ground, the tinkling of glass, and hollow metallic thuds. For a long while, she heard nothing more. She was about to peer around the tree trunk when she realized someone was walking very close by. She held her breath and listened as the slow, even footsteps grew fainter.

When the forest had returned to its usual background sounds of animals scampering and leaves rustling, Lori stepped out and walked to the clearing where the woman had stopped. With eyes down, she walked its perimeter slowly, not sure what she was looking for. There was nothing, she decided, until a bird swooped in front of her and her focus shifted to a muddy area just beyond the grass that had been used as a dumping ground, littered with empty jars, cigarette butts, package wrappers, and discarded shopping bags. And one patch, over which some of the trash had been laid, had fresh footprints.

Lori used a stick to clear away the empty aluminum cans and glass jars, and studied the impressions left behind by someone's shoes. Eventually she saw patterns that made sense. The toes of the woman's shoes pointed to a central spot, which had been smoothed and patted down. The sharp edge of a nearby stone was muddied, and Lori used it as it had just been used: to dig up what the mystery woman had dug up. A few inches below the surface, she found a locked metal box. She thought she could break it open, but she knew there might be more to gain if no one realized she had been there. Instead, she picked it up and shook it. It wasn't heavy, and when she shifted it, there seemed to be two things inside—something small and metallic, and something large and soft.

Before burying the metal box again and scattering some trash over the area, she held one of her own feet above a footprint. It was smaller, stretching from her heel to just where her toes began, and the right sole had a nick at the toe.

Lori pulled out her cell phone and texted Anton. *Meet tomorrow instead. Same time. Same place.*

And she headed back to Comunidade dos Reis to look for a woman wearing a blue shawl and muddy shoes.

It was close to eight that night when Anton and Catarina returned to their room, and it felt almost as if they had never left Terceira. They were young, newly married, and sharing news, dreams, ideas, and plans while they made dinner together.

Catarina placed an onion on the cutting board. "Do you think we should we have asked Felipe to join us?"

Anton knew the onion needed to be chopped and took out a knife. "He might prefer some time away from us."

She added a couple of carrots to the cutting board. "I know what you're hoping for," she teased her romantic husband.

"Felipe would be so much happier if he had someone special in his life." He slid the onion pieces into a skillet his wife had heated, and she stirred them around in olive oil.

"Gabriela's a lovely woman," she said.

"We wouldn't have come as far as we have without her, that's for sure." He sliced the carrots, added them to the skillet, and started dicing the potatoes Catarina had just peeled.

"She and Felipe seem well suited to each other."

Anton was glad to hear that. His wife had an understanding of people so uncanny that she often knew their innermost feelings better than they did. He chuckled. "I believe I have another assignment for the two of them tomorrow."

She smiled. "That's nice." She handed him the salt and pepper. "Did you hear that senhor Machado is retiring as school principal?"

Of course he had heard. Anton knew about most things that happened on their home island, either through official channels or through casual contacts. People called, stopped him on the street to say a few words, and flagged him down as he drove around in his old Volvo wagon. He seasoned the vegetables. "I heard. Maria Rosa said they want the replacement to start two months before this school year ends. What do you think that means?"

She, too, had her sources. A good one was Isabella, who co-owned Water's Edge, the restaurant where many on Santa Maria got together. "Isabella overheard some teachers at dinner one evening saying there may be extensive changes at the school next year. They'll need more time to prepare."

"Changes? What changes are needed? That's the best school on the island."

"It hasn't changed much since senhor Machado became principal twenty-five years ago."

"There's nothing wrong with that."

His remark wasn't unexpected from a man who valued the past as he did.

Catarina started to set the table, and Anton took out greens for a salad. "I know someone who'd be perfect as the new principal," he said.

She put two wine glasses on the table. "Who?"

He poured the wine and lifted a glass. "You."

It had once been her dream to run a school. She had thought through its philosophy; she had imagined her students growing from the first day they greeted her to the day they graduated; she had looked forward to working with other teachers to create a special place and time in children's lives. But her parents had not accepted Anton, or her refusal to attend the university they had chosen for her, so that she could be near him in Lisbon. With the death of his parents, the young couple had been left with no financial support and, having to work while going to school, it had taken much longer than expected to finish their education. Already in their late twenties when they finally graduated, they had both put other plans on hold and done what they agreed was most important to them: start a family.

While the stew simmered, they called their beloved Liliana and Toni to hear their news and to say goodnight, quite content with the way their lives had turned out.

As they ate, they turned their attention to the television. Tiny changes in atmospheric pressure, brought about by Earth's spin on its axis, had changed the trajectory of Hurricane Mimi. The Azores had been placed under a *red alert* for the weekend, signaling the possibility of dangerous weather conditions, including sea waves of up to ten meters, thunderstorms, hurricane force winds, and widespread flooding. This would be the first such weather to hit the islands since they moved back, and they were worried. It wasn't their children they were concerned about; Maria Rosa, who was one of the island's safety officers, would probably have them at the new clinic in town along with her own children before the first raindrops fell. It was Casa do Mar that was on their minds. With Beto's method of restoration, the renovated guesthouses were as likely to survive intact as they had been when new—and they had made it through such weather for a hundred years. It was the barn with the two small spaces at either end, the small spaces they called home, that was most vulnerable.

As they washed up after dinner, they went over the day's developments: the empty house that was tied to a child with a halo of golden curls; the revelation that some of the settlers spent time in Santa Clara, and the animosity some villagers felt toward them; and the promise of pictures taken the day Dawn disappeared. Lori's last minute postponement made them more than curious; it made them uneasy, and they were anxious to see her again.

Before turning off the lights, they made plans for the morning meeting with the people who had dedicated themselves to rescuing Dawn. Then they snuggled close. Anton breathed in the scent of his wife's hair, Catarina listened to her husband's heart beat, and they fell asleep.

Living in the community had taught Dawn to trust everyone, so she hadn't hesitated when her hand had been taken and she'd been led away.

You're coming with me for a while.

She'd been relieved to put space between her and… Was that her father?

Your mother asked me to take care of you.

They'd gone further than she ever remembered going, across that flat gray road, down the hill toward the ocean, and further still to an empty house.

You'll be safe here while I get your mother.

They went down the stairs to a room that was smaller and darker than her room at home. She had waited until the sound of footsteps faded and tried to open the door, to find her own way back to Mama. But as hard as she pulled and as hard as she pushed, the door wouldn't open.

Dawn held her breath at the sound of a key turning in the lock. Mama?

Come here.

She said she wanted her mama.

Come here, and we'll go to meet your mother.

She hugged Bobey. Mama had told her that Bobey would always take care of her.

Come!

She watched a sweaty hand coming towards her face and felt her nose pinched hard. She tried to suck air but there didn't seem to be any. Dizzy, she gasped, then retched on the cloth stuffed into her mouth.

6

It hadn't been necessary to find AJ's mother; she had found them and was waiting at the police station when they arrived the next morning.

Jacqueline Bennett was the sort of woman who would be referred to as handsome. The dark brown page boy that Anton had seen in photographs had grown out and been lightened, but otherwise she looked much like she had when she was younger. Not particularly feminine or notably beautiful, she was tall and lean with strong, regular features. She was dressed simply, but everything from her pantsuit to her shoes was of the highest quality.

She got to the reason for her visit while they were still standing in the reception area. "My lawyer was contacted by your police on São Miguel. Apparently my son has been found dead, and his daughter can't be found." Somehow the way she said it seemed more appropriate to complaining that her dry cleaning had been lost or a restaurant was out of salmon.

"I'm sorry to tell you that is true, Mrs. Bennett," said Catarina.

She didn't even blink. "It's Ms. Bennett."

"Forgive me, Ms. Bennett," she apologized in the formal English she had learned as a child. "We are all very sorry for your loss."

"Yes." It was an afterthought when she added, "Thank you."

Under most circumstances, there would have been several minutes of small talk as they settled into a nearby reception room, but not so with Jacqueline Bennett. Offers of a cup of coffee and to adjust the blinds to screen out the sunlight were summarily turned down; in fact, she pointedly looked at her Rolex several times, waiting impatiently for the formal interview to begin.

"We apologize for having to ask you questions at this time."

"I understand it must be done." Her voice was level and her face composed. She was either a woman who chose not to display emotion or one who had little to begin with.

"We need to talk for two reasons. We do want to find out who is responsible for your son's death. More urgently, we want to find your granddaughter."

"You think the two are related?"

"At this point, we do."

"Please continue." She seemed more detached than defensive or confrontational.

"Sometimes the most seemingly inconsequential detail can help." Catarina tried to build rapport with neutral questions before getting to those that were most important to ask. "I'd like to get some background information first. Where in America do you live?"

"I live in Florida."

"Was Alexander an only child?"

She tightened her mouth. "Yes, he was my only child."

Both the phrasing and her tone made Catarina think she was withholding something. "I was an only child, myself," she said conversationally. "I would have loved to have siblings, even half-siblings. In some families, there is no distinction between half-siblings and full siblings, and in some there is."

Her nostrils flared, and abruptly she changed the subject. "What can you tell me about my son's death?"

Jacqueline wanted to avoid talking about something. Catarina and Anton had already decided which details of AJ's death to tell his mother and which to withhold, and she was given only a vague statement that he had been killed last Tuesday morning. "Do you know of anyone who would wish to harm your son?"

She hesitated. "I didn't know much about the life he chose. He's been away so long. Perhaps you should ask the people he lived with." There was no acknowledgement that he had a family, just *the people he lived with.*

Anton spoke for the first time, his English simpler and slower than his wife's. "You came to the Azores because of the custody hearing?"

She raised her eyebrows, indicating that the answer should have been obvious. "Yes."

"AJ had asked for your help?"

"He wrote to ask for money to hire a lawyer." She was being careful with her answers.

"You wanted to help him get custody of Melody and Dawn?"

She didn't seem to know how to answer.

"You *didn't* want to help your son get custody of Melody and Dawn?"

She raised her eyebrows. "It really doesn't matter now, does it? Maybe the girls would have been better off with AJ, maybe with Janine. We'll never know. Now they will stay with her."

"Could you tell us about your son's finances, Ms. Bennett?"

She took a moment to compose her answer, sighed deeply, and said, "AJ's father settled a modest sum on him when he was born, and he's been receiving income from that since then." She gave every indication of speaking the truth.

"What's the name of AJ's father?" Anton asked, picking up a pencil.

Her eyes narrowed. "I've been AJ's only parent since he was born."

"Yes, we understand this." Anton repeated, "What is the name of AJ's father?"

"I really don't see that has anything to do with why we are here." She barely contained her anger.

"I need the information."

"Jeremy Alexander." She looked at both of them expectantly.

Were they supposed to recognize the name?

She was relieved by their reaction—or the lack of one.

"Perhaps you can help us to find your granddaughter," Catarina shifted to the most pressing matter.

"I really don't know much about her."

Or care much about her. "When was the last time you saw Dawn?"

Color rose in her cheeks. "I've never seen her."

"And the last time you saw AJ?"

"The last time I saw any of them…" She cleared her throat and straightened her shoulders. "AJ and his wife brought the older daughter to my house in Palm Beach before they left for Nigeria."

That was nine years ago.

"You have to understand that AJ and I were never close. I was young when he was born, and he was raised more by my late mother than by anyone else."

Her blasé attitude about her own son and his family unsettled Catarina. She sat back and took a deep breath, and during the lull in the conversation, her mind poked her by recalling a BBC show on the Arab billionaires of England—and she made the connection Jacqueline Bennett had hoped no one would. "Is AJ's father the same Jeremy Alexander who owns Rifai Global?"

Jacqueline Bennett was livid. "How many times do I have to tell you? They never had any interaction."

"We only—"

"Any other questions will have to be directed to my lawyer."

Anton slid a pad of paper across the table to Jacqueline. "Please write his contact information here, as well as Mr. Alexander's information. We will need to inform him of his son's death."

She opened her mouth to protest but took a Mont Blanc pen from her purse and angrily scribbled what he had asked for.

"Thank you, Ms. Bennett," he said coolly, "Chief Madruga will escort you back to your car."

Over tea in Anton's office, Catarina remarked with a sad smile, "So, thirty-two years ago a son was born to Jacqueline Bennett and Jeremy Alexander."

"I wonder whether his name, Alexander Jeremy, was a tribute or a taunt."

"Based on how she dealt with AJ from an early age, my guess is that he was no more than an inconvenience for her."

"Or possibly a convenience? Jacqueline is a self-centered, coldhearted woman, who I don't see choosing to raise a child unless by having him, she benefitted financially. Remember that at least when he was young, she got the trust fund income. His name may simply have been a reminder of that deal."

"Why keep his birth a secret all this time? Presumably paternity could be established, and with Alexander's wealth, it would certainly result in an income greater than the few thousand a month Janine mentioned."

"That's what we have to find out." Anton felt a sadness descend on him. "We have to find out so much and so quickly. Dawn…"

Padre Henriques, the elderly priest on Santa Maria, held the confidences of four generations, so Anton had not hesitated to tell him about Lori's role in trying to find a missing child. Despite the way he teased Anton about the misadventures of his youth on the island, he was fond of him and proud of the man he had become. When Anton had called him for help, he'd been happy to oblige with an introduction to an old friend.

Catarina told Gabriela she was taking a walk, and she was the first to arrive at a private patio behind the rectory in Santa Clara. There she greeted Padre José Santos, a native of Brazil, whose Amerindian heritage was written in his short stocky body, black hair, flat face, and hook nose. His eyes glittered with excitement when he saw her. "I've been waiting for you. No one will discover our secret, senhora. This place can't be seen from any road."

She looked at the potted saplings standing by the holes he had been digging around the patio. "I hope I'm not interrupting your work, Padre."

"Not at all. I'm in no rush to finish. I won't even be around to see them grow large enough to provide shade," he said without a trace of sadness, "but one day someone will appreciate them." Although no one was in sight, he put a finger to his lips and lowered his voice. "Come this way," he said, and he led her to the rectory parlor.

The room was crammed with what Catarina imagined were gifts from generations of churchgoers: furniture of many styles and ages; small rugs atop larger ones; shelves filled with vases, statues of saints, and porcelain candy dishes; and wall to wall paintings of religious scenes.

"You're lucky you arrived when you did. I just got a cake from one of my parishioners, and it smells too good to last long."

"That does smell good," she said, sniffing the butter and sherry rising into the air above a small golden round. He cut wedges for both of them and poured steaming tea from a pot. Catarina could tell he'd been looking forward to his role helping a police investigation. "We really do appreciate having a private place to meet with our friend."

They had a pleasant time sharing their affection for Terceira and memories of Padre Henriques. Then, with second slices of cake on their plates, Catarina asked Padre Santos about how Comunidade dos Reis was seen by the villagers. "Have you heard about bad feelings?"

"Yes, but that's to be expected."

"Because of how the community lives?"

"Because we are human. You may find it unusual for a priest to quote evolution, but early humans could only survive if they lived together. Just as people everywhere, the villagers here were born with a yearning to belong to a group. And just as people everywhere, they look to what they have in common—language, customs, location—and they use that to identify themselves as belonging to their group…and others as not belonging."

"Does that mean some people in Santa Clara want to force the community to leave?"

"It may be natural for humans to want to band together, but what we do with that inclination is different for those who are good and those who are bad. The people of Santa Clara are basically good. Some talk about the settlers leaving, very few want it, and I know of no one who would actually do harm to force them out." He grinned. "And remember I hear everyone's confession."

Anton told Norberto that he wanted to look around Santa Clara again, and he asked to be dropped off there for a couple of hours. For good measure, he sent the young officer to Angra on an assignment that would keep him out of the way for a while. By the time he arrived in the rectory, Catarina and Padre Santos had become good friends—and half of the cake had been eaten. At any other time, Anton would have regretted missing such a treat, but his only thoughts were about Dawn, and now Lori. In the twenty minutes during which they waited for her to arrive, Catarina agreed with him about a growing discomfort with their friend's role in the investigation. If it had been anything less than a child in danger, they would have resisted her idea of infiltrating the community more strongly, and with AJ's murder, they wanted her out.

When she finally arrived, she was greeted with long hugs. Padre Santos brought her hot tea and a large slice of cake, before settling on a small sofa against the far wall, eyes bright and mouth slightly open with anticipation. He may have held an open book in his hands for the next hour, but he wasn't trying to lead anyone to believe he was reading. He was captivated by everything his guests said.

Catarina filled in Lori—and Padre Santos—on what they had learned so far. Lori did the same, entering the information for them on the laptop Anton had brought as she spoke. She told them about the only six people who Kate had said were in the hamlet the day Dawn disappeared and AJ was killed: Millikan, Vera, Helena, Amal, Reggie, and Kate herself.

"Millikan's a difficult man to assess," Lori remarked, "perhaps because the role he plays is almost always associated with charlatans, but he seems to be less a political leader than a parish priest."

Padre Santos choked on a crumb and said with mirth, "Who knew I had a colleague nearby?"

"Vera drinks—I think she has liquor locked up in a trunk in the room we share—and she's so devoted to the community and infatuated with Millikan personally, I wonder what she would do to protect both. Helena's a crackpot. I can't wait to tell you everything she believes in."

The priest chuckled again.

"Right now I'll just say that she comes and goes pretty freely, so she could have been in the forest that morning. Reggie has uncontrollable rages, and he left the settlement early that morning—about the same time AJ did. He could have killed him, waited in the forest, and taken Dawn. Also, both he and Kate have good reason to do what they can to make sure Comunidade dos Reis doesn't close down."

"What reason would that be?" asked Anton.

Lori gave him a sad smile. "For many of them, it's their only home, the only place they feel at ease."

"What about this Amal? You didn't talk about her."

At first she simply didn't know what to say. "It's just that she's known so much pain, I can't see her harming anyone. Also, she's tiny, and it seems to me that AJ could have overpowered her. Come to think of it, he could have overpowered any of them but Reggie."

Padre Santos spoke with a full mouth. "Most people can find the strength to kill if the motive is strong enough." He swallowed quickly and added, "That's not always a sin, you know. Sometimes, it's a regrettable necessity to save another life."

"True." Lori wrapped up, "If what Kate said checks out, with everyone else from the community so far away in the vineyards, this should narrow the field of suspects tremendously."

"Good work," Anton said crisply. "Then there's no need for you to remain there."

"Nice try, but I'm sure there's a lot more to be learned. For one thing, I still haven't found a woman with blue shawl and muddied shoes who was sneaking around the forest, burying a locked box."

Their back and forth continued until it was agreed that Lori would stay just two more nights.

"Take care of yourself. A storm may be coming," he told her.

She was worried, but not for herself. "Most of the settlers have no way of knowing that. According to what you said, Millikan may have accessed weather forecasts on his laptop—he may even be using a phone when he's home—but whether he would tell anyone, I don't know."

Anton moved them along. "If Lori insists on going back today, I don't want her away too long. I've texted Felipe to take four officers out to Comunidade dos Reis to check on alibis for those who supposedly were working in the vineyards that day. We're still confirming the Maiers' movements, and we also have to consider AJ's parents. Just like the Maiers, neither showed any interest in their granddaughters until the issue of custody was raised."

"I'll start looking into Jeremy Alexander right now," Lori said, and she settled in to do what she did so well: uncover information. It didn't take her long to put together a summary of the businessman's life. "For several reasons, he's a very public figure, so this was an easy search."

Anton stopped her with a question, "Why is he such a public figure?"

"To begin with, because he's been quite successful, even more because he married into a large, colorful, and fabulously wealthy family. Some of its younger members have been party to scandalous escapades, like hosting a rave that destroyed fifteenth century frescos, using piles of cash as fuel for a beach bonfire, and being drunk in a mosque—when drinking is forbidden by their very conservative family's religion."

Anton raised his eyebrows, discouraged that such things could happen at all.

She read from her screen. "Jeremy Alexander was born sixty-one years ago to a London print shop manager and a housewife. His father died of cancer at the age of thirty-six, after which his mother moved into her sister's house with her five-year-old son. He showed academic promise at an early age, and with scholarships he received a degree with highest honors in economics from a top university. He had a fellowship in applied economics at Wharton thirty-two years ago. That would be…"

Anton knew. "That would be when AJ was conceived."

She continued with significance, "He must have turned down offers from top firms when he went directly to Rifai Global, a midlevel business in Qatar that had started with oil export and moved into shipping in the 1950s. Let's just say it changed after Alexander was appointed COO in 1986." She looked at a few pages and continued, "He modernized, got rid of nepotism, invested in technology, hired the best talent from competitors, acquired subsidiaries, and built it into a major player on the global economic scene, with holdings in banking, aeronautics, and real estate. Alexander made Rifai Global into what it is today—large, diversified, and very lucrative—and he made himself into the envy of Wall Street in the process."

"A very important man," commented Padre Santos from across the room.

Lori looked up and smiled at him. "The business is worth—"

"Yes?" The priest was on the edge of his seat.

"—many billions."

"The business is worth billions, but is Alexander himself worth that much?" asked Anton.

"As far as I can tell, the answer is no, and for several reasons. It's rare for such a large corporation these days, but Rifai Global is still privately owned by Nejim Rifai, so Alexander wouldn't have been offered stock options as he rose to the top. Also, the extended Rifai family is insular and influential, connected to two royal houses, and Alexander's an outsider, perhaps just tolerated for his expertise. His personal assets seem to be clustered in Qatar, and those could be embargoed by the government at any time with just a word from Nejim Rifai. In fact, he could even be deported at any time with no reason at all. Finally—and remember I'm no expert here—I don't think that at his age and with his one-company background, Alexander could make a go of it anywhere else."

"Could Matthew know more?" Anton asked about the owner of a successful New York investment firm who had come into their lives a year before.

"I'll email him right now," said Lori, tapping on the keyboard.

Catarina changed the subject. "What about Alexander's personal life?"

"Now that's where it really gets interesting."

"Yes. Yes." Padre Santos's cheeks were flushed with excitement.

"Jeremy Alexander has been married to Nejim Rifai's only child, Farah, since 1985."

"Are you sure?" Anton flipped through the pages of research she had prepared for him before he left Santa Maria. "AJ was born in…1984."

"You look disappointed, Anton."

"I had a thought that the secrecy surrounding AJ's birth might have been because Alexander was already married to Farah at the time."

She checked her screen again. "No. AJ's birth date is verified in several places, including on his passport, and the Rifai-Alexander wedding was covered by the press of three continents."

Anton was thinking hard. "Would AJ have been able to inherit some of the Rifai wealth?"

As she slowly worked her way to that answer, she gave a history of Jeremy and Farah's betrothal. "It's complex, but I don't think so. Although tabloids and paparazzi pointed to their having met on many occasions—some claiming that she was infatuated with him, some that she handpicked him as a husband—their marriage was a traditional Qatari one in the sense that it was entirely arranged by Nejim Rifai. The formal agreement was signed at an extravagant celebration during which the groom shook hands with his future father-in-law, and the marriage became official." Padre Santos got up to look closely at the pictures she showed.

"Sharia law is followed in Qatar, and as I said, the extended Rifai family is quite conservative, so Alexander had to formally convert to Islam in order to marry Farah Rifai. As is becoming more common, the marriage contract has clauses restricting multiple wives, stipulating that both Farah and her children will carry the Rifai surname, and stating that should there be a divorce—which technically could result from Alexander simply saying *I divorce you* three times—any children must remain with the Rifai family."

"Is there any mention of financial loss or gain for Alexander should that happen?" asked Anton.

"None." She shook her head and thought aloud, "The most perplexing thing to me is that Alexander was the groom at all. These marriages are usually alliances to cement family relationships and redistribute wealth, and he was born a Christian and relatively poor at the time. Maybe Farah really did love him and got her way."

Padre Santos had a very good question. "How long after the wedding was the first child born?"

Lori suppressed a grin. "Exactly one year. Farah wouldn't have been pregnant already."

"Who will inherit the Rifai money when Nejim Rifai dies?" Anton asked.

"The last generation of Rifais was not a fertile one, especially by the standards of their society. Nejim Rifai has three great-nephews, all of whom have blown through their own inheritances, disgraced the family at one time or another, and been publicly disowned by him. According to press releases, the entire Rifai fortune will be inherited by his only grandson, Amin Alexander Rifai.

"What do we know about this grandson?"

"If he's followed in the footsteps of other young Rifais, those antics have been kept out of the press. From everything I find, his grandfather and the rest of the family in Qatar think of him as the model Rifai. That would make Amin Rifai worth billions one day."

"I need to contact Alexander," said Anton, "if only to let him know his son is dead."

"He may not welcome knowing," cautioned Catarina. "He may not even acknowledge him as a son."

"I still have to explore every possibility when it comes to finding Dawn. Even if he's in Qatar, I have to talk him."

"He's not in Qatar," said Lori, bending over the laptop. "He spoke at a banking conference in Zurich on the thirtieth of last month, and he's cruising across the Atlantic right now."

Anton was immediately suspicious. "Across the Atlantic? Exactly where across the Atlantic would he be cruising?"

A few minutes gave her the answer. "Two of his crew posted from Angra last week. Anton, he's somewhere in the Azores."

"Of course he is." Anton shook his head at the absurdity of that being a coincidence. "So now we have yet another grandparent who never showed any interest in Dawn or even in his own child, and he's in the vicinity of where one was kidnapped and the other murdered."

"I'm setting up alerts for you, Anton." The blank looks she saw on all three faces prompted her to give a simple explanation. "A notice will be sent to your phone if there's any mention on the Internet of Alexander or his yacht in the Azores. That's how, for instance, you'll find lots of fans showing up at a celebrity's hotel or paparazzi meeting them at the airport. You can set it up to ping you whenever there's a mention of someone, and you can make it specific to their location, their finances, their parties, or whatever you're interested in."

Lori's last task was to look into the trust fund both Janine and Jacqueline had mentioned. Using AJ's social security number and the information on his passport, she located two New York bank accounts in his name. Neither was tied to trust funds, however. One was a joint account with his mother that received about thirty-five thousand dollars every month from a Zurich bank. Contrary to what Jacqueline had said, those deposits hadn't begun until AJ was a year old. Every month, she then transferred three thousand dollars into the second account in AJ's name and the remainder into an account in her name alone. They were all quiet—and a little sickened—by the implication. Had AJ had been cheated by his own mother for the past thirty-two years?

Anton settled everyone into seats quickly. With all the activities of market day in Santa Clara, he had cancelled yesterday's evening debrief to allow the team to catch up on assigned tasks. Now, there was a lot to get through. Just as he started to speak, the Chief Rocha walked in.

"This was delivered to me, Cardosa." He approached Anton and held out a folder from the medical examiner. "I thought you might need it tonight."

"Thank you, Victor." Had his responsibilities for the coming storm made him feel less threatened by Anton? "This is going to help. Would you like to join us?"

To Catarina and to half the people in the room, it was plain that he wanted to stay. But accepting the invitation would mean admitting someone else had control over an investigation in his own jurisdiction. "No, Cardosa. You carry on. I need this investigation off my plate. I have so many important matters to deal with right now, you know." And with that, he hurried off, his ego intact.

Anton did his best to understand and summarize the medical examiner's report for his team, but it was a struggle. As taciturn as the doctor had been in person, he was a wealth of words on paper. The toxicology report alone filled five pages. It seemed that every body part had been meticulously examined and weighed, and every body fluid had been sent for analysis. Sadly, none of it yielded much by way of clues. Fingerprints and dental records conclusively identified Alexander Jeremy Bennett. He was a healthy thirty-two-year-old with several minor and healed fractures, and no evidence of drug or alcohol use. Dr. Nunes hadn't found any unexpected hairs or fibers, any foreign substances, or any wounds other than the single one that had ended his life. He confirmed what he had said in the forest: AJ was facing his attacker when a knife was quickly thrust in and up, splitting open his torso from the groin to just below the heart. He had fallen backward and died within minutes as a result of hypotension brought on by severe blood loss, and his body had lain in the forest for approximately four days before the examination began.

Around the conference table, the team sat grim-faced. Anton let a few moments pass in silence. "We will find the savage who did this."

Tight-lipped, Rosa and Sousa nodded. Norberto drummed his fingers on the table with some anger.

Anton moved on to four reports that would narrow the field of suspects considerably. "Felipe, what did you find at Comunidade dos Reis this afternoon?"

"We talked to every adult, sir, and unless several of them are colluding to provide alibis, all but the six people you mentioned left as a group early that morning, and they were too far from the compound to have returned and taken Dawn. Two of the six, Vera de Melo and Helena—no last name—joined them shortly after noon and were there for the rest of the afternoon."

One more possibility crossed off the list, thought Anton. "Norberto, did you find out about any places near Comunidade dos Reis that we may have missed searching?"

"I talked to my cousins—"

"All two hundred of them?" interrupted Gracia, and all the Terceirenses laughed at the inside joke.

"Well, eight of them," he chuckled, "and no one knew of anything reasonably close, other than the four houses we already know about. Also, all of them said the same thing about feelings towards the settlers. Yes, there's talk, but it's mostly like the talk you would hear about opposing sports teams or rival schools: us against them; we're normal, they're strange. That sort of thing."

Much like what Padre Santos had said, thought Catarina.

"In any case, they'd rather have the community there than to see it developed as a shopping area or a factory, or even…" he grinned knowingly, "to have it abandoned again, and become a place where teenagers hang out and get in trouble."

"Felipe, were you and Gabriela able to check the movements of the Maiers?"

"I talked to private plane operators and to the larger airlines. They came and left Terceira as they said, but the hotel manager can't vouch for what they did while here. Apparently, they stay in most days but leave—presumably to eat out—midday and evenings."

"We'll talk to the Maiers again and see if they can account for those times. At the same time, let's search their rooms."

"Yes, sir." He started to write the assignment down, but his pencil broke. Gabriela gave him a new one, and he gave her a shy smile.

"Would you also like us to ask around to see if they've rented any other space on the island?"

"Good thought. Yes." He then eliminated the next suspects himself. He had confirmed with immigration authorities that a yacht registered to Rifai Global had passed through Angra on the way to Horta, but that was before AJ was murdered and Dawn disappeared. According to the Judicial Police, none of its registered passengers returned to Terceira until after the Qatari lawyer was informed of AJ's death. Then, still on the high seas, the yacht's captain filed papers to return to Angra. "It's docked here now, and we'll be talking to Jeremy Alexander tomorrow."

The next report gave everyone hope. As assigned, Rosa had gone through the pictures of Santa Clara on the day Dawn had been taken. She turned on a laptop that she had connected to a television against the wall and opened two files. "In the background of both pictures, you'll see a small child who could be Dawn Bennett."

As unclear as the images were, Anton's eyes clung to them. "She's blond, and the top she's wearing appears to be brown." He got up, walked to the screen, and leaned in, looking more closely. "Does anyone see anything that might confirm this is Dawn?" He wasn't sure.

"Sir, wait," Rosa said. "Those are just what we started working with." She reached over and opened another file. "This," she said triumphantly, "is what my sister did with one."

"Dawn," Anton said almost reverently.

"Dawn," repeated Catarina and Felipe, and others.

The child stood beside a mosaic inlaid on the sidewalk in front of the municipal building, looking right at them with her big blue eyes.

"What about the people around her?" Anton asked anxiously.

Rosa looked down. "Sorry, sir, the camera was pointed down at the mosaic. All the adults around her were cut off at the waist."

"What about other pictures taken at that time?"

It took her a few minutes, but she found five other pictures stamped at about eleven that morning. Three were taken by the same woman who had inadvertently taken Dawn's picture, and all were focused on the same mosaic. The remaining two were taken by another tourist just a couple of minutes after the one that showed Dawn. They showed a colorful village scene, with a pushcart heaped with produce, two dogs begging for treats, and a café waiter pouring wine at an outdoor table. Anton tilted his head right then left, trying to make sense of an area behind the waiter, where someone sat in front of an open laptop, lifting a sandwich to his mouth. "There, at the back of the café," he pointed at the screen.

Rosa changed the exposure, the dimly lit interior gradually grew lighter, and a pale face floated in the darkness: Millikan. For a moment no one spoke. "Shall I pick him up, sir?" she asked.

Discouraged, Anton slowly shook his head.

"No?"

"No."

"But…sir…he was there."

"Where was he, Rosa?"

"In Santa Clara, at exactly the time when Dawn was there."

"If I remember the layout of the town correctly, Dawn was by the municipal building. This picture shows Nuno's Café, four blocks away and across the square."

"Perhaps he moved quickly?"

"Perhaps, but that wouldn't have mattered." Around the table, the police officers looked at one another. No one could understand why that wouldn't have mattered. "He's in the middle of a lunch that had to have been ordered and brought to him and partially eaten, all while Dawn Bennett was standing by the mosaic in front of the municipal building." And hope was replaced by disappointment.

Anton ended by sharing his thoughts on what had happened to Dawn. "Did she wander away? I don't think so. It's unlikely that she would have gotten so far on her own, and there's the matter of the charred paper that was found at the empty house in Santa Clara." He pointed to the evidence bag at the center of the table. "Was she taken by someone with a grudge against Comunidade dos Reis? That's doubtful. We've heard that sentiment against the settlers isn't strong enough to warrant kidnapping or murder on the small chance that it might be effective in getting them out. Could she have been taken by another stranger? I also don't see someone hanging around the forest waiting to take a child who might happen to come by."

He paused, took a deep breath, and ended, "No. The likelihood is that someone who knew Dawn took her. If we can find a reason for taking her, we might find the person who did it—and we might find Dawn."

He felt for Bobey's ear in his pocket. "One last thing," he said with all the gravity it deserved. "If the storm does hit Terceira, she'll be in even greater peril."

Anton and Catarina reclined next to one another in bed, he making assignments for the next day, and she looking at the drawings Melody had done in his office. She laid them out on the quilt. They weren't at all like the early drawings of either her very talented Liliana or her less artistically inclined Toni. Almost all were details of what normally would be a more complete picture, not faces but eyes, not flowers but petals, not trees but leaves, all disconnected from their whole.

Catarina remembered the college lecture in which she had seen drawings like Melody's. The professor had talked about Nadia, an autistic savant who at the age of three-and-a-half had picked up a pencil and started drawing extraordinary, realistic sketches of horses after having seen them for mere seconds. At first she had drawn only isolated parts of the horses—an ear, a jaw, a tail, an eye. It wasn't until long afterwards that she connected those isolated details to draw complete horses and their riders. At that time, she couldn't even use a fork or dress herself. With intensive treatment, she improved somewhat—but as she improved, she lost her remarkable artistic ability.

Nadia's symptoms matched Melody's symptoms in some respects. Like Nadia, Melody had problems interacting with others, rarely making eye contact; she, too, seemed indifferent to the feelings of others; she, too, engaged in repetitive play; and, like one in ten with autism, she showed savant behavior, in her case in art, rather than music or math.

Janine must surely have read that medical science now acknowledges autism is a spectrum condition with a wide range of severity, and that for many such children, symptoms improve over time and with new treatments. Had she also read about the special gift her daughter stood to lose if that did happen?

"Anton, what do you think of these drawings?"

He picked up several of the pages. "You're the artist in the family, darling. To me," he pointed to three disembodied fingers, "these are amazing. I can't tell them from the drawings in da Vinci's notebooks."

"I can't either," she said sadly.

Lori returned by a different route than the one she had taken to the rectory. Her story was that she had gotten lost while trying to find her way to the stream to wash her clothes, and she had even taken the precaution of hiding a few pieces of clothing behind a bush. She walked out of the forest and directly into a group of settlers talking to Millikan. "Thank goodness," she groaned, throwing her head back and letting the clothes drop. "I thought I'd never find my way back home."

Cassie was the first to run up to her. "You poor thing." Kate came next, picking up her clothes, and two or three others talked about how they had been lost in the forest themselves. Only Amal stood back, looking at her, and Lori wondered if she knew the truth. Millikan also seemed suspicious, and the first thing he did was to signal Vera and exchange a few private words with her. Lori may not have been able to hear what they said, but she saw them glance at her before walking away.

That evening, Comunidade dos Reis gathered to share a meal in celebration of the birthdays of three of its members. Although Lori could only identify about fifteen of them, those she lived with and worked with most closely, the others—about thirty in number—greeted her warmly. Again she felt that nothing was what one might expect of such a group. The settlement wasn't populated by disaffected youth or aging hippies living some cartoonish, romanticized version of what they thought life had been for the people of Terceira in the 1800s, nor was it populated by weak-willed, gullible simpletons. There were middle-aged women who she could easily see at PTA meetings, families with children, and a number of intelligent young couples, each with their own reasons for being there. As Millikan had said on her first night there, a broad interpretation of what it meant to live as one of them seemed to be tolerated. Some women wore their hair loose, others in buns or pony tails, and one had just cut off her hair close to the scalp. There were bearded men and clean-shaven ones, and those who shaved their heads. The clothes she saw were all discreet, but they included long flowing dresses, shifts, pants, a pair of culottes, and Amal's hijab. There was no slavish devotion to any one person or ritual. Comunidade dos Reis could not be called a cult.

They gathered around the central fire pit, ate chicken stew, and drank wine that had been made from the grapes they grew. And they told stories of the lives they had left behind.

> *I was with others but I was alone.*
> *I had food but was always hungry for more.*
> *The words of love I heard most often were* Look what I got you.
> *I lived in shame for what I had while others suffered with none.*
> *I was only pretending to enjoy what I didn't enjoy.*
> *I lived as others expected.*

Lori tried to concentrate on what she was there to do—gather information to help find Dawn Bennett—but their words seemed to speak directly to her. She had felt that way in New York; her career had conscripted her time, determined how she lived, and limited the time she spent with those she loved. Listening to the people around her, she fully embraced her decision to return to the Azores for the first time.

She watched Millikan talking privately with Vera, and she watched Helena and Amal, both of whom seemed particularly tired. She watched Janine, who sat apart deep in thought, and Melody, who was mesmerized by the fire. She watched Kate, rocking Sally in her arms and looking concerned, and Reggie, nervously gulping tea and drumming his heel on the ground. As she had since following the woman through the forest, she looked for blue shawls and muddied shoes, but there were none of the former and far too many of the latter. Her next step, she decided, would be to search as many of the homes as she could.

The fire snapped. Reggie jumped to his feet and let out a yell. "Run! Everybody run!" He lifted Sally off the ground with one arm and pulled Kate up with the other. "Gotta go. Gotta go. Run!"

Sally screamed, and Reggie dropped her. Still being tugged away by her husband, Kate remained calm, whispering, "It's over, honey. Look. Look around."

Others were startled, but no one moved, no one even seemed frightened; they had been through this before.

Then Sally whimpered and Reggie whipped around, knocking Amal to the ground. Her head hit a rock and began bleeding. She rose very slowly, looking Reggie in the eyes, smiling all the while.

Once on her feet, she held out her arm. "I'm fine, Reggie, just fine."

Lori knew she wasn't fine. Her voice had wavered, and she was struggling to keep her balance. Soon, the fire light caught rivulets of blood trickling down her face.

Reggie wrapped his arm around Kate's waist and lifted her off the ground, fury about to erupt.

Kate allowed herself to hang almost horizontally. "It was only Sally, darling." She lightly touched Reggie's back. He flinched. "Shall we put Sally to bed?" He set Kate down but moved a hand to her neck, tightened his grip, and choked off her next words.

Sally sobbed, which set off Reggie again. He reached into the fire with his free hand, pulled out the end of a half-burned branch, and raised it over the child's head.

Amal and Vera moved so quickly they seemed to fly. Vera whisked Sally away and into the arms of an older woman standing nearby.

Amal faced him, looking even smaller next to the strapping man. "Reggie, look at me," she said quietly. She reached up and took his chin in her hand, and he let her turn his head. She spoke slowly, softly, firmly. "You are safe. We are all safe."

Vera had returned, and one by one she gently pried his fingers from around Kate's neck.

Amal repeated, "You are safe. We are all safe."

Instead of moving away, once Kate was freed she pressed herself closer to him. His eyes flicked back and forth as he struggled to make sense of his thoughts. Then he shook his head quickly as though trying to clear his thoughts, his muscles relaxed, and he took a deep breath. As quickly as it had started, it ended. "I'm sorry, everyone." He hung his head. "I'm so sorry."

The community made light of it, only nodding to acknowledge his apology or waving a hand to let him know they weren't upset.

The instant Reggie vanished into the darkness, Lori shot up and grabbed Amal. She felt the tiny woman crumple against her. Together with Vera, they helped Amal back to their house. As they settled her on Cassie's bed, Lori said, "You could have been hurt even worse. Why, Amal? Why even get near him when he's in that state?"

She smiled feebly, "I would have done the same for my brothers. I'd rather have them like Reggie than not at all."

Helena washed the blood from Amal's wounds and wrapped her wrist in a tight bandage. "Would anyone like tea? It will help us all to sleep."

It took a while for everyone to settle down, and the five women who shared adjacent cottages talked long into the night. Lori found herself feeling affection for them—or in the case of Helena, at least acceptance. She struggled with deceiving them every time she referred to the fictitious life that had brought her to them, and she had to remind herself that the deceit was for a good cause. While part of her puzzled over who among them could have done those terrible things in the forest, most of the unvoiced conversation she held with herself defended each of them.

7

Norberto met with Anton's approval as he sped along the two-lane coastal road, swerving around slower cars, and neatly pulling up to within three feet of the gangplank. Catarina was used to such driving, although not by someone other than her husband, so she was relieved to leave the police car and put her feet on the firm dock of the Angra marina.

Far from being awed by Jeremy Alexander's luxury yacht, the *Qasr*, after having been guests of Matthew Cunningham aboard the *Casa do Mar,* they expected most of what they saw. Escorted by two security guards, they crossed highly-polished mahogany decks to the main salon. A crewman used a remote control to open a twenty-foot expanse of retractable glass doors and Alexander stepped in, his face arranged to show mild surprise at their presence. That didn't fool either of his visitors. Not only had they been expected from the moment the official police car reached the dock, but everything from the heavily-muscled man in the background to the attendant with a hand poised over a tablet seemed staged.

Compared to his picture on the home page for Rifai Global, Alexander's wrinkles were deeper and he had less hair, but he was still quite fit for a man in his sixties. Tall and straight, he had an angular face, ice-blue eyes, and metal-rimmed glasses resting on a thin nose. Both Catarina and Anton had the same passing thought: the frames were probably solid gold.

Catarina underlined Anton's authority when she introduced him as Minister Plenipotentiary Cardosa of the Azores, representing the Presidente on an urgent matter. It was a line Lori had used to great effect on more than one occasion; the difference this time was that it was the truth.

"You are welcome here, Minister Cardosa," Alexander started in Portuguese. "Sadly, I know little of your beautiful language, so we must continue in English. I am Jeremy." His handshake was firm, his voice warm, and his manner approachable. "This is my son, Amin."

A slender young man on a white leather Eames chair at the back of the room slowly unwound himself from a relaxed position and rose to greet them. Like his father, he gave the impression of being well cared for in his perfectly trimmed dark hair, glowing tanned skin, manicure, and bespoke shirt and pants, but he lacked his father's hard edges, so the grooming gave him a somewhat effeminate air.

Anton was about to speak when Alexander slightly raised a forefinger, setting off a flurry of activity. A pretty woman wearing a conservative white shirt, black pantsuit, and traditional black hijab on her head stepped forward and, with the touch of a button, raised a low coffee table by two feet. In less than a minute, she had set the table with Majolica china, gold spoons, and gold-embroidered napkins taken from shelves hidden behind an ebony panel in the wall. Three similarly uniformed women entered with silver trays adorned with a jewel-like array of tiny pastries, and a teenaged boy wearing a perfectly pressed *thobe*—or long white dress—approached with two large silver pots.

Alexander asked Catarina, "May I offer you and the Minister refreshments?"

Anton pulled his gaze away from the tempting sweets that had been laid out. "Thank you for the offer, Mr. Alexander, but as Mrs. Vanderhye explained, my mission is urgent and we must talk now."

"Of course. You have my full attention, Minister Cardosa. Please sit." The food was whisked away, all the attendants except the man carrying a tablet disappeared, and Alexander gave a nod to his son, who came to sit beside him.

On white suede sofas, they talked for the next thirty minutes. Alexander's manner was confident, his speech was educated, and never once did he refuse to give an answer. In fact, he was so accommodating that it set off alarms in Catarina's mind. She suspected he had planned to say exactly what he knew they wanted to hear—nothing more, nothing less. After all, decades of doing just that with extended family, colleagues, and clients had rewarded him richly. But any ulterior motive for being guarded remained unclear.

"I know the British consulate in São Miguel has told you of your son's death, and I offer my condolences," Anton began.

"Thank you, Minister. My wife and I thought it best to return to Terceira as soon as we received the news. You may speak freely in front of my son, but I trust you understand the delicacy of the situation concerning the birth." Catarina wondered if his wording was intended to avoid using AJ's name or even referring to him as a son.

Anton had been raised in a conservative Catholic family, and he did understand that out-of-wedlock birth was seen very differently thirty years ago, and continued to be viewed with disapproval in other cultures. "I have no intention of making anything public unnecessarily. Right now, my primary concern is locating your granddaughter, Dawn Bennett."

"Yes. Terrible thing. Terrible."

Catarina wondered if she was seeing the reverse of an Englishman's stiff upper lip; to her, he seemed to be a man arranging his features to show concern, when in fact he felt nothing.

"I would like to ask you several background questions," Anton began.

"Of course."

"When did you last see your son?"

"Sadly, I have never met him."

Anton managed to stop his eyebrows in mid-rise. "Yet your lawyer has been interested in his whereabouts."

"I'm not a heartless man, Minister. Family is very important to me, so when I learned that my son was in danger of losing his lovely daughters, I asked one of my company's law firms to monitor the situation and reach out to him if warranted. I'm only sorry I was too late."

Thirty-two years too late. "When did you last see Jacqueline Bennett?" Anton asked. Amin shifted positions.

"Now let me see…" he scratched his forehead and appeared to think. "It was some time ago. I'd have to check my calendar and get back to you." He leaned forward and whispered in a way that probably would have convinced other men they were special friends, "You understand, I don't want say anything incorrect."

"You were in the Azores at the time of AJ's death?"

"I was. The *Qasr* put into port on Terceira two days before his death. I was hoping to see him, but sadly business took me away quickly. I had planned to return, just not under these circumstances." He raised a finger, and the man with the tablet stepped forward. "In the interest of helping your investigation, I've had an account of our whereabouts prepared." He took the tablet and handed it to Anton, who glanced down but nothing more. "You will find the particulars of our itinerary, as well as the names and contact information of people who were on board, both when we arrived and when we left Terceira."

The man anticipated needing an alibi for his son's death. Anton handed the tablet back to Alexander, with his own business card. "Thank you," he said. "You can have the file sent to me. Now, who are you traveling with?"

"Other than crew and occasional guests who I helicopter in, only my wife and son."

"Have you had any guests aboard since entering the Azores?"

"No. I had so much to deal with in Zurich—one false step and tens of thousands could be thrown out of work. I just wanted some quiet family time—well, as much of that as I can ever have."

Catarina heard how carefully he worded everything he said. As a powerful man, he dealt with important issues. As a caring man, he did so with the interests of tens of thousands in mind. As a busy man, he should be given consideration. He was very good at presenting the persona of a well-intentioned, successful businessman, someone who you would want on your side. But she knew that, although he had expressed disappointment in not having met his own son, he was a calculating man who cared more for himself than for any family he had.

Anton probed further. "I understand that you took care of AJ financially."

"I did. That is only right."

"Could you tell me what those arrangements were?"

"He received an annual sum of approximately half a million American dollars since his birth—and of course I took care of all taxes."

Of course. "And will his children now receive any money that would have gone to him?"

His hands stiffened, but he said coolly, "I have not yet considered what I will do."

"Of course, when a child is taken, we have to consider the possibility of kidnapping for ransom—"

"Let me stop you there, Minister. Beyond the fact that the Rifai family has made very clear in the past that no such demands would ever be met, Jacqueline has been extremely careful about keeping her son's paternity private. My life is the subject of constant scrutiny. Have you ever seen a single word about this—anywhere? No."

"Can you think of other reasons for taking your granddaughter?"

Catarina saw Alexander flinch when he heard Dawn referred to as his *granddaughter.*

"I cannot. But I have every confidence in you, Minister. I'm sure you will leave no stone unturned to find the person who did this terrible thing…both terrible things."

"Would anything be gained by AJ's death?"

"If we are talking about any gain to be made by my family, the answer is no. He was to receive no inheritance, he had no voting shares, and let me assure you that the amount he received each year is small for us. I strongly suggest you look elsewhere." He spoke calmly, but the pulsing in his neck betrayed his rising irritation.

Anton nodded thoughtfully. "I do understand this is a delicate matter, but it may become necessary to talk to your wife."

"Not a problem at all, Minister. Just let me know. He rose and looked down at Anton. "I'm sorry to cut this short, but I had no idea you needed this much of my time. I have an important call coming in from London. I'd be happy to answer any further questions at another time." He wanted to leave on a cordial note. He bowed his head slightly to Catarina. "A great pleasure, Mrs. Vanderhye."

Anton and Catarina both stood and shook hands with Alexander.

"Amin, you have work to do, as well." Alexander walked away swiftly, replaced almost immediately by one of the security guards. Amin moved less decisively than his father. As he passed Catarina, she pretended to stumble and reached out to him. His immediate reaction was to step back. She righted herself and sounded flustered when she said, "I'm so sorry. I guess I don't have my sea legs."

The *Qasr* was as steady as land.

"Quite alright." His English was even more educated than his father's. "Allow me," he said, extending his arm for her.

"I should move more slowly." And that was what she did; she walked beside him quite slowly, and they made what on the surface was just small talk—but to Catarina it was a goldmine. "How are you finding our islands, Amin?"

"They're lovely. It's our first cruise here, and I'm sure we'll return."

"Had you planned this visit for a while?"

He missed a beat before saying, "No. It was last minute. In my family, everything revolves around business obligations, as it should."

Was he parroting his father or was he just as committed to Rifai Global?

"That must be hard for you and your mother."

For a moment he didn't understand what she was saying. "Yes," he replied without conviction.

"Where will you go from here?"

"We head to Morocco for a week. It's one of our favorite spots. Then we join Father in New York and return home."

The *we* going to Morocco did not include his father.

"Did you have a chance to tour Terceira?"

His arm dropped slightly, and he was slow to respond. "I'd like to see more of the island." Clearly, he didn't want to say either no or yes. If he hadn't left the *Qasr*, why not say no? That their stopover had been too short was enough of an explanation. If he had left the *Qasr*, why not say yes? The only reason Catarina could think of was that Amin didn't want to admit to having left—but didn't want to risk lying about it.

They had reached the gangplank. Amin offered a cool, moist hand and said a formal goodbye.

On the dock, Anton saw three men taking pictures of the *Qasr*. They didn't look like tourists. Within moments, their cameras were trained on Anton and Catarina, who were then surrounded and bombarded with questions.

Can we get a statement?
Were you talking to Jeremy Alexander?
Has a crime been committed?
Can I get your name?
Why are the police here?
Is Amin on board?

They were still yelling for answers as the police car raced away.

When they returned, the municipal building was lively with activity. Two fire trucks stretched across half of the spaces in the visitors' parking lot, two ambulances stood by the back door, and boxes were being unloaded from trucks and stacked in the lobby.

"What's going on?" Anton called out to Gabriela, who was watching from the first floor landing.

"The hurricane is gathering strength. It's now just five hundred kilometers west of Madeira. They say it's only a matter of time before it hits the Azores. The Island Guards have been called in for support after the storm strikes, and Emergency Services are meeting in your conference room right now."

He and Catarina stood in the doorway to the packed conference room, where an unfamiliar voice was speaking. "We're not sure which islands will take the brunt of the storm, but right now winds of 130-150 kilometers per hour are expected, and sea waves of 10-15 meters are projected. We're preparing for rescue operations and airlifts of injured people from other islands to our hospital here on Terceira."

Chief Rocha took over. "Schools and businesses will be closed, roads are being blocked off, nonessential public services have been suspended, and all flights have been cancelled." As Anton listened to details of the chief's plan, he heard another side of the man, a competent, methodical, thorough commander. For whatever reason, his better qualities were flawed by an unwillingness to share authority or even collaborate with anyone else.

As the meeting drew to a close, Anton was conflicted. Local police, including the team he had assembled to find Dawn, were needed to prepare for the storm. The communities they were familiar with had to be alerted. The roads they patrolled had to be blocked off. The public areas, marinas, and airports they knew had to be shut down. He was painfully aware that Dawn was in serious danger, but there were many other lives to consider, and he wasn't sure if he should call the team away from other duties.

Just as he decided to rely on Felipe alone until the next day, he heard a commotion in the hallway behind him. The Island Guards had arrived—and thirty-six hours before the storm was projected to hit. A last-ditch plan formed in Anton's mind.

He called Presidente Moniz. "Dawn has to be somewhere on the island. Just thirty Guards, sir, please," he pleaded, "and if the prediction of when Hurricane Mimi will hit is moved up, they'd be released immediately."

In the end, he got what he asked for. Every known space for rent would be searched—rooms in private homes, bed and breakfasts, hotels, houses for lease. Boats and storage units would be searched. Cars would be searched. Parks and nature preserves and recreational areas would be searched. Every place that Anton could think of would be searched.

Still, he worried. *That might not be enough to save Dawn.*

Lori had promised Anton that this would be her last day at Comunidade dos Reis.

She set three tasks for herself before leaving, and a golden opportunity for the most challenging of them presented itself when Millikan announced he would be away for the rest of the day on community business. She waited until she saw him heading into the forest with a small bag, presumably on his way to Santa Clara to use the laptop she was certain he had concealed inside.

She slipped into Millikan's cottage, thankful that most of the community were starting a day of work in the fields, but wary of the bright morning sun streaming through the open windows. On the surface, the small house was as simple as every other place in the community. Despite that, there were many places where something might be hidden, so she moved slowly, not even knowing what she was looking for. She methodically and thoroughly searched each area, and returned everything to its original place, before moving on. She started with more obvious hiding places, looking on shelves and through drawers one by one, and found only household goods and a few items of simple clothing.

In the middle of rooting through Millikan's trash, she heard footsteps on the porch and held her position, waiting for silence. Then she carried on, digging her fingers into the toes of boots, looking through the dirty laundry that filled a basket in the corner of the room, reaching in the pockets of jackets hanging on hooks, and fanning out the pages of the three books on a table—

the *Bible*, a prayer book, and *A Cultural History of Europe 1820-1920*. There was nothing.

She headed to the curtained alcove that served as an office for community business, wincing as floorboards creaked underfoot. In one drawer of an old wood file cabinet, she found work rosters, a list of community members and their birthdays, and hand-drawn maps of the fields and vineyards, labeled with the names of crops and dates. She was about to close the drawer when the front door latch jiggled. Could Millikan have returned so soon?

She tried to slide the open drawer back without making a sound but the old wood jammed, and she just managed to slip behind the curtain before feeling a breeze from the open door. From what she could tell, someone was doing what she had just done, ferreting through things in the outer room. She prepared the most reasonable excuse for being there that she could come up with—that she wanted to talk to Millikan—and she waited, but soon the sounds faded, and the front door squeaked shut.

Quickly, she returned to her search of the file cabinet. The next drawer was filled with bank statements, stacks of passports, a receipt for the annual payment on a post office box, the deed for Comunidade dos Reis, and correspondence—including the papers she had brought with her. The community had two bank accounts, one set up seven years ago, with Wallace Jenkins as the primary trustee, and a second one opened three months ago, with Henry Patrick Millikan as the primary trustee. The balances never exceeded five thousand dollars, and several others in the community were also listed as trustees. Nothing seemed out of order, but she took pictures of two statements; some of the information on them would help her to look into the community's finances more closely.

The third drawer was locked, but it was nothing that Lori couldn't get into with a kitchen knife and a little time. She found a small envelope stamped with the numbers one-seven-two, and inside it there was what looked to be the key to a safe deposit box. There was also a large accordion folder stuffed with legal papers, including marriage certificates, divorce decrees, birth certificates, adoption papers, custody agreements, deeds, and wills. It was far too much to read through carefully, so she scanned for the Bennett name, which she found on two documents. The first was dated thirty-two years ago, just before AJ's birth, and it both acknowledged Jeremy Alexander as his father and stipulated that child support would begin on his first birthday. The second was signed by Alexander Jeremy Bennett, endorsing the transfer of twenty-seven hundred dollars each month from his bank account to another account in Henry Patrick Millikan's name. Her initial thought was that the paper pointed to a motive, but the fine print pointed a finger in the opposite direction. The agreement expired on AJ's death.

She took a few more pictures and messaged them to Anton. Smiling to herself, she sent another message. *Having a wonderful time. Wish you were here!*

Next, Lori set out to find the woman who had buried a locked box in the forest, an unsuccessful effort that took her from one cottage to another, casually chatting about shawls in the occupied ones, and surreptitiously looking for shawls in the empty ones.

Discouraged, she returned to her own house, where her hopes for finding the mystery woman skyrocketed. Two minutes after sitting on the edge of her bed, she heard erratic pounding at the bottom of the door, and she opened it to find a grinning Cassie holding a basket of yeasty rolls in one hand and two cups of hot tea in the other.

"Sorry for the weird knocking," Cassie said, holding the cups out to Lori. "My hands were full, and all I had was my foot."

Lori missed a beat before taking the tea from her. "Ah, thanks, Cassie."

She waved the basket under Lori's nose. "A treat from Kate for those of us staying close to home today."

"Mmm." Lori was distracted. "That's a lovely shawl, Cassie. I haven't seen it before."

"Isn't it beautiful? Such a cheerful blue and so soft." She gently squeezed a corner of the shawl. "But I can't take any credit for it. It belongs to someone who left us. It's become sort of a communal shawl, passed around more than a newborn baby."

"That's nice. I think I saw someone wearing it the day before yesterday."

"Hah. Just one person? I know I handed it over to Kate before lunch that day to use as a blanket for Sally. After that, who knows? It's popular, so you have to get in line! Now let's eat before everything cools."

Lori ate quickly and made an excuse to leave Cassie. She had one more thing to do before meeting Anton and Catarina at the Santa Clara rectory in an hour.

She retraced her steps along the overgrown path, through the lilac grove, and to the grassy clearing where she had last seen the woman in the blue shawl. This time, she found the metal box easily, although in a different position from the one she had replaced it. She shook it. It still seemed to have both a small, metallic object and something large and softer. If she could open the lock, she might be able to re-lock it after taking a peek inside.

She reached into her pocket and took out the thin nail she had brought with her. *Now what?* She pursed her lips, squinted into the lock, and sighed. *It'd be nice if I had a clue about how to do this.* She inserted the nail into the lock and wiggled it around for a few minutes—and a few more minutes. *Well, that isn't working.* She wrapped the box with her scarf to protect it against dents and picked up a nearby rock. *Here goes nothing.* She struck the lock, hoping it would somehow pop open. Surprisingly for what seemed to be a flimsy box, it held.

Lori considered her dilemma. If she did any more, whoever had buried the box would know it had been tampered with. If she took the box to someone who actually knew how to open the lock, the owner of the box might notice it was missing before she had a chance to return it. In the end, she replaced it as she had found it and hurried out of the forest to meet her friends.

Anton enjoyed driving for the first time since he arrived; the focus he needed to speed along winding, narrow roads took his mind off Dawn for a short while.

The second time they all met, it was in an empty rectory, where Padre Santos had left a note apologizing for his absence, atop a box of pastries from the bakery in Santa Clara.

"How's life in the nineteenth century?" Anton joked when Lori walked in.

"As problematic as life in the twenty-first century," she laughed.

Catarina handed the pastries over to Lori and poured her a cup of hot, black coffee from a thermos.

She groaned with pleasure after taking her first sip. "I never thought I'd miss coffee so much."

Anton started with what was uppermost in his mind, "You agreed last time that tonight would be your last at Comunidade dos Reis."

"I remember."

"Seriously, it's time to leave. He looked at the overcast sky with concern. Hurricane Mimi is moving closer and getting stronger with every passing hour."

Her first thoughts were of the community. Would they be safe in their old cottages? Did they have emergency supplies? Should she warn them?

"There isn't much else to gain by your staying there," insisted Anton.

"I'm finding out more every day. Besides, how can any of us quit while Dawn is still in danger?"

"Lori," Catarina tried to gently persuade her, "this storm may be the worst to hit the islands in many years."

"That's all the more reason to stay. Dawn might be somewhere nearby. She might need help. Besides, aren't you always telling me about how the hardy settlers of the Azores survived?"

"That's different," Anton said.

"How?"

He lowered his head and smiled to himself.

Catarina answered for both of them, "It's different because you are our family. We worry about you."

"I'm only doing what you would do. I'll leave Comunidade dos Reis Friday morning. Promise."

There wasn't a trace of the typical cheeriness on his face when he said, "If you don't, I'll come to get you."

"I love you, too, guys." She changed the subject by tempting them. "I have news."

Catarina pulled out her pad of paper, ready to add to their notes.

Lori led with her search of Millikan's cottage that morning. "There's a locked drawer in his office that's filled with all sorts of interesting legal papers. Did you get the pictures of the paternity paper and the agreement to transfer AJ's monthly deposits to Millikan?"

Catarina answered. "I looked at them while Anton drove here."

Lori couldn't resist. "You had enough time in the thirty seconds it took the demon driver to get here from Angra?" They shared a laugh at his expense.

Lori swallowed a large bite of a pastry before going on. "So, AJ was helping to finance the community."

Anton rubbed his head, frustrated. "The problem is that according to the agreement, AJ's death means less—not more—money for everyone in the community. It would have been to everyone's advantage to keep him alive."

"*If* they knew about this," cautioned Catarina, "and even then, there might have been a more pressing reason to want him dead."

"I also sent pictures of two bank account statements. One was set up by Wallace Jenkins, the other by Millikan. The balances are what you might expect, modest cash deposits going in each month, presumably from the sale of their crops or crafts, and the same amounts being withdrawn for community expenses. Still, I think they should be looked into."

"There aren't too many banks on the island, and none are in Santa Clara. It shouldn't be too hard to check on that."

"Now, I found what I'm pretty sure is a safe deposit key in an envelope with the numbers one-seven-two."

Catarina added that to the list of things to follow up on.

Anton nodded. "What else, Lori?"

"A lot that hasn't led anywhere. I had hoped to find the woman wearing a blue shawl, who I followed through the forest, but that may be a dead end." She paused to start a second pastry. "I tried to open that locked box, but the lock's deceptively strong. I'm going to need a key," she grinned, "or lessons in how to pick locks."

"As soon as you're out of Comunidade dos Reis—and that will be *Friday morning*," Anton said firmly, "we're going in. Then I can order the box dug up and opened by force if necessary."

Lori ignored what he said about her leaving. She added one more small piece of information, "It's hardly a game changer, but I doubled back to my cottage right after leaving this morning and looked through the window. I could see Vera unlock her trunk and start her day with a long drink of cheap rum. Not a surprise, really. We all thought she drinks."

She had left bringing up Reggie's outburst until last, and somehow telling them about it felt like a betrayal.

Anton's heart dropped when he heard. "Could he have lost control and killed AJ...maybe even Dawn?"

"I hate to say it, but it's a possibility. I also have to tell you that after Reggie exploded last night, I saw a side of people—Vera in particular—that makes me question whether any of the others could have harmed a child."

Catarina reminded her of what Padre Santos said: anyone can find the strength to kill if the motive is strong enough.

After another cup of coffee, Lori's investigative skills were put to good use looking into Amin Rifai. "At the age of thirty, he has yet to be tagged with any distinctive label—not the astute businessman, not the superficial playboy, not any type at all. In fact, he's not in the press a lot, which in itself is a bit odd. He just seems to blend into the background of his father's life. Some reporters say he's a mama's boy, rarely seen far from her.

Others claim he's gay or just completely dominated by his father."

Anton couldn't add much to that. "Matthew said Amin doesn't have any role at all in Rifai Global, unexpected for someone who will inherit the empire one day. He told me what some respected businesspeople think: Alexander's success came as much from extraordinary luck as extraordinary ability. He also talked a bit about Nejim Rifai's character. Matthew quoted Rifai's mantra," Anton read from his phone, "'Act honorably, and I will support you; act dishonorably, and I will destroy you.'"

As they cleaned up and left a thank you note for Padre Santos, the three agreed: all they had for their efforts was a growing collection of seemingly useless facts about people whose intentions and behavior contradicted everything that made sense. The Maiers had washed their hands of Janine, yet had come thousands of miles when the custody of her children was in question. Jacqueline Bennett had a document acknowledging a very wealthy public figure was the father of her child, but had kept that a secret. Jeremy Alexander was perfectly at ease with his own family knowing about AJ's existence, while fiercely guarding that fact from a twenty-first-century world. Millikan lived a life that both seemed irreproachable and raised suspicions. Those closest to AJ formed a cast of damaged people, who conveniently corroborated each other's alibis. And Dawn remained missing on an island where a blond child carrying a red elephant should have been noticed.

At two-forty, Lori hugged them goodbye and retraced her steps down the steep hill and around the western edge of the rectory. Anton and Catarina waited for another few minutes, talking about how Casa do Mar might weather the approaching hurricane. Then they left, taking the route Lori had taken towards the edge of town. They saw senhora Brum tipping back the last of a cup of espresso at the café on the corner and waved. When they reached the main square, they made eye contact with the grocer and one of his patrons, and everyone exchanged nods. As they passed the bakery, the church bell—now electronic, like so many church bells around the world—started ringing, and by the time the third peal had faded, they too had reached the main road. From there, they had an unobstructed view of the route Lori must have taken to return to Comunidade dos Reis, and both Anton and Catarina instinctively scanned the area for her bright orange scarf, but neither could see her.

As Dawn came to, she heard a chain clanging against metal. Then absolute silence. She was in a different place, a darker and colder place. And she was alone with Bobey. Fear cloaked her cold body like static electricity, prickling her skin, carried in the air she took into her lungs, making sharp points of light in front of her eyes, and tingling in her ears.

After a while, she stopped screaming. She knew no one could hear her.

8

While the guardsmen carried out their assignments, Anton's focus remained on those who were most closely associated with the Bennetts. He sent Felipe off to bring in suspects for questioning, along with their passports and visas.

For the most part, Catarina led the questioning. She excelled at getting the most from every interaction, phrasing questions in the best possible way, and gleaning as much from what was not said as she did from what was said. She had a knack for putting people at ease and never was that more needed than with the first person she talked to. She looked over what Lori had said about the woman before the door opened, and Amal stepped in. "Hello, Miss Hukan. Thank you for coming to help us find…" She looked down at her notepad, as if trying to find the name.

"Dawn," she said in a whisper. "Her name was Dawn Bennett." She looked even smaller than she was, her head hung low and her hands folded together over her stomach.

Catarina pulled out a comfortable chair that Gabriela had found and moved into Anton's office for the afternoon. "Yes, of course. Dawn Bennett. Please have a seat."

Amal sat quickly, keeping her eyes lowered. Anyone could see the woman was more than a little frightened.

"Would you like some hot tea?" asked Catarina.

Amal said no, but in a way that made it seem like a plea not to have the tea.

Catarina watched as Amal wrapped her shawl tightly around her arms and sat perfectly still. The reason for the young woman's dread suddenly came to her, and her heart broke. "Anton, could you give us some time?"

He didn't have to know why. His wife had a reason, and he trusted her instincts completely.

She squatted beside Amal. "There's no need to be afraid."

Her eyes filled with tears but she said nothing.

Catarina slowly reached out, put her hand over Amal's arm, and left it there, light and warm, for a long while.

Eventually, Amal looked at her, into her eyes, trying to read her.

"I promise no harm will come to you. I promise this in the name of my family."

Amal took in a shaky breath and nodded.

"The only reason you are here is to help us find Dawn. After we are done—any time you want—you can return to Comunidade dos Reis. I will drive you myself, if you like."

Amal gave several quick nods and sniffled.

"Could I ask you about the day Dawn disappeared?"

"Yes."

"Do you remember seeing her?"

"She was sitting on the chair in front of the Bennett's house." Still overwrought, large tears rolled down her cheeks.

Catarina patted her hand but said nothing.

Amal recalled that morning, "She was sitting the way small children do, with her legs straight out in front of her on the seat, talking to Bobey. Melody was there, too, scratching the ground with a stick, as she sometimes does. The next time I saw them, they were walking hand in hand towards the forest. Dawn loved the forest."

She spoke in past tense, but with her history, who could blame her? Disappearing usually meant death. When Catarina was certain Amal had nothing more to say, she asked, "Did you see anyone else around that day who might be able to help find Dawn?"

She tried to picture the scene that morning. "It was market day, so both AJ and Reggie left very early. Helena and I helped Kate prepare the evening meal. Vera was working with Pat on community business in the morning, but then she and Helena went to join everyone else in the vineyards." She was silent for a long while, shaking her head side to side. "I can't remember any more." She looked up apologetically.

Catarina stood by Amal's side and wrapped her arms lightly around the frail young woman. "Thank you. Thank you for having the courage to talk to me." She couldn't let her know that Lori had already told part of her story, and that she had guessed more when the woman, already on edge after being brought into the police station, had been driven to tears by the offer of hot tea. To her, it was a threat, the same threat of burning that is made to girls who are kidnapped by ISIS terrorists.

"I brought no passport. I have no papers." Fear, desperation, and defeat permeated her voice. "I'm not here legally. I came as a cleaner on a boat. I got off and never went back. If anyone finds out…" Her words caught in her throat; she thought she had made a mistake.

"I'll never tell anyone…about anything."

While they waited for Felipe to return Amal to her home and bring in the next person, Catarina told her husband that Amal had confirmed what Kate had said. Reggie and AJ had both left the compound early in the morning; Vera and Helena had gone to the vineyards about noon, the same time that Millikan had left for Santa Clara; and Kate, Amal, and Helena had worked together on and off to prepare the evening meal.

"Carlota Zubiri," Felipe introduced the next person he escorted into Anton's office.

"You can call me Helena. It is my true name." She spoke in a deep, slow voice, the portrait of a mysterious woman. She looked deeply into Catarina's eyes. "I know you don't believe as we believe," she said, with her features fixed in place, "and that is fine."

"Please sit down," Catarina said without comment.

"My papers are in order." She slipped a passport and resident visa out of a deep pocket in her skirt, placed them on the table, and tapped them slowly with her hand.

"I see you are from Spain."

"I was. I am now one with my community."

Anton had far less patience than his wife did when it came to tolerating the likes of Helena, and his desk quivered as he jiggled his leg underneath it.

"What brought you to the Azores?" asked an unruffled Catarina.

"I was called here to help my community."

"How did you hear of Comunidade dos Reis?"

She could have been trying to remember during the short pause that followed, or she could have been crafting an answer. "I was passing through Angra and heard my calling carried on the wind."

The desktop shook more rapidly.

"I see. Could I ask what you do as a member of your community?"

Helena's response proved not only very detailed but— when she started to talk about her psychic abilities—capable of rattling Anton's nerves. While he made a note to check on Carlota Zubiri's past, Catarina continued to listen, nodding at appropriate times.

After Helena came to an abrupt stop, Catarina smiled and said, "They're lucky to have you. I love using herbs and mushrooms in my cooking, and I wouldn't want to go to bed without my cup of tea."

Helena looked pleased.

"We're asking everyone who stayed behind at Comunidade dos Reis what they remember about the day Dawn Bennett disappeared."

"I will call on the spirits to help me find answers."

Anton's pencil snapped in half.

"Do you remember seeing the Bennett children that morning?"

"I do. Lovely children, both of them. I had picked mushrooms early in the morning, and I saw them go into the forest just after I came out. Who would take an innocent child from us!" She pulled a handkerchief from her sleeve and cried into it.

Catarina looked at Anton, who had tightened his jaw so much there were bulges on either side of his face. When Helena had composed herself, she asked, "Did you see anything unusual while you were gathering mushrooms?"

"I was only in the forest a short time. I wish I had seen something," she said sadly.

"Where did you go after that?"

"I remember it was an especially busy day for me. I went to start a batch of soap at the northern edge of the forest, on the other side of our settlement. I helped Kate with the evening meal, and then I went to the vineyards with Vera, where I was for the rest of the day." That was all in line with what both Kate and Amal had said.

"Can you think of a reason why someone might take Dawn?"

"Children have a special role in our universe; they balance chaos. Look to people who are in chaos now, and you may find the reason Dawn is missing."

Anton loudly scraped back his chair and stood over Helena. "Are you are one of the members who occasionally leaves the community with senhor Millikan's blessing."

Color drained from her face.

Until this point, Anton had just been gathering information, but an idea was forming in his mind. "Where have you been recently?"

Catarina saw her hold her breath for a moment.

When she answered, her mouth was dry. "I don't go often, but Pat thinks it's important that occasionally I represent us in other communities—an ambassador for our beliefs, so to speak."

Anton would make a bet that she was the woman who villagers had seen at the grocery store carrying a large cloth bag and wearing a scarf. "And what do you do as ambassador?"

"I offer my gift to help people reach their spiritual side."

In Anton's mind, he could see her hunched over a crystal ball telling widows how to communicate with their dead husbands and teenage girls how to make love potions. "Were you in Santa Clara the day that Dawn was kidnapped?"

She seemed offended by the implication of his question, but she controlled herself well. "Absolutely not. I told you I rarely go, and only when Pat asks me to."

"Well, that was twenty-five wasted minutes," Anton said the minute Felipe left with Helena.

"I know listening to her was hard on you," Catarina massaged his shoulders with a grin.

He let out a long breath. "She did answer every question, and for the most part—although she's peculiar—she was cooperative and at ease."

"Perhaps, she's simply a very good actress."

"That's possible," he returned, "but her account of where she was when AJ was killed and Dawn was kidnapped is perfectly in line with everything else we've heard."

"With so many people vouching for each other, it's getting to the point where they'd all have to be involved in a conspiracy for anyone from the community to have been involved."

And neither of them believed that.

"Vera de Melo," Catarina read from the citizen card. "You're from São Miguel."

"It's better than some of the other places a person could be from."

Catarina wasn't sure how to take that remark. "Could I get you a cup of tea?"

She looked like she wanted one but said, "I only drink the tea God has given us."

Anton worked hard not to roll his eyes. *How does that tea differ from the tea grown anywhere else on God's earth?* He was about to take a hard line when he saw his wife warn him with a small shake of her head.

"Do you grow tea at Comunidade dos Reis?" she asked.

"One of our members selects and dries leaves from plants she knows. It's her contribution to our community."

Catarina picked up on her slightly slurred speech and delayed reactions, and she wondered if the woman had been drinking, perhaps to give her the courage for the interview. "I imagine it's delicious."

"It really is. I could bring—" She was about to say more when she stopped and tightened her lips, truculence reappearing on her face.

"Minister Cardosa wants me to ask you some questions."

She snorted softly. "The *government minister* wants to ask some questions."

"He is looking into the disappearance of Dawn Bennett—"

"I don't know anything," Vera cut her off.

"Sometimes we know more than we realize."

"In the community our lives aren't cluttered with so much that we lose sight of what is around us." She gave a defiant look.

"We're just trying everything we can think of to find her. It's terrible to think of a child suffering."

Vera's face softened a bit.

"I'll just run down the list of questions quickly, then. How long have you lived on Terceira?"

"I moved here last December."

"What brought you here?"

"I came with my group from Flores, with our leader, Patrick Millikan." You could hear the pride in her voice.

"How many of you came from Flores?"

She didn't seem to know how to answer. "Um...there were two of us. Two of us were...are...deeply committed to our way of life."

"Who are the two?"

"Me and, of course, our leader."

"You joined another community here on Terceira?"

"It is our community wherever it is located."

Anton shifted positions, trying to control his reaction to the illogic of her remark.

Catarina understood that Vera's devotion was to Millikan himself as much as to the community. "What was the name of the person who headed Comunidade dos Reis when you came to Terceira?" She shuffled some papers, pretending to look for it.

"Jenkins," she swallowed the name. "Wallace Jenkins."

"He left soon after you arrived?"

"Yes, he did." There was an element of triumph in her voice.

"It's a difficult role to fulfill, helping a group of people live together in a different way—"

"Oh, we're not the ones who are different." The chance to talk about her beliefs animated her. "It's everyone around us who's different...who became different over the years."

"Nonetheless, it's a challenge to live as you do. How is everything going?"

"We'd be just fine if everyone left us alone, but it's the nature of your society. You have to keep trying new ways to fix the mess you've made," she huffed. "The answer is right in front of your faces: just return to the way life was before all your problems cropped up."

Catarina understood that each period in history had problems, some different from those of other times and some that only appeared to be different. But it would be counterproductive to argue the point. Gradually, she eased into what she really wanted to ask, and gradually Vera's responses became slightly less confrontational and more informative. Ten minutes later, she asked, "Did you happen see Dawn the day she disappeared?"

"She's hard to miss, such a sweet little child carrying her bright red elephant around all the time," she said tenderly. "I saw her and Melody in front of their house after everyone else had left for the vineyards." Much as Padre Santos had said was true of all humans, she couldn't resist presenting the case for the superiority of her own group yet again. "Unlike people who've accumulated money easily and just throw it around buying everything they see, we all work for what we need."

"That's a good way to live."

"Good? It's more than good. Those of us who can do for ourselves will survive. If there's an earthquake or a tsunami or even a nuclear war, we will have food. And we'll have the satisfaction of knowing we didn't survive on the backs of others."

She nodded thoughtfully, as if seriously considering what Vera had said.

Anton's reaction was different. *How is living off the land going to allow anyone to survive a nuclear winter?*

Catarina took Vera off her soapbox and brought her back to what she wanted to talk about. "Do you remember what time it was when you saw the children?"

"We live without constant reminders of time passing, like calendars and clocks."

"Mmm." She waited.

"Since work had started, though, it would have been about nine."

"And where did you go after you saw them?"

It took a few moments, but slowly she said, "I'm not sure."

Was it understandable forgetfulness, or was she trying to be difficult? "Since it was market day, could you have been helping senhor Millikan with business?"

"So, you do keep an eye on us," she said as though she had proved a point. "Market day. Yes, I remember now. I had a quick talk with Helena as she was returning from the forest with some mushrooms. We all contribute in our own way, you know."

"Do you remember what you talked about that day?"

"We just had a few words agreeing about how well everything is going for us this year. Then I went to ask Kate Tuttle if she needed any help, since her daughter was sick."

"Did she need help?"

"No. She had made a little play area for Sally near our oven, so she could watch her while she baked the bread."

"Did you see anyone else before you joined senhor Millikan?"

"I think Amal was there, too. You could ask Kate."

"What about after you finished helping with the community business?"

"I went to join everyone else working in the vineyards."

Anton spoke up for the first time. "What do you do with senhor Millikan?"

Vera's nostrils flared. "I help him with the *private* paperwork of the community."

Catarina wasn't sure if her short, shallow breaths were because she saw the question as an intrusion, or because there was something in the paperwork she wanted to remain hidden.

Anton set his jaw. "Please give me examples of the paperwork you handle."

Silence.

Catarina waited and watched. She thought about the two different faces of Vera she had seen in the course of half an hour. Her devotion to Millikan seemed as strong as her aversion to Jenkins, and her affection for Dawn seemed as strong as her resistance to helping outsiders to find her. Catarina's best guess was that a shaky self-esteem inclined her to be overly generous with those she had loyalty to and overly defensive with anyone else, the very embodiment of the survival mentality Padre Santos had talked about. She made eye contact with Anton, and then looked at the picture of Dawn on the table.

Anton understood. He turned the picture around to face Vera and slid it across the table.

Vera did battle with herself over whether or not to cooperate and give him the information he had asked for. Ultimately she took a breath and listed everything Lori had told them about, along with details on additional bank accounts, legal papers that made Comunidade dos Reis beneficiary of several IRAs and 401Ks, three overseas properties that had been deeded to the community, and more. Individually, none was worth a fortune; together their worth must have totaled over two million U.S. dollars.

"Thank you so much," said Catarina, smiling.

Catarina had become an ally, so Vera smiled back—after scowling at Anton, the outsider.

"I imagine you take great care with all those documents."

"We do. Senhor Millikan keeps the key with him at all times."

Anton took over. "Going back to senhor Bennett's agreement to have his monthly income transferred to one of the bank accounts—"

"That's perfectly normal," she interrupted. "After all, he got his house and everything that comes from community lands. Besides, his father has plenty of money, and you can be sure that came from working people like us. It's only right that it's returned to us."

"How do you know that AJ's father has money?"

She thought. "It was one night when a few of us got together. Janine was upset that determining the custody of the girls had become so complicated. 'It's because his father is loaded,' she told us. Apparently, a few months earlier AJ had figured out that his father was a wealthy businessman. But Janine didn't give us his name; maybe she didn't know it herself."

He tested her to see how carefully she had read the papers that Millikan kept under lock and key. "Will his death affect the community finances?"

She colored deeply and stammered, "Ah...I...I'm not sure."

It was clear that she had not only seen the financial agreement turning over AJ's monthly income to the community, she had also seen the acknowledgement of paternity. She knew that with his death, the community would lose its monthly contribution—and she knew the name of his father. Anton decided not to push her further on that point. He needed something else from her. "I understand that some people can leave the community from time to time."

The artery in Vera's neck pulsed rapidly. "Anyone can leave. It's just that no one wants to," she said angrily. "Senhor Millikan wisely advises some that they would not be well served by leaving."

"Who does he feel can leave without being harmed?"

Resigned, she gave four names through clenched teeth: AJ, Reggie, Helena, and herself.

The Tuttles came in holding hands. Looking at the fear in Reggie's eyes and the uncertainty in Kate's, Anton didn't insist on questioning them separately.

Catarina greeted them. "Thank you for coming in, Mrs. Tuttle. And you, too, Mr. Tuttle. We appreciate your help."

"Will this take long?" Kate asked anxiously, glancing at her husband. He was nervously clenching his hands and taking rapid breaths through an open mouth.

Catarina remembered what Lori had told her. "I wonder if you would mind talking outside? I've been cooped up inside for so long, and it's much more relaxing in the park."

Reggie broke out in a wide grin. "I agree. It's much more relaxing outside."

They walked on the narrow path that looped around the park behind the municipal building, Catarina pairing herself with Reggie, and Anton following next to Kate.

"We're hoping you can help us to find Dawn and return her to her mother," Catarina said to Reggie. She avoided mentioning AJ's violent death. "What do you remember about that day?"

"I took the cart to Santa Cruz for their market day," Reggie answered in his halting voice. "I load it the night before and leave it to the side of the road, just beyond the bend. I left when the sun was just coming up." He stopped and took a deep breath. "It was still pretty dark, and I had to go on the path through the forest, because I was bringing the donkey..." he stammered, "...so...so...I didn't see her."

"Did you see anyone else?"

"I saw AJ."

Anton couldn't help moving up between them. "Where?"

"Leaving the forest." He replied as though that should have been obvious.

Anton could picture exactly where Reggie had seen him. "Did you see anyone else there?"

"No...no one else." Reggie pulled away from Anton and looked at his wife.

"Did you notice which way AJ turned?"

Catarina saw Reggie's increasing anxiety in a widening of his eyes, and looking over her shoulder, she saw Kate getting ready to intervene. She moved aside to let his wife walk next to him, waiting to follow her lead on when to start talking to him again.

A few yards further down the path, Kate dropped Reggie's arm and let him walk ahead slowly on his own. "Thank you," she said quietly to Catarina.

"Perhaps we could talk for a while," she shifted her attention from Reggie. "By any chance, did you see Dawn that morning, Mrs. Tuttle?"

She repeated what she had told Lori, "Dawn stopped by the oven, where I was putting the bread in to bake. She asked if Sally could go into the forest with her and Melody, but I explained she was sick that day."

"I understand. Could anyone else have possibly seen Dawn?"

"As Reg just told you, he left early for Santa Cruz, just like AJ went…started off to Angra. Helena went into the forest for a short while to get the herbs and mushrooms that I wanted, and Amal was with me much of the day, helping with community chores."

"I believe Vera de Melo and Patrick Millikan were also there."

"That's right. They were working in the office until he left for the village about noon, when Helena and Vera went to help everyone in the vineyards. We're a small community, senhora Vanderhye, and we've all talked about this. No one saw anything."

Anton tapped his wife on the shoulder, and she moved up, letting him replace her by Kate's side. He slowed his pace to put distance between them and Reggie. "I have to ask you about Reggie's arrest records," he said quietly.

She was expecting the question. "What do you want to know?"

"The arrests were for violent behavior—"

"And all four were before we came here. He's been fine here."

"He hasn't, Kate." He knew of two outbursts in Angra that hadn't resulted in an arrest, because Reggie had been able to get himself under control.

She started to deny it but couldn't. "Those were just passing feelings. We all get them. It's just harder for him not to show those feelings."

"That's what I'm concerned about. Is it possible that he wasn't able to control himself, and he overreacted with AJ?"

"No. Absolutely not. Do you think I'd risk my child's life if I didn't believe that?"

He said nothing, and they walked on together.

It was time to get back to what Reggie had said. "Isn't it a nice day?" Catarina looked around her. "I've always loved the way plants and animals somehow know when summer is coming."

Reggie turned around. "Many plants will only flower if they survive enough adversity in winter."

"Reginald Tuttle," she said lightly, "that's the most interesting thing I've learned today."

He smiled.

"The most helpful thing I've learned came from you, too. I never imagined that someone saw AJ leaving the forest that morning."

"Well, I did. And when I reached the edge of the forest, I saw him again at the intersection, looking down the main road as if he was waiting for someone."

AJ had left the forest—and returned for some reason.

Anton received the file from Alexander's lawyer. Point by point, he checked the itinerary with the port authorities on both Terceira and Fayal, the *Qasr*'s intended destination. Everything was in order. He looked at the names of those who vouched for the whereabouts of the yacht and those aboard her on the day Dawn had been kidnapped: Jeremy Alexander; his wife, Farah Rifai; their son, Amin; Alistair Jones, the captain of the *Qasr*; and a man with the title of Senior Security Chief for Rifai Global. It was a small group, each one providing alibis for one or more of the others, but he wondered if that could be otherwise with the few people aboard.

A security guard aboard the *Qasr* escorted Anton to the pilothouse, introduced him to Captain Jones, and stepped back—but stayed in the room. The captain was a tall, lean man in his fifties, and both his thick hair and his small eyes were the same silver gray as the MacBook open in front of him. Standing in front of a large bay window, periodically looking down at a state-of-the-art console that monitored and controlled the ship's activities, he answered each question in the same way: neutrally. He showed no curiosity about why he was being questioned, no indication that the interview was a nuisance, no irritation over the nature of the questions. He was perfectly accommodating—as he might have been told to be.

"It's just a matter of accounting for everyone who was aboard on certain dates," Anton said.

The captain nodded his impassive head. "It's standard practice to account for all persons on board before leaving port and when docking, and that was done."

"How do you verify that everyone who should be on board is on board? A visual check?"

"For the crew and staff, yes, a visual check. In the case of Mr. Alexander and his family, the head steward calls for verification."

"So an audio check?"

"Yes."

"Would everyone who works on board have been on duty at one time or another between your departure from Terceira and your return?"

"You could verify that with the first mate, but I would think so." He tapped one of six touchscreens and soon pages were ejecting from a printer under the console. "This is the account I have for all crew and staff on those dates." He handed the pages over to Anton.

"Would the family have been seen by the crew during the voyage, for example, during meals?

"When no guests are aboard, the chef usually has meals taken to the private family quarters."

"I'd like to talk to the stewards who delivered meals in the past two weeks."

"Certainly. The head steward brings all meals to the family when they eat in their quarters." He picked up a receiver on the console and quietly asked for Jacques. "He'll join you shortly," he told Anton.

It *was* shortly—in fact just a matter of a minute—that the head steward appeared, and it crossed Anton's mind that perhaps those who might be questioned had been forewarned of his visit. Jacques was not of much use. He could look up every menu and every request from fresh pillowcases to a masseuse for Madame Rifai, but when it came to exactly whose faces he had actually seen on which dates, he said he drew a blank.

Whether by design or otherwise, speaking with Farah Rifai proved to be a far more difficult undertaking than any other interview Anton had conducted. The same man with the tablet who had provided information about alibis on Anton's last visit met him in a feminine office, filled with French country furnishings in powder blue, white, and gilt. He explained that by custom and by law, Anton would not be allowed to question Madame Rifai without a male relative present, and neither Jeremy Alexander nor Amin Rifai were on board. From what Anton could remember of the online pictures Lori had shown him, the woman was active socially and often seen in mixed groups of men and women, but he decided that with time running out for Dawn it wouldn't be wise to press the issue. He could be given information freely long before he could coerce it from Alexander and his family.

"Would it be possible for a female representative of the police to speak with Madame Rifai?" he asked. "It's an urgent matter, and any time she gave us would be appreciated." Twenty-five minutes later, he had an answer.

Farah Rifai didn't so much speak with Catarina as grant her an audience; however welcoming her words were, she made clear that she was doing a favor that could end at any moment. She sat in front of an exquisitely carved tigerwood screen on a private deck off the main salon, facing a manicurist who was preparing to paint her nails a subdued shade of pink. Where Jacqueline Bennett was well-groomed, Farah Rifai was striking. Stylishly dressed in white linen pants and a silk top, she was long-limbed, slender, and had perfect alabaster skin as a setting for large almond eyes and full lips. And she was probably the only Muslim woman aboard who wore her black hair uncovered and loose in the sea breeze.

It didn't escape Catarina that the manicurist was still laying out her tools or that the tall glass of iced tea by Farah's side hadn't even had time for condensation to form yet. Just as when she had met Jeremy Alexander, Catarina got the feeling that the setting was designed to impress, almost a backdrop waiting for a director to call *Action*. "I'm sorry to interrupt your day," she said, doing her best in words and tone to acknowledge the position the woman clearly enjoyed having.

Farah pulled her oversized sunglasses down her nose enough to peer over the top, looked Catarina over from top to bottom, and in French-accented English asked a question she must have known the answer to. "Who are you?"

In this woman's world, some social standing would help—as long as she believed there was no question of her own superiority. "I am the wife of Minister Plenipotentiary Cardosa. I understand you have been gracious enough to find time to help the Government of the Azores with an important matter."

"Please sit down, senhora Cardosa. I hope you are enjoying your time aboard the *Qasr*." She said something in Arabic to the manicurist and then to another female attendant who stood nearby. Both left immediately. With offers of refreshments declined, she sat back, took off her sunglasses, and said, "I will first tell you that I am aware of the circumstances surrounding the birth of the man who died here last week."

"Thank you. That does make it easier for us to talk openly."

"It's a sad story, both about his birth and his death. Unfortunately, though, men do such things. Do they not?"

Catarina gave her a sympathetic smile but fiercely thought otherwise. *My husband would never do any such things.* "I understand you were on Terceira recently." She waited for a response but got none. "Were you able to see much of our island?"

"I did take a short tour, and I walked around the downtown area a bit. Yours is a lovely island." Her compliment seemed hollow.

"I imagine Mr. Alexander is kept quite busy. Was he able to get away at all?"

"No. Sadly."

"What brought you to Terceira?"

She didn't like the question. "We were in the area, and we had not seen it before."

"Did you, your husband, or your son see Alexander Jeremy Bennett while you were here?"

"We did not. And—as I would have thought your husband told you—all three of us were at sea when he was killed."

"I understand, Madame Rifai. It's simply protocol to confirm all this." She brought up something that might make an impression on Farah. "Minister Cardosa wants to be able to clear suspicion from everyone who is innocent, in case there are questions—from the *press*, for example."

Farah gave a tight smile.

Touché. "So, is there anyone who can vouch for your presence on the *Qasr* the day after you left Terceira?"

She used a cell phone to make a brief call in Arabic. Soon the manicurist re-appeared with two other women. "This is my husband's translator, Noha," she introduced one of them to Catarina. "She has excellent command of English. Please tell her what you want to know."

As it turned out, the manicurist also did hair and gave massages, and she vouched for Farah's presence on board every day since they left Zurich.

"Madame has a massage every evening and is also telephoned by her father frequently during the day," reported Noha.

Looking at their faces, Catarina had no reason to think either the manicurist or Noha was lying.

The other woman, who had the job of attending to the wardrobes of all three family members, responded to Noha's inquiry by taking a small notebook from the pocket of her uniform and leafing through the pages. There was some confusion as Noha translated what she said, though. "Mr. Rifai asked her to provide certain items of clothing on the evening of the second."

Catarina was about to explain that she only wanted to hear about the time *after* the *Qasr* left port about midnight on the second, when she caught Farah's expression: a blend of anger and embarrassment. She decided to pursue what the woman had said. "What items of clothing?" she asked.

The woman in charge of the family's clothing colored when Noha translated the question, and she lowered her voice to say something in Arabic directly to Farah.

Farah drew her lips into a reserved smile and explained, "My family is constantly in the public eye, senhora Cardosa, and we occasionally resort to disguise to be left in peace by the paparazzi. My son had the uniform of a crewman brought to him, so he could go out for the evening."

Noha translated a few more questions and reported that Amin had returned the uniform to the woman the following morning, and that both Amin and his father had requested specific items of clothing on the third, the day AJ had been killed. As far as Catarina could tell—and she was very good at spotting liars—everything had been truthfully answered and faithfully translated.

When she tried to direct the conversation to business, Catarina was stalled by Farah, who claimed to know nothing about such matters. While possible, it wasn't in line with what she knew of her: a Muslim woman from a powerful conservative family who had managed to have her marriage to a poor

Christian approved, who socialized frequently and openly with Westerners, who had been left on her own to deal with police questions about her husband's illegitimate son, and who spoke daily with her business tycoon father. No, Farah Rifai was a strong woman who knew something about Rifai Global's financial empire.

As Anton and Catarina were leaving the *Qasr*, they became aware of an uproar on the dock below. A knot of people, who Anton recognized as the same paparazzi who had hounded him the day before, was moving towards the ship, tussling and shouting. Followed by two security guards, he and Felipe hurried down, expecting to find Alexander or Amin in the middle of the group. As it turned out, however, they found the Maier brothers.

Felipe sent the paparazzi away with threats of arrest if they appeared on the dock again, and the gentle man was met with a barrage of camera flashes and verbal abuse in at least three languages. Anton stood back and watched as one of the security guards tried to turn away Franz. "I'm sorry, Mr. Maier, but Mr. Alexander is a busy man. An appointment is needed before you can board."

Franz and Horst vigorously argued the point, until both guards turned their backs and retraced their steps up the gangplank.

Anton joined the Maiers. "You wanted to speak with Mr. Alexander?" His tone said he was suspicious of the reason.

The twins looked at each other, guilt written on their faces. Befitting his role as the lawyer, Franz spoke, "We have business with Mr. Alexander."

"What business is that?"

"It's private," he bristled.

Given how both men had behaved in past interactions, Anton had every reason to believe they wouldn't be anxious to cooperate now. A hard line was needed. "I'll be the judge of what's to be kept private."

"I have numerous complaints about your lack of progress in finding Dawn Bennett," Franz protested.

His grievance, clearly a distraction from Anton's interest in why they were there, fell on deaf ears. "Mr. Maier," he looked at Horst, "you were concerned about having your lawyer present the last time we spoke, so I'm glad that's not an issue now."

"Now just a minute here, Mr. Cardosa—" protested Franz.

Felipe interrupted with a growl, "It's *Minister* Cardosa."

Franz's jaw slackened, and his voice lost most of its fire when he continued, "My client has already answered every question you asked."

"Now I have more questions…which can be answered at the police station or here."

The brothers looked at each other. "We have time for a few questions here," said Franz.

"Fine, and if time runs out here, we can continue at the police station." Anton looked at Catarina, and she stepped forward.

"What's she doing here?" Franz challenged.

"She's here so I'll know if you're telling the truth."

Both brothers pursed their lips.

Anton had only one question before turning the interview over to his wife. He had caught the fact that one of the security guards addressed Franz by name. "How many times have you talked to Mr. Alexander?"

Horst pretended not to understand the question, but an involuntary swallow gave him away.

Finally Franz answered, "We have met once. More than that, I will not say. You will understand; it's a matter of legal confidentiality."

Anton said nothing.

Catarina's aim was to find out more about what had made Horst so uncomfortable the last time they spoke. "You were hoping to claim custody of the Bennett children," she said to him in German.

"I already told you that."

"What made you decide to take an interest in them after seven years?"

"Janine wrote to us for help."

"I believe she asked for a place to stay while she found a job. Were you—*are* you—willing to provide that now?"

He didn't want to commit himself to anything. "It's a parent's responsibility to provide financial support."

"Are you talking about Janine's responsibility to her children, or your responsibility to her?"

He was indignant. "I accepted my responsibility to her, and she repaid me with…with…inappropriate behavior."

"Let's move on to relevant questions here." Franz lifted a scolding finger to Catarina, which prompted Felipe to take a step in his direction and slap his hand against his thigh.

Catarina gave her protector a smile and turned to Horst. "What did Janine tell you about her husband's financial situation?"

"Nothing," he replied.

Franz interjected, "Nothing specific. Only that his family might be able to support the children."

"His family being Jacqueline Bennett?"

Horst flicked a glance at Franz and said very slowly, "Yes."

Franz took over. "Yes, his mother. She has money."

"What did she tell you about his father?" she asked Horst.

"Nothing."

Franz felt the need to clarify again. "She gave no details."

Catarina took her time looking over the *Qasr* from stem to stern.

The Maiers knew they had just been painted into a corner. She looked Horst in the eye. "Do I remember correctly that you are here to talk to Jeremy Alexander about a business venture?"

Franz swallowed hard, and Horst turned pale.

She carried on, "How did you find out about the connection between AJ and Jeremy Alexander?"

Horst started to protest but clamped his lips shut.

With a gesture of defeat, Franz said, "That is the job of a good lawyer, Frau Vanderhye. I started with Alexander's name on the paternity papers we were about to file. Then I noticed some resemblance between AJ's face and the billionaire's, so I looked into where Jeremy Alexander was when AJ was born, and I made some educated guesses."

Franz was quite proud of his explanation, but Catarina had picked up on an anomaly, which she brought up to Anton after the dockside interview ended. "Why would the Maiers have any interest in filing papers that revealed the identity of AJ's father? All that might have done would be to show that AJ had a steady source of income, making him *more* likely to be granted custody."

One motive came to Anton's mind immediately. "A man who had so carefully hidden the existence of his own son for over thirty years might pay someone a price *not* to file those papers."

As the evening debrief started, storm warnings were being posted around island, and the wind was picking up. Anton led with what Reggie had said and asked everyone to consider a question. "If AJ had already left the forest, why did he return?"

The number of answers was a testament to the value of teamwork. The group ultimately dismissed most of the ideas, such as being forced back or returning for something he had forgotten, as implausible. They were left with two possibilities: AJ had been leading someone through the forest—to Comunidade dos Reis—or he had seen something important enough to let someone know immediately. For everyone sitting around the table, frustration came with not being able to connect either scenario with what had then happened in the forest.

Felipe had found damning records on two of the settlers. "Not unexpectedly, sir, when we looked into *Henry* Patrick Millikan, we found he is wanted for questioning in three American states."

"For what?" asked Anton.

"The specifics differ, but in each case people—a church group, a home for the elderly, a farm cooperative—have accused him of deceiving them into giving him money."

Catarina was able to contribute to a fuller picture of Millikan. "As you asked, I spoke with Wallace Jenkins, the former leader of Comunidade dos Reis. He sounded quite happy and said more than once that leaving was the right decision for him. Reading between the lines, however, I gathered that he and Mr. Millikan had disagreed over the direction the community should take in terms of membership."

"How so?" asked Anton.

"He made a couple of remarks about his own belief that anyone should be able to join the community, as opposed Mr. Millikan's feeling that those who joined should be able to contribute to the 'growth' of the settlement."

"I think we know what he meant by 'growth,'" he returned with a sigh. "Felipe, would you visit banks *early* tomorrow morning? The storm is expected to hit in the afternoon, and they may close at noon. Try to find which might have given out a safe deposit box key in an envelope numbered one-seven-two."

"Yes, sir. Moving on to the self-named Helena, the owner of the grocery in Santa Clara has returned and confirms that Helena is the woman who goes in quite a bit."

"What does she buy there?"

Felipe laughed. "Other than the same thick linguiça sandwich, a bottle of wine, and magazines every time? Well, sir, the grocer says she buys," he consulted his notes, "'every box of tea in the store. Doesn't matter what brand or what size.' He's had to order more stock because of her."

"Let me guess," said Anton, amused and relishing the prospect of confronting Carlota Zubiri. "She also buys herbs and mushrooms."

"And every bar and bottle of soap on the shelves." There wasn't a straight face around the conference table, and the laughter felt good. They had their answer about whether or not Helena was just an eccentric. She was a very clever charlatan.

"I also looked for records on Carlota Zubiri and found a long history of activity that bordered on the criminal but never crossed the line. She's been cited six times in France and Spain for fortune telling without a business license; she's been implicated in fraud; and charges of pickpocketing in Italy were dismissed twice. She has a pattern of preying on marks, mainly tourists, and leaving town. She entered São Miguel on a cruise ship, and then disappeared from the system. She seems to have been making money from the gullible here, spending a portion at the grocery store, and hiding out at Comunidade dos Reis."

So, both Millikan and Helena were frauds…but did that make either of them a kidnapper or a murderer?

The search by the Island Guards had yielded nothing; there was no record of Dawn leaving Terceira and no trace of her on the island. The day's work by the team seemed only to eliminate suspects. Reggie Tuttle had been seen by several other vendors at the Santa Cruz market from eight in the morning until late in the afternoon, and the Maiers' rental car had only enough mileage to account for their first visit to take the custody papers to Janine for her signature.

"What about taxis?" asked Anton.

Norberto had handled that. "Taxis recorded five trips to Santa Clara on the day the little girl was taken. Normally that would be five more than expected, but it was market day and all five pickups were at hotels—tourists, the drivers remembered. None recognized the Maiers."

Typically thorough, Felipe was able to expand on that. "The Maiers spend most of their time on Terceira in the hotel, and they were identified by their pictures and CCTV as walking to the same three restaurants many times. A second man, who was described as looking just like the first man, joined them a couple of times."

Catarina added one more line of inquiry, "I'm curious about where Amin Rifai went on the night the *Qasr* left for Fayal. When I first talked to him, he didn't want to either confirm or deny that he had left the ship. Then, when I talked to his mother, I was told he had asked for a crewman's uniform, so he could leave the ship that evening."

Anton assigned that task to Norberto and Rosa. "Again, with the storm expected, everything could be closed tomorrow night. It's best to ask around tonight."

"I'll put on my dancing shoes," joked Norberto.

"Is this a punishment, sir?" laughed Rosa.

That ended the meeting on a lighter note, but it was somewhat forced. Everyone knew that by the end of the next day, a six-year-old child could be in the greatest danger of her life.

Ten minutes later, Anton was sitting in the conference room wrapping up the next day's plans with Felipe, when Gabriela showed up at the door. Anton looked up. "How can I help you?" he asked.

Felipe stood and cleared his throat. "I believe senhora Viveiros is here to see me, sir."

Anton just nodded and went back to his paperwork. Then his eyebrows drew together and he raised his head, processing what he had just heard. "To...see..."

"I can stay if you need me, sir."

"We can both stay," Gabriela added.

"No. No. Not necessary." A wide grin split his face. "Where are you two going?"

Felipe shrugged his shoulders.

"An Italian restaurant nearby," Gabriela answered. "Italian is Felipe's favorite food."

Well, I didn't know that. "Have fun, you two."

Anton paced the empty conference room. He was about to receive a call from Presidente Moniz, and the only thing he could tell him was that hope of finding Dawn Bennett alive was all but gone.

The Presidente got to the point quickly. "Anton, this is becoming a bigger international incident with every passing day. Jeremy Alexander's lawyers have described us—you—as harassing their clients, who have cooperated fully and given a detailed account of their whereabouts on the day the child was kidnapped and her father was killed. They also say that with the press following their every movement, Mr. Alexander and his family would like to—or, as they put it, '*expect to*'—put out to sea immediately after the storm passes. Franz Maier has also been in my office twice this week, complaining of incompetence and intimidation. And there's the matter of publicity with these paparazzi."

Thanks to the alerts that Lori had set up on his phone, Anton knew there was speculation about a missing child and a murder in the same place where Jeremy Alexander's yacht was docked. "I understand, sir, but my main worry now is the welfare of Dawn Bennett. Frankly, she may not even be…" He couldn't bring himself to finish that thought. "The storm will put her in greater jeopardy."

"Anton, I gave this responsibility to you because I knew I could trust your judgement. I still do."

In the park behind the municipal building, the night air was eerily still. Anton let his mind wander from one thought to another, memories of voices and images replacing one another randomly. He had searched every place he could think of searching, examined every piece of evidence he could think of collecting, talked to everyone he could think of talking to. Dawn's fate lay in putting it all together. He was close. He could feel it.

For the next hour, he tried to figure out what his mind was trying to tell him, but each time he was on the brink of a breakthrough, it all slipped away.

Light came through her closed lids, and water dripped somewhere in the distance. She was very thirsty. She tried to hug Bobey, but she could only move her hand.

9

Anton and Catarina spent the night in the conference room, lying on cots that had been set up for the weather emergency. Neither slept. They thought about their children, safe with Maria Rosa. They thought about Casa do Mar and hoped it would come through the storm without major damage. They thought about their neighbors on Santa Maria, certain to suffer varying degrees of loss from Hurricane Mimi. They thought about Lori on what they expected would be her last day at Comunidade dos Reis. And they thought about Dawn.

At seven in the morning, Gabriela came in carrying toothbrushes, toothpaste, and a comb. Fifteen minutes later, she re-appeared with a pot of hot coffee and a bag of sweet rolls. "Come on, you two, you have to eat," she said as she filled two cups.

"Thanks, Gabriela," Catarina said numbly. She picked up a cup, felt the heat rising from wisps of steam, and put it down before it reached her lips. "Any update on the storm?"

Gabriela frowned and looked out the window. "It's closing in on us."

"Who else is here?"

"Chief Rocha is here." She saw Catarina's raised eyebrows and added, "Even when there's nothing urgent to deal with, he does that. His work is his life."

"He has no family?"

"He did once. They say his wife left him and took the children with her, and that's when he got even more difficult to deal with."

She thought about Felipe and how being without a family had engendered the same devotion to work in him; his personality, however, had made a man who cared deeply for those entrusted to his care. "Is Felipe here yet?"

"He's just freshening up before heading to the banks with Norberto. Like you, he's been here all night."

"So have you, I think."

She nodded and started to fold the cots against the wall.

Gabriela made neat stacks of photos, interview transcripts, and meeting notes down the center of the table. Rosa added a report on Amin's activities the night before Dawn was taken: a few hours in cafés and bars, during which he flirted with other young men, one of whom waved goodbye to him as he re-boarded the *Qasr*. Catarina wrote up a summary of what they knew and left copies at everyone's places. Gracia and Silva came in and left three times. It was all any of them could think of doing.

Deep in thought, Anton walked the length of the room many times, looking at what was laid out on the table. By the time the pot of coffee was empty, his thoughts about Dawn's kidnapping had started to come together, and he called for his team. He took his one tangible connection to Dawn out of his shirt pocket and stroked it gently with his thumb. *Are you still there, child?*

The first squall line was already moving across Terceira, skies had darkened, and rain beat against the glass as everyone settled into place. Anton was about to send Felipe to bring Lori back, by force if needed, when a singular sight appeared in the doorway: a tall blond, not just soaked but dripping wet, holding a metal box to her chest. If that wasn't enough to capture everyone's attention, the reception Anton and Catarina gave her was.

As expected, Gabriela had Lori dried off, in a spare police uniform, and sipping hot tea within ten minutes. In the meanwhile, the metal box was pried open to reveal a thick bundle of cash and a large key, both of which shortened the list of suspects Anton was considering.

"Why take Dawn?" he began. Catarina and Lori knew from the tone of his voice that he had realized something important. They waited. "Why take Dawn?" he repeated, slowly the second time because he was still thinking it through. "What was there to gain by taking her from the forest?"

"With her father dead, someone might have thought she would come into a lot of money," offered Lori.

"Again, why take her? No one could claim that money without having Dawn, and anyone who had Dawn would be admitting they had kidnapped her and then lied to the authorities about it."

There were a few moments of silence while they all considered that.

Catarina had an alternate motive for taking Dawn. "One of her grandparents might not have wanted to risk letting the courts decide where Dawn would live—not out of love, I know—but for the money that might come to them through her if another court system decided in their favor."

Anton shook his head. "How would they be able to take Dawn with them? We're on an island, and they had to have known they would be searched more thoroughly than anyone else, whether at the marina or at the airport."

Lori said what no one wanted to, "There are other, terrible reasons for a stranger to take a child."

Anton drew a deep breath. "I know. I know. But the forest is remote. How would they know that Dawn would be passing through at that time? I can't picture someone pulling to the side of the road at just that spot, climbing up to the forest, happening to find Dawn, and taking her away. So again, why take her?"

"So she *couldn't* claim the money?" suggested Lori.

Catarina's heart sank. "You think she was killed?"

"No! That's just it, you see," explained Anton. "If someone wanted to kill her, why not just do it in the forest? There'd be much less chance of being seen, much less chance of leaving evidence behind, much less chance of running into problems elsewhere. Not to mention that Melody would also have to die if the motive was to prevent the money from being inherited by Alexander's grandchildren."

"What reason does that leave?" asked Catarina.

"The classic reason. The reason the children of wealthy parents are sometimes taken by strangers."

"She was kidnapped for ransom?"

"I think so."

"But there's been no demand for money. And I don't see Jeremy Alexander or Jacqueline Bennett paying ransom for a grandchild they didn't care enough about to have ever seen. AJ was the only one with money who would have cared enough to pay a ransom, and he's dead."

"That's the point. If we stop looking at the two crimes together, it becomes much simpler to figure out what happened. If the kidnapper didn't know that AJ was dead…"

Lori was following his train of thought. "He had gone into the forest so much earlier than Dawn did, so it makes sense that he was already dead when she was taken."

"She must have been taken by someone who knew that AJ had access to money—perhaps because of who his father was, perhaps just because he was able to give so much to the community—but someone who didn't know the whole story, someone who didn't know AJ was already dead."

Lori picked up the thread. "So she was taken to the house in Santa Clara—"

"—but when AJ's body was discovered, the kidnapper knew there wouldn't be a payoff—"

"—and his murder had brought so much attention to the area—"

"— there was no easy way to return Dawn."

"Don't we still have the problem of who would have known she would be in the forest at that time?" asked Lori.

"We have the answer," said Anton. "One of the people at Comunidade dos Reis who had access to the documents in the locked file cabinet was waiting for the opportunity that arose that morning."

"Two problems, Anton," Lori challenged him. "How did the kidnapper know about the empty house? And if it was someone in the community, wouldn't Dawn have been able to identify her kidnapper?"

And with those two questions, Anton knew who had taken Dawn.

He rose and said to the team, "Let's go." *I just hope we're not too late.*

Norberto screeched to a stop beside the forest. Anton was as fast as he had ever been as he climbed the muddy rise, and as angry as he had ever been as he raced between trees. Community members were outside, taking advantage of a letup in the storm, when he burst out of the forest, followed closely by the men and women who had dedicated the past week of their lives to finding Dawn.

Amal and Cassie looked up, smiling before they saw the looks on their visitors' faces. Kate walked slowly to a startled Reggie and wrapped her arms around his waist, soothing him with soft words. Alarmed, Vera turned one way and another before running off in search of Millikan. Helena raised her arms to the sky and uttered some gibberish with closed eyes. Janine left Melody on her front porch and walked to them, anguish and anticipation written on her face. Millikan took center stage in the clearing and was quickly surrounded by about half the community, the rest looking on while they gathered together their children. Rather than fear, most of their faces reflected sorrow.

Walking behind Anton, Lori felt her betrayal keenly. She knew what the people of the community were thinking. Was their community and their way of life about to be taken from them?

No one said a word as Felipe stationed the police to encircle the group and Anton claimed their attention. "Ten days ago, Comunidade dos Reis suffered two losses. Janine," he held out his hand to her, and she joined him, "has lived every moment of that time wondering what happened to her daughter that day. Your own way of life—a way you have every right to choose— has been challenged by these events." Members of the community moved closer to him, now listening more intently.

"Here are the facts. One, several people saw Dawn in the settlement until about nine that morning, and we have photographic evidence that she was in Santa Clara—less than half an hour away—two hours later."

Helena and Kate nodded.

"Two, we know only six of you were not working in the vineyards at that time."

Amal shrunk into her clothes, a faraway stare in her eyes.

"Three, Mrs. Tuttle and senhora Hukan say that, with the exception of brief periods of time, they were within sight of each other all morning."

"Four, according to several people, senhora de Melo did not leave for the vineyards until close to noon, when senhor Millikan also left the compound." When he looked at Millikan, Anton's feelings were a mixture of satisfaction at exposing him and disappointment that he was no longer implicated in the kidnapping. "And we know he was enjoying a meal and using his laptop at a café in Santa Clara, when Dawn was being taken to the house where she was held."

Murmurs arose from the group.

"Then, perhaps you'll leave us alone," Millikan angrily challenged him. He looked around at everyone. "They will say anything, do anything to get us to abandon our rightful place."

"I have no intention of disturbing Comunidade dos Reis," Anton calmly said. "You, however, are not off the hook. Henry Patrick Millikan is wanted for questioning—"

"Just another case of the authorities using their power against people like us," he turned his back on Anton and addressed the community.

Anton, too, directed his next remarks to the community. "Henry Patrick Millikan is wanted for questioning about *fraud* in *three* American jurisdictions." He continued more emphatically, "A church group, a home for the elderly, and a farm cooperative have all accused him of deceiving them into giving him money."

He stubbornly defended himself. "I was helping those people. You all know how I've helped you. We've thrived since I took over leadership."

Some looked at each other, unsure, and Anton heard whispers. *Perhaps those charges are trumped up. It's true: we've done well recently. They might say anything to get us out.*

"Senhor Millikan has taken money from a number of you—"

Again Millikan interrupted, loudly declaring the aphorism above his front door, "Those who have should help those who have not!"

Anton's objective was to save Dawn—if that was still possible—but he knew he might need the community's help, so he made one last effort to bring them together against Millikan and in support of what he needed. "How many of you have given Comunidade dos Reis money? How many of you have turned over social security checks, veteran's benefits, disability payments, child welfare money?"

Hands went up slowly, until all but a few were raised.

"And how many of you were told your money stood between survival and defeat of this endeavor?" The hands remained raised. His contempt was clear when he said to Millikan, "You wanted everyone to give to the community financially, but you didn't use what they contributed for them; it ended up in your own safe deposit box, number one-seven-two."

"You had no right! That money is mine. I knew I hadn't forgotten to lock that drawer."

In truth, although Felipe had located the box, he hadn't been able to have it opened yet. Still, Lori's information had done the job; guilt bloomed on Millikan's face. One by one, the settlers turned their backs on him, ignoring his increasingly feeble attempts to explain, and they rallied around Janine.

Vera stepped in front of Millikan. "You weasel! I've been worrying myself sick over you and how to make your dream come true!"

"Henry Patrick Millikan, extradition papers have been filed, and you will be turned over to American authorities." He nodded to Felipe, who took such pleasure in his next duty: handcuffing Millikan.

"This is a good place to hide," Anton addressed all of them, "and a good place to find people like you, who are trusting and well-intentioned." Everyone knew there was more coming, and they hung on his every word. "Carlota Zubiri, you are also a fraud. You weren't about to stay on this island for the rest of your life, making a few Euros telling fortunes to tourists who you deceived into thinking it was a local tradition, and then spending most of it to buy tea, soap, and herbs from the local grocer."

Muttering rose from the group.

"I bet you were thrilled when you broke into the file cabinet in the office and realized there was money to be had from AJ. When you saw the name of his father, I imagine you realized immediately just who Jeremy Alexander is—perhaps from all the magazines you bought with your lunches in Santa Clara." He pointed his finger in her direction. "So you made plans."

Anton heard angry whispers. "You were one of just two or three people who could have known about the empty house in Santa Clara. After all, you were there quite a bit, and you talked to people in the village."

She stood without expression and said nothing.

"Everyone here is used to seeing your comings and goings through the forest, and it's only a matter of twenty or thirty minutes to that house. You waited for the perfect moment, took Dawn there, and returned to the other side of the forest, where you were supposedly making soap. Your plan was to leave as soon as you got the money from AJ, so it wouldn't matter if she was found and identified you."

"Then it all fell apart. AJ was dead, and his death brought attention to the community and its people. You had to burn the ransom note and move Dawn. With all flights off the island cancelled because of the storm, though, you couldn't leave and disappear to another place, as you've done more than once before. So you just left the child there."

Janine charged, almost knocking Helena to the ground. She pulled her head up by her hair and screamed, "Where's my daughter?" At the same time furious and feeble, she beat against Helena's chest. No one stopped her. "You killed her, didn't you? You killed my baby."

Catarina didn't need much strength to pull her away. Janine collapsed to the ground, her open mouth contorted in agony, her throat tight with sobs she couldn't release. Then she choked out over and over, "My baby. My baby." Catarina wrapped Janine in her arms until her primal screams died to whimpers.

Anton glared at Helena. "You have one chance, *one* chance, to tell me where Dawn is."

She smirked and rolled her eyes to the heavens. "Well, you have me on charges of fraud, Minister. I guess I'll have to plead guilty to...what? Oh, right, telling fortunes without a license. And providing tea and soap...without even charging for them."

Her response—or lack of response—was what he had feared. There was little to hold over her head in exchange for information about Dawn. He pleaded with the people around him. "Where would she have hidden her? Please, help us."

They tried. Some named places that had already been searched. Some offered to look in the forest again. Vera examined the key Lori held up, hoping to think of a lock it might open. Cassie offered to take Helena to the forest and force her to talk. Anton was ready to do that himself. Through gritted teeth, he growled at her, "You will tell me where Dawn Bennett is, or I will bury you, too."

She snickered. "How the hell am I supposed to know where the girl is?"

Catarina caught an expression, so meaningful and at the same time so brief that if she had blinked, she would have missed it. Helena had opened her eyes wide just as Anton finished talking. She signaled for Anton to join her. "What did you just say to her?" she whispered.

"I just let her know that I'd do whatever it takes to find the child." Anton had meant what he said.

"No. What were your exact words?"

"Ah," he ran his fingers through his hair and rubbed his scalp, trying to remember. "I wanted to let her know that if she did kill her, Dawn wouldn't be the only one to die. I said I'd bury her, too. But you know it was just a figure of speech—"

"Anton, when you said that, she looked as though she was amazed you knew something." Catarina glanced at Janine, who stood weeping next to Amal, and she trembled. "I'm afraid Dawn is already dead, and she's been buried somewhere."

Anton hung his large head. When he turned around, he willed himself not to look at Janine. If she saw his face, she would know what he was feeling. He fixed Helena in his sights and walked to her slowly. He could at least try to find Dawn's body.

Ignoring everyone else, he grabbed her arm and pulled her towards the forest. "Move!" he bellowed, and she flinched.

It was one of those moments when the mind makes a connection between seemingly unrelated thoughts. Anton looked ahead to where Melody was gently stroking a small black dog, and he realized two things at the same time. He knew where Dawn Bennett was. And he knew Dawn Bennett might still be alive.

He left dealing with Helena and Millikan in Felipe's hands, and charged into the forest with Norberto on his heels. Trees were swaying in the quickening wind, and here and there a tree branch snapped as it broke to the ground. "Monte Brasil!" he called out when they reached the road. By the time the car had turned around, Lori was reaching for a back door handle, with Catarina and Janine on her heels.

Dark thunderclouds filled the sky as they raced down the hillside towards Angra, careening around slower cars, shooting through traffic at intersections. In the back seat, Catarina wrapped her arms around Janine and explained, "Monte Brasil is a tiny peninsula just outside the capital. It has a long history of being associated with ancient peoples."

A flicker of hope lit Janine's eyes. Breathlessly, she stammered, "I think Helena's mentioned it before. Some temples and burial chambers carved out of the rock?"

"That's the place. There are manmade caves, known as hypogea, that archeologists tell us have been there for thousands of years."

"Anton thinks Dawn is in one of them?"

"He's talking to a professor at the university in Lisbon, the leading expert on the hypogea, right now."

Janine squeezed her eyelids shut and grabbed Catarina's hand.

Flashes of lightening sparked at the horizon, the temperature dropped, and the roar of the surf nearly drowned out Anton's conversation. Along the coast, crashing waves reverberated in the low clouds, sounding like thunder overhead. The rain started suddenly, with heavy drops beating on the car windows, and within minutes the car was churning through inches of water. That Norberto made it to the hill without an accident was remarkable.

Anton listened on his phone and directed Norberto, "Turn right ahead." The road ended at a small overlook. He turned to the back seat. "The most likely place is ahead. It's isolated, and it's one of three hypogea with a door across the entrance."

Every piece of their clothing was drenched before the car doors closed. Lanterns hanging around the overlook had switched on in the darkness, making shadows swoop as they were blown around. They each turned on a flashlight and followed Anton along an overgrown path that ended at a wall of impenetrable brush.

He bent over pulling the neck of his jacket over his head to shield his phone. "Which way now?" he called out over the wind. "Okay. Okay." He pointed to the left, along a ridge that parted a wilder area of the hill. They stopped at a rocky outcrop draped with vines that hung from a half-dead tree above. He grabbed a handful of the stems whipping in the gale and pulled them aside to reveal a small arched doorway that had been carved out of the rock. The recessed iron door had been chained shut.

Lori pulled the key she had taken from Helena's box from the pocket of her borrowed police uniform and handed it to Anton. Everything conspired against them. Seconds after Catarina positioned the wavering beam of her flashlight over the lock, it dimmed, flickered, and went out. Working with Norberto's flashlight, Anton started again, only to lose his grip on the wet key and drop it somewhere in the mud. More time was lost pulling wind-driven vines away from the door, wiping away sheets of water, and working the key around in a rusty lock…until…at last…the chain rattled through the door's handle to the ground.

Anton and Catarina's eyes met. If the worst was inside, neither wanted Janine to see it. "I'll be right back," said Anton, and Catarina replied, "We'll wait for you."

First, there was only blackness and the sound of dripping water. As Anton's eyes adjusted to the darkness, he made out a low ceiling, then the walls and ledges carved into them. He swept the small cave with his flashlight. An unopened box of cereal. Plastic water bottles, all filled.

Dawn, are you here?

He realized he hadn't said it out loud. "Dawn, are you here?" He spoke softly; he didn't want to frighten her.

He swept the cave with light again. A lantern, either turned off or burned out. A blanket, flat on a ledge.

"Dawn? Your mama is outside." Silence. "Dawn?"

Tears rolled down Anton's cheeks. The flashlight beam caught something red at the back of the cave, and he held it in the cone of light. With each step, he could see more: a trunk, four legs, a tail, and, on Bobey's other ear, Dawn's chubby hand.

She felt a warm hand on her head. She remembered where she was. *Don't move. Just listen. Now peek.* Her eyelashes fluttered, and her eyelids opened partway. There was a man with tears brimming in his large brown eyes, and he felt…safe. She snuggled against his chest. *Maybe it was all a bad dream.* And she fell asleep again.

10

Driven by a strong offshore wind, the clouds that had gathered over the past week were clearing, and after days of chilly damp, the air was warm and bright.

The island had taken a savage beating. Everywhere Anton looked, there were shattered windows, roof tiles on the ground, and uprooted trees blocking roads. But there had been no serious injuries, and for that he was thankful. His eyes followed the line of white wake being left by a motor boat. He imagined himself on the water rowing his own boat and released a deep breath. After rescuing Dawn, everything else seemed doable: finding who had killed AJ, saving Casa do Mar, even creating the historic trust he hoped would preserve the culture of his beloved Azores.

Climbing the steps to the police station, Anton had a good idea why AJ had been murdered, but he didn't know yet who was responsible. He sat at the head of the long, age-darkened table in the conference room, and for several seconds he could only look straight ahead to the nineteenth century fresco of Angra, sad that his islands had been stained by evil, and sad that AJ and his family had been hurt by that evil.

Reactions to being summoned to the conference room were varied and expected. Agneta was wide-eyed and timidly looked to her husband. The Maier brothers exchanged guilty glances. Jeremy and Farah sat together, he covering anger with an expression of disdain, and she holding herself aloof with the same expression. Jacqueline waited tensely for what was to come. When Amin walked in, uneasy and pale, his father gestured to the empty chair next to him. Catarina could follow the silent conversation that followed, the son not wanting to sit where he was told and the father insisting. She could see Amin—a man in his thirties—weigh his resistance to his father and ultimately capitulate.

Anton addressed no one in particular when he started. "Collectively, you can put together a picture of the first days of AJ's life and his last days, and you can explain how events surrounding his birth led to his cruel death."

He turned to Jacqueline first. "Ms. Bennett, you met Mr. Alexander in Philadelphia, where he was studying economics at the Wharton School."

"Yes." She steeled herself for the questions that might follow.

"And it was there that AJ was born."

"Yes."

"Before your son's birth, Mr. Alexander provided you with a legal document acknowledging paternity."

"I don't see how any of this is relevant. So what if he acknowledged paternity?"

"That same document stipulated a very generous financial settlement to begin on AJ's first birthday," he paused a moment, "although at that time Mr. Alexander was not in fact a wealthy man."

The front of Jacqueline's silk blouse quivered as her heart beat hard and fast.

The last piece of the puzzle to fall into place in Anton's mind explained something that had nagged at him ever since Lori told him that Alexander and Farah were married *after* AJ's birth. If not to cover up a marital affair, what was the need for such secrecy about AJ's existence? He realized it was because Alexander actually *was* married at the time of AJ's birth—but to Jacqueline.

He turned to Alexander. "When Nejim Rifai proposed your betrothal to his only child, you were already married. But you and Ms. Bennett saw a golden opportunity. By concealing your marriage and your son's existence, you could marry into the Rifai family and the Rifai business, with all the wealth and power that would come with it. And you, Ms. Bennett, would have a portion of that, knowing full well that if the money ever stopped coming, you could reveal his secret."

No one said a word. Anton looked at Farah, coolly observing the scene. "When did you find out about this?"

The smile she returned carried no emotion. She had no intention of answering.

"You got the marriage you wanted, one in which you had your own power to reveal secrets if your desires were not accommodated."

She smirked with superiority, Amin squeezed his eyes shut, and everyone else tried not to betray what they were thinking.

Anton took a long breath. "Let's move on. All your fortunes are tied to the success of Rifai Global."

"Rifai Global is doing quite well, Minister," said Alexander.

"Exactly. It is to your advantage, Mr. Alexander, to remain associated with it." He waited a moment before quietly continuing, "But you personally are not Rifai Global."

Alexander exploded. "I *am* Rifai Global!"

Amin hung his head. *Was it a line he had heard too many times?*

"It was nothing more than a family business, doomed to fail in the modern world, until I came along." Alexander pounded the table with his fist. "*I* made it what it is today."

"But it was never truly yours," retorted Anton.

Farah languidly stretched and said, "Rifai Global belongs to my father, and it *will* belong to my son."

Anton glanced at Catarina, and she gave him one slow nod of her head. She had seen the small shifts in position, the dry swallows, and the short breaths. They were all getting nervous. He was on the right track.

He continued, "From what I've gathered, Rifai Global is to be inherited by *legitimate* male heirs."

"That is standard in my culture, Minister." For the first time, Farah's voice carried some emotion: anger.

"I do understand that, Madame Rifai, but if your father found out about Mr. Alexander's marriage, Amin's legitimacy would be in question, wouldn't it? Then Rifai Global might not be inherited as everyone wants."

Alexander attempted to make light of what Anton had said. "Nejim Rifai is quite familiar with the gossip that follows our family. He wouldn't give a second thought to innuendoes coming out of an insignificant island in the middle of nowhere, and neither would anyone else."

Anton waved one of his cell phones in front of them. "Recently, this was set up to alert me if there was any mention of one of you by certain news outlets. It's remarkable how quickly an innuendo is passed along and becomes a story of major significance. I would imagine that's especially true if what's being passed along comes from notarized court documents."

Alexander's mouth hovered between smile and grimace. "Eventually, people forget and move on. After a while, they have a distant memory of some story they aren't sure was ever more than salacious gossip cooked up by the tabloids to boost sales."

It was Anton's turned to smile—enigmatically. He would return to that point soon enough. "Money had no attraction for AJ Bennett personally but—as his wife explained—he was glad to have it when he thought it might be a factor in getting custody of his children. He intended to use the document that showed his paternity and the income he received every month. Surely your lawyers explained that those papers would be in the public domain as soon as they were officially filed. You all knew that the paparazzi would be alerted to any mention of Jeremy Alexander in the custody hearing, and you all dealt with that in different ways."

Anton's first target was Jacqueline Bennett. He fixed her in his sights and—with more than a little contempt—said, "Just as you had since his birth, Ms. Bennett, you put your financial gain above your son's welfare. As soon as he wrote to ask for your help in keeping his children with him, you contacted your—I guess I should say your husband—so he could become involved. After all, you didn't want risk the lifestyle you took at your son's expense." Her jaw tightened so much the tendons in her neck stood out.

He turned to the Maier brothers. They looked at each other. "When you found out that Mr. Alexander was AJ's father, your first plan was to gain custody of his grandchildren and make sure the child support was generous, wasn't it?"

"It's not illegal to ask for child support," Franz defended himself. "In fact, as a lawyer, I would be derelict in my duties if I didn't try to get as much as I could for those poor children."

"Then why did you suddenly stop trying after the first of the month?" He answered his own question, "Janine showed you the papers AJ was about to file. His income was not at all what you thought it would be—given his paternity—and you could hardly compel Mr. Alexander to give more...or could you?" Agneta's tears betrayed them. "Your silence about AJ's paternity could be worth quite a bit more than child support. Of course, silence would be worthless if AJ filed those papers."

Franz held in a short breath and looked ahead at the wall. Horst closely examined his hands. Anton got their attention by slapping the table with a heavy folder. "You knew AJ would be leaving for Angra early that Tuesday morning, and you passed that information on to Mr. Alexander, so he could convince his son to drop his custody suit. When AJ was found dead, did you wonder if Jeremy Alexander or one of his family had killed him? Now that would really be worth a fortune. Is that what you returned to the *Qasr* to talk about, on the day I found you surrounded by paparazzi?" He looked at Horst, wiping the sheen from his upper lip with a forefinger.

Anton picked up the thread he had suspended. "Mr. Alexander said that eventually people forget and move on. But that's not true of all people, is it? A friend of mine quoted the mantra that drives Nejim Rifai's dealings with people: *Act honorably, and I will support you; act dishonorably, and I will destroy you.* Among you, one person stands to lose everything because of acting dishonorably." He looked at Jeremy Alexander. "You couldn't take the chance that he would dismiss those *innuendoes*."

Anton pushed his chair back and stood. "You left the *Qasr* when it was in port and spent the night in Angra, perhaps in a hotel, perhaps just at a club. You took a taxi to Santa Clara and met AJ as he was leaving his community, at exactly the time Horst Maier told you he would. You convinced him to return to the forest, perhaps saying you wanted to meet his wife and children. I want to believe that you only intended to convince your son to drop the custody suit, but you were certainly prepared for his refusal, prepared to permanently remove the chance that something like this would happen again."

Alexander looked at him with curiosity but nothing more.

Speaking almost to himself, Anton asked, "How could a man kill his own son?"

"There could be many reasons, Minister," Alexander smiled as if he pitied Anton's weakness in thinking otherwise. "Perhaps—purely theoretically, of course—it would be to save something more important, something such as a business that is irreplaceable. I, for example, have such a business." He looked at Amin. "And I do have another son." He turned to his wife. "Farah, we've accommodated these people long enough. It's time to return to the *Qasr*."

"Neither one of you will be leaving."

"What do you intend to do, Minister? You have only speculation."

"I'll let the courts decide how much is speculation and how much is fact. We've already located the taxis that went to Santa Clara on the day you killed your son. It will be a small matter to have the driver identify you. Your picture will be posted around the island. Someone will recognize the man who stayed at their hotel or partied at their club that night."

"If...*if*...I did stay here, I'm only guilty of wasting my time in an abysmal place."

Anton's eyes went to Felipe, and he saw what he knew he would: a man trying very hard to control his temper. "Mr. Jeremy Alexander, by the authority of the President of the Azores, I am placing you under arrest for the premeditated murder of Alexander Jeremy Bennett...your son."

"Call our lawyers, Amin."

Amin started to walk out of the room. Farah reached out to stop him. He shrugged her off.

Alexander jumped to his feet, took two long strides, and grabbed his son. "You stay right where you are."

Amin roughly pulled his arm away.

Farah stood and took slow steps towards the door.

"You won't be leaving, either, Madame Rifai. You were complicit in this. If AJ had gone ahead with his plan, your marriage contract would be void, and your sham marriage would be paraded in front of the world. Your son's inheritance might be in jeopardy; your own lifestyle might be in jeopardy if your father discovered the role you've played in hiding the truth." Perspiration made her makeup settle into creases around her eyes. "You were well aware that your husband wasn't on board the *Qasr* the night before AJ was murdered. You both knew we would contact him about his son's death, and the ship could be directed to return to Terceira, so he could slip on board again. Did you cover for him by simply saying he was there, or were you more deceitful, perhaps playing a recording of his voice? We'll look into that, too."

Alexander protested and demanded to speak with his lawyers.

"Enough!" Amin's cry was somewhere between a plea and a demand. Then he drew himself up and seemed to find a strength of character no one had seen before. "You both disgust me." He looked Anton squarely in the face. "Minister, please give Mrs. Bennett my deepest condolences and my deepest apologies. I can only hope that she—and you—understand that what was done is contrary to everything my family stands for, and I will do whatever I can to make amends."

Anton extended his hand. Amin shook it and left.

Felipe handcuffed both Alexander and Farah, and led them out through the front door of the municipal building. The paparazzi had gathered again, shouting questions and snapping pictures. And Felipe didn't even try to stop them.

Miriam Winthrop

Comunidade dos Reis had been devastated by the hurricane, fields flattened, roofs torn away from stone cottages, both donkey carts shattered by the same fallen tree, and the stream—swollen threefold after the storm—muddied and thick with fallen leaves. The community was gathering for lunch when the people who had saved Dawn came through the forest to accept Janine's invitation to meet her daughter and to hear two words: thank you.

Voices hushed as Lori entered the center of the hamlet, unsure of how she would be received. She glanced at one person and another, trying to gauge their feelings about her.

"I could use a little help with this soup pot," Cassie said loudly to her. "If you're not going to work, you're not going to eat."

Lori smiled with relief and took one handle of the large pot.

Kate was the next. "Thank goodness you gave us some warning about the storm. Otherwise, this soup would be even thinner."

"It made a difference," an elderly man asserted. "We stocked the storage cellar with water, some food, and lanterns—just like we used to do when I was a boy."

"I wonder if this is the end of what we started," a young mother said with a trembling lip.

Vera firmly declared *no*, and Catarina gave the settlers hope when she told them, "I think you'll find that your neighbors outside the community aren't as hostile as senhor Millikan said."

Anton added, "Running this place isn't as much work as senhor Millikan led you to believe, either; you don't really need any special knowledge of law or business.

"Have you thought about who will lead the community?" asked Lori.

Kate answered, "Many of us have asked Amal and Vera to help us."

Janine and her children joined everyone gathering around the fire pit, fragility and suffering still plainly written in her silent expressions.

"Have you decided where you will go now?" Catarina asked her.

"We'd like her to stay right here," said Amal. "We don't turn our backs on family just because they have a different point of view."

"No, we don't," seconded Vera.

"The community is allowing us to stay," Janine explained. "For the time being, Dawn will go to school in Santa Clara. And I can consult with specialists about Melody."

In front of the community, Janine thanked the team who had saved Dawn's life.

Anton added his own thanks. "From Norberto's many cousins to Rosa's sister, from Felipe to Gabriela, from my wife to Lori, your dedication and hard work have saved a child." There were quiet words of gratitude and raised cups before the soup was ladled out.

Heads began to turn toward the forest. Led by Padre Santos, villagers from Santa Clara emerged carrying clothes, blankets, and large baskets brimming with food. Amal was the first to walk forward and greet them, and others soon joined her.

An hour later, Reggie had struck a deal to supply the Santa Clara grocer with fruit in the coming year, Dawn had made a new friend, and Anton had eaten the last of his favorite dessert: the traditional Dona Amelia tea cakes, made with molasses, cinnamon, and raisins. Padre Santos took his leave, whispering happily to Catarina as he passed, "I told you: people come together to survive."

Anton's eyes found Dawn, sitting by the oven, wrapped in the soft blue shawl. Bobey was on her lap, and Melody was by her side, content to draw what she saw in her mind. He took Bobey's ear from his shirt pocket and held it out to her. She looked up, first at the red wool ear, then to fix her large blue eyes on Anton. His stomach lurched when he saw her swollen cheek and the bruises on her arms. In the softest voice he had, he said, "I think Bobey lost this."

She didn't blink. "I saw you in the dark place."

He nodded. She smiled.

As he walked away, he heard a testament to the resilience of children: "Now, Bobey, your ear will hurt for a few days, but then you'll be fine."

Lori said her goodbyes. She would feel the loss of Comunidade dos Reis for a long time. Like her, they were people in need of others, and in need of a place in life. Living as they did only served to draw them together with common struggles and common victories. It was no different than what she enjoyed with her new family.

At the edge of the forest, Anton, Catarina, and Lori paused to look out over the island of Terceira and the endless Atlantic Ocean beyond, each one grateful for the others.

11

On the way back to Casa do Mar, Anton was replenished by the beauty of his island. His eyes lingered on white sand beaches, towering cliffs, and billowing hydrangea bushes. He swelled with pride at the sight of the stone buildings and roads that were a testament to the determination of his people to make a home in the middle of a fierce ocean. He smiled at fishing boats setting out to sea, as they had for centuries, and carpets of agricultural fields, planted as they had been for generations. He waved at one neighbor taking a cartload of oranges to market and another driving his cows to pasture. He knew there were other cultures—and he would never say that his was better—but it was *his*, and he didn't want it to be lost.

The family—and of course that included Lori—was sitting around the old oak table at Casa do Mar. The stories of their time apart had been told, second cups of coffee and hot chocolate had been poured, and all that remained of the sweet rolls made by the young baker in Santa Clara were crumbs.

Toni was showing his papa pictures of the whaling boat races when the phone rang. Everyone expected it would be more congratulations on finding Dawn or another offer to bring something to the welcome home party that evening.

When Anton saw who was calling his official government phone, he put it on speaker for all to hear. This time, the Presidente had called early in the morning.

"Anton," the Presidente began as he usually did—without preliminaries, "we've had more crime since I appointed you Minister than in the thirty previous years put together." His good humor came through as he continued, "It's a good thing we have the Trinity Detectives on the islands." In the past, Lori, Catarina, and Anton had quipped that they should name themselves the Trinity Detectives for the different but equally important talents they brought to solving crimes.

After thanking Anton in the name of the people of the Azores, Presidente Moniz asked, "How did you know where to find the girl?"

"I saw Dawn's sister pat a little black dog just as my daughter pats our little black dog, and I remembered that Liliana wants to see the hypogea."

"Well, you tell your daughter that she will have a special tour of the hypogea any time she wants." Liliana beamed.

When the Presidente got to the part where he repeated his pledge to support Anton's proposal to create a living historical trust on Santa Maria, the children twitched with quiet excitement. And when he added, "Of course, that means your appointment as Minister of Culture will be extended another year," Lori and Catarina hugged.

Their dream lived—for the moment.

"We have the rest of the day before our friends arrive. What should we do?" And without taking a breath, Anton answered his own question. "We should give Mama a present." Grinning with same sort of boyish excitement he had shown when he brought home Sombra, Anton pulled a small gift-wrapped box out of his pocket and placed it in front of Catarina.

"Is it for me?" asked Toni.

"You?" teased his father. "Why would I get a present for you? Is it Christmas? Is it your birthday? Have you done something wonderful for me?" To each question, Toni giggled and said no.

Catarina sat quietly with a smile on her face. "Who would it be for, then?"

"It is for you, my love." He could barely keep himself from unwrapping the box himself while she untied the red ribbon and took off the silver foil paper.

"Hurry, Mama, hurry," said Liliana, now standing beside her mother.

She lifted the top off the box and wrinkled her brow. "A key?"

Anton tried to keep a straight face. "Yes, a key, but a key to what?" And with that began a treasure hunt at Casa do Mar. Laughing, racing, yelling with excitement, the five of them went from lock to lock, trying to open trunks in the barn, cupboards in the guesthouses, doors to outbuildings, and gates to pastures. When the key slipped into the lock of a storage room beside Catarina's bedroom door, everyone held their breath, and when the key turned, the children and Lori grabbed each other's hands.

Catarina smiled at Anton. "What's this? That door hasn't been locked since we moved in." The room had been used to store furniture that couldn't fit in the tiny spaces the family occupied in the old barn.

"Papa," Liliana scolded, "Did you just give Mama a key to lock up our old things?"

"She will have to see."

Catarina knew from his expression that her husband had a special surprise behind the door, but nothing prepared her for what she found. "Oh…"

"Oh…" repeated Liliana and Lori.

"A tub!" squealed Toni.

An alcove under one of the barn's many windows had been finished with white marble tiles, and at its center sat an extravagant new bathtub. On the windowsill, between two small plants bright with yellow blooms, a basket held a collection of fragrant soaps and oils large enough to last a year, and on Catarina's old desk, new pink towels were waiting, along with copies of her favorite magazines and a pair of the reading glasses she'd recently started using.

"Me first!" squealed Toni.

"No," said Anton, drawing the curtain Beto had hung across the space to screen the new tub from the jumble of dusty, old furniture. "This is for Mama. Maybe she will share it on special occasions and maybe not."

Catarina hadn't said a word. Then again, words were seldom needed between her and Anton. She laced her fingers with his and squeezed. He knew how much this meant to her, and she knew he had received her thanks.

Another surprise awaited them at the end of the day. Just as the garden in front of the Casa do Mar barn was slowly filling with party-goers, Anton's nephew, Ethan Monise, and his parents from America arrived. Lori spotted the tall, rugged adventurer practically running down the long driveway, shining green eyes fixed on her as he waved enthusiastically. She had felt something special for him in the past but, with Carlos courting her and Ethan far from the islands, her attraction to the quiet, dark-haired man had overshadowed her attraction to the exuberant, fair-haired man.

In rituals that crossed cultures and generations, hugs and kisses were exchanged, children's cheeks were pinched and heads were ruffled, gifts were opened and thanks were given, and everyone was updated on the latest news of family and friends. Ethan's job had sent him to Italy for what he hoped would be the next two years. "I plan to indulge in a lot of diving and eating," he told them, adding, "and visiting nearby relatives."

It wasn't lost on Anton that he said that while looking at Lori.

It was a diverse, sociable group: Matias, Isabella, and Estela from Water's Edge; the elderly Dr. Leal and the even older Padre Henriques; their neighbor, Maria Rosa, and her children; the Monise family; Felipe and Luis, the young policeman from Faial who had recently joined the Santa Maria police department; senhor Machado, the outgoing school principal; Beto and his wife, Emanuela; Carlos and his mother, who was a cousin of both Matias and Dr. Leal; about thirty other friends; and, fresh and fragrant from her bath, Catarina.

Food appeared on the tables and slowly disappeared. Conversation bubbled here and there in both Portuguese and English.

Felipe, when will you be inviting Gabriela here?
Here's to the end of Hurricane Mimi.
Who do you think will replace senhor Machado?
Santa Maria did well in the boat races.
Did you see Matias and Isabella holding hands?
Beto did such a good job with the old cart house.
Cheers to finding Dawn Bennett!
It's good to be home.

Under a dome of sparkling stars, everyone danced to music of the islands, and with every new song, Lori found both Carlos and Ethan vying for her attention. Her feelings for Ethan were rekindled, but her mind kept returning to the conversation Carlos started on Terceira.

Children eventually wandered off to play by themselves. Maria Rosa put her two in bed across the road and returned to the party knowing they were safe. Estela's son, Nuno, bedded down with Toni, and Liliana read a book to Sombra, who found her favorite spot on the bed, smiling in that dog way, then—after a long day of romping, exploring, and socializing with guests—fell asleep.

With many stories told, many laughs shared, and many bottles of wine enjoyed, the party ended at about two in the morning, everyone a little bit giddy and more than a little bit happy.

Coming in 2017 from Miriam Winthrop

GARDEN OF DUST

Maryam was born in a house on the banks of the Euphrates River in Syria, the daughter of an Arab woman caught between the traditions of her past and a future she would not live to see. Her American father severs all connections to the society he holds responsible for the death of the woman he loved. Maryam becomes Mary, a child of Western culture and a woman unaware of her mother's heritage.

At a turning point in the history of the Middle East, Mary returns to that house on Euphrates River and is trapped, a witness to noble humanity in the face of inhumanity. On the eve of her escape, she is entrusted with seven treasures—a Neolithic statuette, a Babylonian pot, a Greek brooch, Roman coins, a Byzantine mosaic of the Virgin Mary, an eighth-century Koran, and an Armenian relic—each one testimony to the consequence of her birthplace in human history. Stolen from museums to safeguard them from inevitable destruction, she must decide which to save—and at what cost to the family she never knew but always loved.

From Garden of Dust

I made a leap of faith into the oldest and most fabled of Mankind's homes, reputedly the location of the Garden of Eden. But by the time I left, it had become a Garden of Dust.

If I had not gone, if I had not been born, these irreplaceable objects would have met a different fate—and different people would have died and lived.

Printed in Great Britain
by Amazon

19595161R00132